SPONTANEOUS
COMBUSTION

ALSO BY DAVID B. FEINBERG

Eighty-Sixed

SPONTANEOUS
COMBUSTION

DAVID B.
FEINBERG

VIKING

VIKING
Published by the Penguin Group
Viking Penguin, a division of Penguin Books USA Inc.,
375 Hudson Street, New York, New York 10014, U.S.A.
Penguin Books Ltd, 27 Wrights Lane, London W8 5TZ, England
Penguin Books Australia Ltd, Ringwood, Victoria, Australia
Penguin Books Canada Ltd, 10 Alcorn Avenue, Suite 300,
Toronto, Ontario, Canada M4V 3B2
Penguin Books (N.Z.) Ltd, 182–190 Wairau Road,
Auckland 10, New Zealand

Penguin Books Ltd, Registered Offices:
Harmondsworth, Middlesex, England

First published in 1991 by Viking Penguin,
a division of Penguin Books USA Inc.

PUBLISHER'S NOTE
This is a work of fiction. Names, characters, places, and
incidents either are the product of the author's imagination
or are used fictitiously.

In different form, "The Age of Anxiety" first appeared in *Mandate*
and in *Men on Men 2: Best New Gay Fiction* (New American Library); a portion of "The Week of the Floods" in *Mandate*; "Despair"
in *The James White Review* and in *The Gay Nineties* (The Crossing
Press); "Breaking Up with Roger" in *Tribe: An American Gay Journal*; and "Appendix: After the Cure" as "Close Encounters of the
Cured Kind" in *The Advocate*.

LIBRARY OF CONGRESS CATALOGING IN PUBLICATION DATA
Feinberg, David B.
Spontaneous combustion/ David B. Feinberg.
p.   cm.
ISBN 0-670-83813-6
I. Title.
PS3556.E425S67   1991
813'.54—dc20   91–50162

Printed in the United States of America
Set in Sabon
Designed by Fritz Metsch

TO
JOHN WEIR
AND
MICHAEL NAVA

Acknowledgments

Thanks to my editor, Ed Iwanicki; to my agent, Norman Laurila; to Freeman Gunter, for discovering me; to ACT UP, for the valiant work it does in fighting the AIDS crisis; to my wonderful friends Mark Bronnenberg, Robert Braun, Terry Callaghan, Michael Dorris, Joe Gallagher, Tom Gladwell, Jim Hubbard, Richard Kahn, Wayne Kawadler, Joe Keenan, Dennis Klein, Roz Lippel, David Mackler, Chris Mathewson, Glenn Pumilia, David Paonessa, Jan Carl Park, Jon Schlissel, Conyers Thompson; and to my family.

In memory of Michael Altman, Tucker Ashworth, Bob Berkson, Jim Bronson, Robert Chesley, Raul Companioni, Joe Concilio, Wayne Cummings, John Fox, Robert Hoppe, Chaz Klein, Peter Lawson, Geoff Leon, Sal Licata, Saul Meissler, Glenn Person, Vito Russo, Kevin Smith, John Sturman, Michael Swart, John Tannenbaum, Dennis Warning, George Whitmore, Jeff Wolfson, and all others who have died of AIDS.

Contents

Contents

SPONTANEOUS
COMBUSTION

Elephant & Castle

JANUARY 1985

Cameron and I were having a bite at Elephant & Castle one Tuesday night in early January. It was about ten P.M. We had been abusing the word "fabulous" for the past hour as we tried and discarded restaurants. "Let's go to Rumbuls," I said, "it's *fabulous*. They have an exquisite fruit tart with kiwis on display; doesn't it look *devoon!*" We went in and sat down. Cameron bantered with the waiter while I checked out the tearoom. There wasn't much action. It was so tiny that the toilet paper was sitting on top of the commode; there was no room to hang it on the wall. I returned, and Cameron told me that the kitchen had closed an hour ago.

The waiter directed us to a chichi French bistro on the corner which we immediately rejected because the appetizers were in our meal price-range and a too-horrible-for-words musician was playing troubadour. "Darling," said Cameron to the glass window, "the Middle Ages are *over*, haven't you heard?" We had to skip Tiffany's because one only breakfasts at Tiffany's. I had always wanted to try Butterfly, in the vain hope that the proprietress, Miss McQueen, would be there to seat us personally. But it was *too too* heterosexual that evening; it was *filled* with screaming infants and broods of breeders, and frankly, I didn't have the stomach for it. To add insult to injury, the blackboard menu in the window announced "muscles marinara" as a special. I peeped in and saw nary a single bodybuilder, although we were a scant block away from the Sheridan Square Gym. "False advertising," hissed Cameron. We were just about to eat at Montana Eve ("So chic with the neon and smoked glass. Darling, it's *Columbus Avenue!*") when I suggested Elephant & Castle.

"Of course! It's perfect! The tables are tiny, and so are the portions, and it's extravagantly overpriced, and the waiters are so terribly attractive. Why didn't I think of it before?" Cameron eagerly concurred. We were seated immediately at (an embarrassment of riches) a *table for four midgets!* which was quite comfortable for two. It was *extremely close* to the kitchen, so we knew that our food would be *fresher by microseconds* and far less likely to experience a radioactive decay. The tantalizing cakes and tantalizing waiters were *en pleine vue,* as were the coffeepots and the steam above the grill. And our particular waiter was *to die for!*

"Why, see how elegantly this attractive young man distributes the menus. I'm in seventh heaven," I gushed. The waiter, whom I shall dub Evelyn for the sake of our narration, was a skinny blond with a British accent that initially appeared to be Bostonian, at least to me. I was too dazzled by his anorectic dancer's physique to concentrate. One of his teeth was capped with silver.

"What's the darkest beer you have?" asked Cameron.

"I'm afraid we don't have any dark beer at all," replied Evelyn.

"Perhaps you have some brown food-coloring or smoked glasses? Never mind, I'll have a New Amsterdam."

I hadn't drunk anything alcoholic for an entire year. Well, since January first, which was about ten days previous. "I'll have—oh, God, I *always* forget what it's called. A spritzer?"

"You mean wine with seltzer?"

"Yes, but could you hold the wine and give me a slice of lime instead?"

"You want a wineless spritzer?"

"You're looking at me as if I'd asked for an eggless pantyhose or a ginless tonic."

"OK, a seltzer, and I'm sorry, we don't have any lime. I'll have to give you a slice of lemon instead."

"Whatever you say." I smiled. I was trying for a coy, demure, reserved, I'll-see-you-in-the-loo-in-twenty-minutes-while-my-friend-takes-care-of-the-check smile, but I'm not altogether sure whether I communicated the full message.

"I don't know why," I said to Cameron. "I always go blank with the word *seltzer*. There's something *extremely vulgar* about it."

"Does it make you think of the Marx Brothers having spritzer fights?" asked Cameron.

"Maybe it sounds too Jewish for my taste. I *am* trying to *forget* my *past*. I can never say, 'I'll have a bagel with a *shmeer*.' It sounds like a test for uterine cancer. Now, club soda sounds much more *sophisticated*. 'Let's go to the Club Baths and drink club soda while we examine brochures for our Club Med vacation.' "

Cameron—who laughs too loudly in public and once at the theater said in an extremely loud voice to the usherette, who just happened to be female, "You don't mean to tell me that I have to sit next to *him???*" but that was after I had embarrassed him about his outfit of the evening, which left far too little to the imagination, by *tweaking* his *nipple*—was telling me about his latest boyfriend. He was in stage one, which is Major Infatuation.

This includes goo-goo eyes, grocery-shopping hand-in-hand at the Food Emporium, discussions of summer shares at the Island, et cetera. After two or three days (Cameron has an extremely rapid metabolic rate) he segues into stage two, Mature Love. Here such a deep understanding has been reached that verbal communication is no longer necessary: Cameron and his intended would finish one another's sentences as if linked tele*pathetically*. They graduate from sleeping face-to-face to sleeping curled up in the same direction (facing a favored shrine or Bloomingdale's), matching spoons of sterling silver from Mother's hope chest.

Stage three, the Fading Bloom (approximately thirteen hours after the cessation of stage two), is the rocky period of the relationship, fraught with the terror of separation anxiety and the banality of household tasks. Laundry will be done. There will be wrenching phone calls at three in the morning. The topic of separate vacations will be broached. When they sleep together, their bodies will migrate to stylized back-to-back with the tension of Egyptian friezes, the repulsion of magnets with like poles. Stage four, Dissolution and Despair (twenty-seven minutes after the cessation of stage three), will be the last gasp of the affair. Futile attempts at recapturing the old passion will be made, desperate appeals to the senses: Perhaps an alternate nipple will be exposed, or a new hair-color experimented with. Inevitably, a threesome will be tried and fail. Fortunately for Cameron, stage four is usually concurrent with a new stage one. The entire process usually lasts two to three weeks. I debated whether to tell Cameron to use an egg timer to help him with his love affairs. As I had heard this story countless times before with a slightly different set of characters, I had one ear on Cameron and all four eyes on our waiter.

"Fred," Cameron was saying, "is *great* to sleep with and *wonderful* to *be with*. He's only a bit dull when it comes to conversation. I mean, he goes *on* and *on* about how his *mother ruined him!*"

"How old is he?" I inquired, wondering whether in the midst

4

of Cameron's narration I would witness the transition between stages two and three.

"*Thirty*. B.J., it's unbelievable! And he's only been in therapy for *three months!* I was *shocked* until he told me that he has just moved here from Texas."

"And *what* does he do for a living?"

"Would you believe it? He's in *fashion too!*"

"That settles it. I'll design the invitations. *Tom* can cater the affair. You two will have to fight it out between yourselves to decide who gets the honor to create the wedding dresses. It's a match made in *heaven!*"

Cameron taught a class at Parsons in seventeenth-century hems. His original proposal for a class had been "How Accessories Changed My Life," but the administration thought that was *far* too ambitious for undergraduates. By days Cameron processed words for a multinational conglomerate; by nights he was a fledgling rock star. I admired his versatility *effusively!*

"But I'm really not sure what to do with Fred. I'm afraid he might latch on to me with a deadly vise-grip. He *misses* his friends from Texas *dearly;* the poor man has only been in New York for five months. But he *is* a terrific dancer. And he *does* have an awful lot of friends here. *I just don't know!*"

I didn't know how to respond. I could give Cameron some serious advice on relationships, but then, my longest relationship lasted three months, and that was only because Richard was experimenting with a new antidepressant medication and his psychiatrist advised against any radical changes for the time being. I could purposely give bad advice because two weeks earlier Cameron had been extremely insulting to me by giving me a year's subscription to *Vanity Fair* for Christmas. It *is* true that whenever I went over to Cameron's for dinner out, I would always immediately gravitate toward the pile of *Vanity Fair*s while he spent *hours* selecting a proper outfit (OK, ten minutes tops). But that doesn't mean that I would *want it in my house!* I am *far too embarrassed* to be caught buying it at a newsstand. I feel less ashamed picking up the latest issue of *Anal Masturbation* on the way to work—wrapped in *The Wall Street Journal,* of course. I mean, *any magazine with Ron and Nancy on the cover!!! Gag me with a silver spoon!*

Furthermore, this present served only to remind me how much I *loathe* and *detest* Christmas. I had actually done quite well this year. I had received only three Christmas gifts in toto and not sent out a single one. Aside from the *ludicrous magazine subscription,* there was a set of espresso cups from Dennis which are extremely handy, considering that not only don't I have an espresso machine, I don't even drink coffee. I suppose they might serve for my Sunday cucumber sandwiches and tea. The third present was a set of *hopelessly tacky* socks from Tokyo with the legend *"Paris Scandals."*

I have hated Christmas ever since I was a child. How *dare* those heathen pagans preempt my Saturday-morning cartoons with their hagiographic extravaganzas and biblical spectaculars! Even the commercials had Santa Claus riding a Gillette razor over cotton-candy snow. Christmas was inescapable. Some dime-store Jews in the neighborhood would put up Hanukkah bushes. Heretics! Assimilationists! Downtown would be ablaze with over-sized plastic wreaths and dangling lights of a decidedly inferior quality strewn across the main drag. And in choir at school they would force us to say the baby Jesus's name—*force* us to sing praise to somebody else's Lord, because he certainly wasn't mine—with the threat of detention heavy on our little heads. Christ! We killed him. What's to celebrate? I must say that my favorite sight of the New Year is a row of discarded Christmas trees on the sidewalk, rotting in the trash.

Anyway, back to Cameron and his current boyfriend dilemma. I decided the *best solution* was to be *completely irrational* and *change the subject.* "Do you like this sweater? It's one hundred percent acrylic. I bought it at *Gimbel's* on *sale.* Thank God the season is over. I can *finally shop.* It's a *madhouse* the entire month of December. Isn't it lovely? I can wash the floor with it when I get tired of wearing it. It has absolutely *no pores*. It just doesn't *breathe!* I shall die in it one day *just* like the girl in *Goldfinger* after she got covered with paint and her pores were *completely clogged*. Won't that be *too glamorous* for words?"

"Have you made any resolutions for the new year?" Cameron asked.

"Well, last year I was being *entirely unrealistic,* what with resolving to end world hunger, stop the arms race, and find a boyfriend. This year, I've decided to be ever so clever and stop drinking coffee and smoking cigs."

"But you don't smoke."

"Neither do I drink coffee. See how *easy* it will be?"

"Well," said Cameron, "I've made a *ton* of resolutions. This year I'm going to floss *hourly*. My oral hygienist will be *so pleased*. I've decided to rid my life of vice. No more calling boys with live-in boyfriends! No more dope! No more booze! No more pills! No more fashionable nightclubs and trendy discotheques! No more cruising Action Down Under at Macy's for hot young Puerto Ricans and bridge-and-tunnelers! No more white sugar! Well, after dessert tomorrow at the very latest. Actually, I'm probably going to end up only keeping the ninety-second resolution."

"Which is?"

"To break the other ninety-one resolutions by February first."

At this point we were interrupted by our extremely attractive, painfully slender young waiter.

"Care to order now?" asked Evelyn.

"Would you recommend the yogurt froufrou? Does it come with fluffy slippers?" asked Cameron.

"No, and it's not pink either," he said, catching on. "It has strawberries and blueberries and apples and whipped cream."

"Is it frozen yogurt?"

"No, it's fresh."

"*Ugh!*" I said. "What about the hazelnut mousse?"

"We're out of it tonight. That rather limits your choices."

"The steamed vegetable. I assume it is either a single pea or a cube of carrot?"

"Tonight it's spinach."

"Darling, have you been talking to my nutritionist behind my back?" I decided to have a brownie. Cameron ordered a Swiss-burger with fries.

"My advice to you is *forget the Texan*," I said between bites. "Have you seen the latest ish of *Newsweek?*"

"Oh, the *coverboy*. I'm quite taken with him. Are you too?" It was *Newsweek*'s annual article on homosexuality. This one was about coming out: one family's story.

"I just *swooned!* I'm sorry, I'm tossing all of my *Torsos* and *Blueboys out the door. Blueboy* always did have bad color sep-aration anyways. This is the *real thing!* I'm quite *smitten*."

"What about the waiter? You *have* been paying more attention to him than me this evening." Cameron was a bit peeved. He wiped some ketchup from his chin.

"I just *can't* be *totally faithful*. It's *against* my *nature!*" I beck-oned Evelyn over. "Can I have another one of those fizzy things? It's OK, he's driving."

He smiled and returned in a jif. "I *must say*, you've been an exceptional waiter. *Top notch* in *my* book," I oozed.

"Thanks," he said. He coughed into the back of his hand. "Actually, it's my last night. I'm taking some time off."

"I don't know that we'll give you permission," said Cameron, disappointed.

"Unfortunately, it's beyond my control," he replied. "I'm start-ing on medical disability tomorrow."

We knew that it could be only one thing. Words were not necessary in this day and age.

"Oh," I said. "Sorry."

"Cheer up," said Cameron.

We overtipped, even though he charged me for the second seltzer, which didn't have any citrus wedges in it at all.

Outside, on Greenwich Avenue, I said to Cameron, "I think we should call it a night. I feel a bit run-down."

"Same here. It's bedtime for Bonzo."

"Could you do me a favor and hail me a cab?" Cameron lived downtown and I lived uptown; it would have been silly to share one. "They never seem to stop for me. I guess I just don't have the touch. I always feel feeble watching them drive by on the other side of the street. And you know how much I hate rejection."

"No problem. Taxi!" I could see one coming down Seventh.

"Take care," said Cameron as I stepped into the cab. We kissed the air and parted, decidedly more sober than when we arrived.

The Age of Anxiety

AUGUST 1985

I blame it all on the existentialists. Before I heard of them—compliments Mme. Escoffier, third-year French—life proceeded as smoothly as the automatic door at the A&P. I would step on the rubber pad outside the supermarket, activating sensors, causing the door to open automatically; I would enter and the door would close silently behind me. I would sleepwalk through life with as little thought as the electric eye on an elevator. I had such confidence! I operated under the assumption that no conscious intervention from me was really ever necessary. My life was a moving sidewalk, effortlessly transporting me from one destination to another.

But then in tenth grade Mme. Escoffier had us read *The*

Stranger, by Albert Camus, and nothing was ever the same. I realized that intention underlay every action. At gym class when Mister D would call attendance, I would be overcome with fear. Suppose I didn't answer "Here" when he called out "Rosenthal"? Suppose that at that moment I were unable to speak, temporarily struck mute? Suppose instead of responding in an appropriate manner I swore involuntarily? And what if I did not recognize my own name? What if I opened my mouth, and a pigeon flew out?

Twenty years later, I stood at the Fiftieth Street IND station. I heard the buzzer; the sign flashed "DOWNTOWN" in dot-matrix red bulbs; I stumbled down the stairs. Although the train was not yet visible, I knew it would turn the corner in approximately one minute and thirty seconds. I could already feel the breeze in the tunnel. I saw the bright lights approaching: the eyes of a snake. The train thundered closer, an unstoppable natural phenomenon, an act of God. I stood transfixed and wondered, would this be the time that the bright lights would hypnotize me into jumping? Would I spring out onto the tracks at the last possible moment, leaving no time for the conductor to pull the emergency switch? I walked backward and clung to a steel girder, grasping it tightly, fearing that the rush of air might suck me onto the track, that the third rail, live with six hundred volts, might erupt in an electrical explosion, shooting sparks on the platform. If I stood in front of the textured line that the Transit Authority has painted parallel to the tracks for the blind, some prematurely released psychiatric patient who ran out of medication might bound down the stairs and push me onto the tracks.

The train pulled in and stopped. One door opened near me (the other was stuck), and I entered the car. The door closed. I knew I had passed the point of danger. Now there was nothing to worry about except whether the man who was smoking a cigarette had a knife and whether the soda stain on the floor would make my shoes pick up the discarded *New York Post* with the latest AIDS-hysteria headline screaming at me and whether the sleeping man with urine stains on his pants was breathing or dead and whether the well-worn cards giving instructions on signing the alphabet the deaf-mute passed out had any contagious diseases and whether the teenage couple of alien ethnicity were laughing at me because they had seen my earring and whether the extremely obese woman who had sat next to me would allow me to exit at West Fourth Street.

Why I Was Upset

I was upset for a variety of reasons, but mainly because my best friend and former lover, Richard, had just informed me that he was moving to San Francisco in two days. I was on my way downtown to see him for dinner and maybe to try to persuade him not to go. Richard had called me that day at work, around noon.

"Hi, B.J. Do you want a cat?"

"What cat?"

"Jessica." Jessica was Richard's eighteen-pound misanthropic cat. She had spent eight months at the Bide-a-Wee shelter on the East Side before Richard rescued her. People would coo, "What a beautiful cat," and try to pet her. After Jessica bit them, they'd decide on some cute kittens or an unhousebroken angora instead. Richard took one look at Jessica and fell for her. He sensed that she too had been abused. I loved to go over to Richard's and play with Jessica; it was always fun watching her squirm out of my arms. Richard called her The Weasel. "Jessssssica," he would sibillate, "come over, sweeetie, Potato."

"Why would you want to get rid of Jessica? Are you sick of her or something?"

"No, I'm moving."

"You're *what?*"

"I'm moving to San Francisco."

"What do you mean, you're moving to San Francisco?"

"I'm moving to San Francisco Friday, and I wanted to know if you would take care of Jessica for me."

"You're moving to San Francisco in *two days?* Richard, this is crazy. You don't just move to San Francisco in *two days!*"

"I've had the tickets since Sunday. You know I've always been thinking of moving to San Francisco. I just can't take the heat any more. Remember last summer, and the summer before, I said I couldn't take another August in New York City? I hate it here. I hate my job. I hate the subways. I hate the noise. I hate the crowds. I've been living in New York for eleven years, and I think it's time to move on."

"But you've never even been to San Francisco! You don't just *move* to a place you've never even visited. You go on a vacation, and then you come back. If you like it, you quit your job, give up your apartment, pack up your belongings, and go. You make arrangements with your gym and your phone and your electric and your cat. You don't just leave on a week's notice."

"I had a feeling you would react this way. I should have known. You've never been supportive of my decisions."

"Have you told any other of your friends? Have you even told your therapist? I bet you haven't, because you're afraid they'll talk you out of going. I think you're just trying to run away from all of your problems, and moving to San Francisco won't help. I think—"

"I think this discussion has gone far enough, and it's quite pointless to continue it. I called to ask if you wanted my cat. I guess you don't. I'll speak to you later when you're more rational. Goodbye, B.J."

Richard himself was no model of sanity. I had met him five years earlier on the street. He had gone home to pee because at the time he had found that he was incapable of performing this bodily function anywhere other than home. Richard had a history of depression that went back ten years. He had an extensive support network of friends and acquaintances who would do nearly anything for him, and for a while he liked me the best because he knew that compassion didn't come easy to me and he saw me as a challenge.

I have a photograph of him on the wall, above the desk. Richard was at the beach, covered with baby oil, reading *The Magic Mountain*. The photo was taken from a skew angle—the camera near ground level, directed at Richard's torso and the clouds above. Consequently, his visible arm was massive, his chest gigantic (a pun on *The Magic Mountain*), and his head unnaturally small in comparison.

Richard went to the gym five times a week, which left two nights for me. He tended to be a creature of habit, settling into patterns quite easily. Before I met him, he would have a cheeseburger and a protein shake for dinner every night. I taught him how to make chicken in a skillet. So he merely switched to chicken every night. There were periods when he would go to AA meetings for support, sometimes as many as three in a day. The year I met him he went through more therapists than I did boyfriends, which was to say, quite a lot.

TROUBLE IN PARADISE

We had a stormy relationship that ended one day in Sheridan Square when he pointed at my thickening waist and then at a display for starch blockers at the General Nutrition Center. "That's it," I said. "It's over."

The problem was where I was compulsive, Richard was addictive. Our relationship had never been properly consummated. Richard refused to sleep over in my apartment because it was too noisy and threatening in Hell's Kitchen and too messy in the apartment. Richard lived in a single-room occupancy residence with a single bed, so when I slept over, it was on a foam mattress on the floor while he would sleep in the bed, which was too tiny to fit both me and a Sheridan Square Health Club ("Exercising and Reducing") gym queen who had used steroids a few years ago to gain friends and influence people like me. Our relationship could have been annulled properly had I been Catholic and asked papal permission.

Richard felt that I wasn't supportive enough of him, and I felt that he wasn't responsive enough to my needs, and he claimed that I was making him feel guilty with my passive aggression, and although I denied this, on some level I knew that I was eating him alive.

Sex with Richard was a challenge. Richard was interested in sadomasochism as a purely theatrical act of the imagination. He had joined Amnesty International a few years earlier just so he could read the actually documented accounts of torture in Third World countries, complete with photographs and illustrative diagrams. Richard would lose his erection fucking me if I moved too much, and I was tired of playing Nicaraguan corpse to his freedom fighter.

I was interested in achieving the type of popularity I had always dreamed of in high school but never imagined would be possible by merely (a) going to the gym three or four times a week, (b) buying a pair of contact lenses, and (c) eliminating the word "No" from my vocabulary. Richard expected me to be absolutely faithful to him on two nights a week, maybe, and I wanted more than two nights a week, maybe. At twenty-three I was constantly horny: Richard was demanding the impossible.

The final straw was when Richard saw *Sophie's Choice* with someone from one of his therapy groups who had been telling Richard how wonderful he was, whereas I was long past the stage of praise unmitigated with sarcasm and cynicism. I had tacitly assumed that we would see it together because we had spent weeks anticipating the movie version (we had both read the book), and I was furious, and my pettiness knows no bounds.

Two weeks after we broke up I was mugged on the PATH train coming back from a New Year's Eve dinner in Jersey City.

Then Richard called me, telling me that his mother had died a few days ago, and could I come over? We were drawn together in a hostile world.

In December of 1982, two years after we broke up, Richard's doctor diagnosed him with lymphadenopathy, persistently swollen lymph glands under his arms and in his groin. He panicked. He went to the hospital for tests. It was benign. He developed night sweats. He switched to another antidepressant and upped the dosage. Richard got a fungal infection on his toes. He had difficulty swallowing. His doctor told him he had thrush and gave him the appropriate medication. His T-cells dropped precipitously. He had ARC. I was inextricably entangled in Richard's life. I helped him through each crisis. We grew closer and closer.

After he told me he was going to move, it felt as though I had lost a limb. I was slowly disappearing, and the next time I tried to look at myself in the mirror, there might not be anything there at all. I took two deep breaths and swallowed. I paused and tried to calm myself. I thought slowly, deliberately, "I . . . must . . . not . . . get . . . upset. . . . It . . . is . . . im . . . per . . . a . . . tive . . . that . . . I . . . not . . . get . . . up . . . set. . . . How can you do this to me, Richard, after all I have done for you? How can you abandon me like this, so easily? And *not when I have herpes.*"

THE LITTLE DISTURBANCES OF MAN

For the past several years it seems that I have turned into a mass of symptoms and inchoate disease. As soon as one minor inconvenience leaves me, another fills its place without a moment's loss. I tend to think of it as some cosmic law, like the conservation of matter and energy in the universe: the conservation of bacteria, microbes, viruses, and disease. In moments of endearment Richard would call me his walking petri-dish.

I've had herpes on the lower lip for about five years. It tends to recur when my defenses are down, when I am overtired, when my resources are low, when I am overdrawn at the bank, when another prospective boyfriend turns out to be living with his lover of ten years and I call by chance at the incorrect time, when I sit and wait for two hours at the dermatologist, reading about Arnold Schwarzenegger and Rock Hudson in *People* magazine, and after being tortured with WRFM's mellow music I'm admitted and he scrapes off some tiny warts from my chin ("We won't need any anesthetic for this," he says, beaming beneath his headlight, a strap-on light I expect coal miners use) and I rush home afterward to get stood up for dinner by a friend who lives down the block whom I haven't seen for about a year who had called me last week saying that he had been diagnosed with AIDS, so how can I possibly be mad at him, or when I sit and wait in expectation of Mister Right to open the door and come into the steam room at the health club and sit across from me and start stroking his dick, all the while not letting his eyes leave mine, and an hour later, having lost ten pounds in bodily fluids, I manage to pry myself off the bench with the last ounce of strength I have and go back to the office from the gym and eat a tuna-salad sandwich in a pita pocket that leaks through the bag because it has too much tahini dressing and sweat through another shirt because my glands have not decided to stop, or when the local from Fourteenth Street turns express one stop before mine and I have to take a local back downtown and it's midnight and it's August and the subway is at least twenty degrees warmer than on the surface and I decide that even though I am dead tired, because I only got four hours sleep the night before, it will be quicker just to walk home from Seventy-second Street, or when my phone is out of service for an extended period of time (e.g., more than fifteen minutes), or invariably after I have sex with the person who had initially given me herpes.

UNNATURAL ACTS, NONSTANDARD POSITIONS

Herpes was just a minor indisposition, a major irritation—hardly cause for alarm. The anal warts were, however, a major source of grief and humiliation. Every two or three weeks I found myself in a nonstandard position on the doctor's padded table—not lying, not sitting. I can only describe it as follows: Imagine that I am wearing suspenders, and a crane has caught them with its hook at the seat of my pants and has lifted me by the ass a foot off the table. My elbows dug in tight to the padding; my hands were clasped behind my head as if I were a hostage in a bank robbery. My shirt was soaked; my pants were down to my ankles, my underwear not far behind. Dr. Roto-Rooter told amusing jokes (about, for example, why warts were not burned off electrically when they occurred in this area—should the patient fart, he might spark an explosion) as he applied the acid with the utmost of care and delicacy. How I appreciated his bedside manner. I closed my eyes and thought of more pleasant things: spinal taps and root-canal work. Dr. R didn't have a particularly busy practice. He waited for flu season the way some people wait for Barney's annual warehouse sale. After I buttoned up and sat on the most extreme edge of the chair in order to minimize contact, I wrote him a check and listened to him talking about the anxieties that accompanied closing the deal for his co-op in the Village. On the memo section of the check I wrote "Real estate: extortion."

Aside from herpes and warts, there was a host of minor dermatological disasters—including psoriasis, impetigo, dermatitis, seborrhea, and dandruff—virtually anything you would care to name that required sixty dollars for a five-minute visit with a skeletal dermatologist who apparently spent an inordinate amount of time in Peru and always had a case of the sniffles. All this was minor.

Except I was also worried that my lymph glands were slightly swollen at the neck. Was this because of the herpes, or did they cause this outbreak? Questions of teleology concerned me deeply.

Which came first, the chicken or the egg? How did the first sheep catch the clap, if not from an errant farmboy? Everything, of course, had a reasonable explanation in the end. The recent unexplained weight loss of four or five pounds became an equally mysterious weight gain the next day. This, due to a faulty scale. The purplish bruise on the arm was terrifying until I recalled the frying-pan accident during Thursday's unsuccessful attempt at Chicken Marengo. Again, the temperature reading of 105.5, which caused severe hysteria (shallow breathing, profuse perspiration, and a host of other allied symptoms) last Sunday, turned out to be the thermometer's only reading. Unlike the stopped clock, which is at least accurate twice a day, the broken thermometer can be wrong indefinitely. And on it went. The sweating at night: Was this pathological or just because of the August humidity?

Nonetheless, my neck ached, and it was 95 degrees outside, with two hundred percent humidity, and the office was littered with Doctor Pepper empties (even my empty calories were directed toward quasi-medicinal sources), and once again I seemed to be without prospective boyfriends, and the thought of reading through ten pages of fine-print personals in search of more prospective boyfriends in the *New York Native* was not at all appealing, and going to a bar would be too depressing, and going to the baths was of course out of the question, and now my head started to hurt, which could be dehydration from the endless series of carbonated beverages I flooded my system with or else could be from the minor case of the runs I've had off and on for weeks or months or years and might even be from the herpes, which also seemed to affect my sinuses, and I didn't know why I should even be *thinking* about prospective boyfriends, considering the state I was in; I should probably be eating more saltpeter, but the equations were just too complicated or maybe too direct and simple for me to comprehend. Sex equals death. Libido equals Thanatos. They used to be flip sides of the coin, didn't they?

I've been convinced that I was dying about three times in the past three years. The last time I was at the gym; my head was pounding, and I noticed a swelling at the side of my neck. I did my fifty push-ups mechanically, thinking, "This is it. The final curtain. The big sleep. The deep six." How gladly I paid Dr. Hurwitz (fee due in advance; no checks or credit cards, please) to tell me that the swelling I was feeling was a subcutaneous pimple, a gathering of pus, not even a cyst. Regrettably, I never believed in an afterlife. If I ever come back, chances are it will be as a strand of worry beads.

I used to think that VD could be eradicated if everyone on the planet abstained from sex for fourteen days and anyone with symptoms was treated. This included sheep. You would only have to wait for the period of transmission or detection. As a precautionary measure, all sexual contacts of those infected would also be treated. And, just to be safe, all contacts of those contacts. With AIDS, we merely had to extend this fourteen-day period to eight or ten years. This might incidentally solve the population-explosion problem—temporarily.

I spent the rest of the afternoon under the desk, doing the *New York Times* crossword puzzle. Somehow I dragged myself through the rest of the working day. I made seventeen promises I knew I could not or would not fulfill to associates and strangers and bosses and underlings, my legions of serfs, typed up a few meaningless memos, and went home to check the mail and lie down.

Be It Ever So Humble

The apartment in a moment of whimsy and miscalculated aesthetics was painted two shades of blue: morose and inconsolable. There was no television in the apartment. Less of a moral stance than a snobbish affectation, this decision to forgo the tube was made when I realized that more households have television than indoor plumbing. The management had chosen to upgrade the apartment with an intriguing avant-garde design concept: exposed plumbing. There had been a leak in the wall. After ripping up a significant portion of the bathroom wall, the super, evidently pleased with the effect he had created, chose to leave the wall in this seemingly unfinished state.

The ceiling hadn't collapsed, so I was grateful. Each day I came home and the ceiling was still there I was thankful, remembering the day four years ago when this was not the case. The phone was working, another one of the modern conveniences I do not take for granted. I seemed to lose phone service about once every three months. Most recently, after the hurricane, my phone had undergone a curious metamorphosis. On pulse I got *nada,* but when I switched to tone, I heard a tiny voice exhorting me to give my soul to Jesus. It was *The Voice of Prophecy,* a syndicated radio show. Like those errant fillings in the mouths of paranoid schizophrenics convinced the CIA is listening in to their thoughts, somehow my phone had become a radio receiver.

I called Richard and arranged to meet him for dinner. I lay down for a few minutes, stared at the ceiling, and pretended I was in Sweden. Then I changed from school clothes to play clothes, found something appropriate to read so the train wouldn't get stuck in a tunnel, and left.

DRIVEN TO TEARS

I went past the oppressive sign flashing "GET RIGHT WITH GOD" on one side and "SIN WILL FIND YOU OUT" on the other, and then the Adonis ("Flagship Male Theater of the Nation"), and went down to the subway at Fiftieth Street. By the token booth there was a little sign: "Courtesy is contagious, let's start an epidemic." I imagined that everywhere people's faces were being replaced by lifesize have-a-nice-day yellow smile buttons, like in *Rhinoceros,* where all the characters turned into rhinoceroses. I caught the train uneventfully, got off at West Fourth Street, and crossed to the uptown-side exit because it always smelled of piss on the downtown Waverly Place exit. I had to call from the corner. I paced back and forth from phone booth to phone booth. A Puerto Rican woman about forty was speaking Spanish rapidly into the working phone; the other had its coin-drop stopped. Richard told me he would be down in a minute.

Jessica was in the window, looking out, in the planter. She ignored me. Richard and I sat down. I could not look him in the eye. "Well," I said in a quiet, even voice, so small it amazed me that it was coming from my mouth, "I hope you know what you're doing. It's rough moving to a totally new place without friends."

"I've thought this through," said Richard in his oddly sane voice. "I know it will be difficult at first, but it's time for a change."

"Are you doing anything about the TV set?" It was rented from Granada TV Rental.

"That's not that important. Paul downstairs will look after things. If things don't work out, I can always come back. You know, nothing is final."

"What about your mail? Are you going to have it forwarded?"

"It's just bills. No. I want to start from scratch. B.J., you're not being totally honest with me now. I want you to look me in the eye and tell me how you *really* feel."

Why are you doing this to me? I thought. Why are you trying to drive me to tears? You *know* how I feel. Do you want me to beg you to stay? Will that make any difference? If it does, does it prove only that you are incapable of making decisions on your own? Are you trying to humiliate me? Why are you doing this to me?

There were a thousand and one reasons why you shouldn't go. I wanted to be calm, rational. I didn't want to start crying. The last time I cried was at a phone booth after another prospective boyfriend jilted me because he was disease-conscious and I had just gotten another herpes outbreak because I was so upset when

I came home to discover the apartment in utter disarray; they had installed new windows and not bothered to clean up afterward and somehow managed to cut my phone wire in the process, and of course it was on a Friday, so I wouldn't get repair service until Monday; I was buying the *Daily News* and the *Post* and the *Times* and saving the quarters for phone calls so I could call people and get their machines from the phone booth around the corner, and I had called up Lloyd to tell him that we could have dinner that night but we couldn't fool around because my face had broken out, and he had said well maybe we shouldn't be seeing each other anymore because he was unable to give me what I wanted, which was to be boyfriends, because that required a time commitment he couldn't really afford because he had this new job that he had to work at sixty hours a week and he was learning to play the piano and in therapy and working out at the gym and he really didn't have time for a relationship, and I knew that his job was more important than me, and the times that I slept over at his apartment he forgot to set the alarm clock to get me to work on time because subconsciously he wanted the extra hour of sleep, and of course he wouldn't sleep at my apartment, so this said to me in effect that he was more important than *my* job, which I suppose totally negated my existence when you put the two together, and I kept on getting these little illnesses, and he was spooked; he had had several friends die of AIDS, so maybe it would be the best thing not to see each other anymore, and I paused, and I kept my voice calm and even and said, "Sure," and then he said those same six words that Richard said, "*Tell me how you really feel,*" and I don't think I will ever forgive him for making me break down in tears at a phone booth in public; I mean, he was crying too after a while, but at least he was home in his apartment, the spineless bastard; the least he could have done was break up face to face, and here my phone was out of order, and I had gone out of my way to please: I had even bought a bottle of Rose's lime juice for his infernal vodka gimlets, which I decided to mail to him, although there was the question of whether I should shatter the bottle before sending it or rely on the United States Postal Service to do my dirty work for me. Five years earlier Richard and I had broken up in the very same apartment, leaving *me* with the ignoble task of returning home by subway, and here I was again. I sobbed to Richard, "I worry about you all of the time."

"You wouldn't know it from that exterior."

"You're my best friend. . . . *Of course I don't want you to go!* I want you to do what's best for you. You know that. But why will telling you this make any difference?" Richard held me, sobbing. He was crying too.

"Emotions are all that matter in the end," he said.

"But don't you see, *I can't get upset.* Not when I have . . . *herpes!*"

Richard laughed. "I can see you in a cork-lined room, far from the world, insulated, like Marcel Proust, taking sustenance from weak tea." Richard, mad as a hatter yet perfectly sane.

About a year earlier Richard invented the "WAAAAAAH" response. When you just feel like crying, you say, "WAAAAAAH." Richard said it was like a doll, Baby-Crybaby, that you would squeeze and tears would squirt from its eyes—hot, salty tears. Not to be outdone, I invented the compassionate response. When Richard was depressed and I was low on compassion, I would hold his hand and pat it, murmuring, "There, there." Out at Jones Beach the rest rooms are called comfort stations. I imagine they have an eighty-year-old Jewish grandmother in an overstuffed chair, patting the hands of strangers and murmuring, "There, there."

Richard and I sat there, screaming "WAAAAAAH, WAAAAAAH" and patting each other on the back of the hand, murmuring, "There, there, there."

We had a terrible farewell dinner at Tiffany's and said goodbye. I went back to the subway to face the lights of the approaching train.

The Week of the Floods

FEBRUARY 1986

EMPIRES WOULD TOPPLE

The day after Richard Burton died, the *New York Post* printed excerpts from an autobiography he had written some twenty years previous. On my way to work on the subway, looking over the shoulder of a fellow commuter, I read the caption "Her breasts were apocalyptic—empires would topple down before they withered" to a photograph of Elizabeth Taylor in all of her voluptuousness taken during the shooting of *Suddenly, Last Summer*. All day at work I wrestled with my conscience whether I should break down and buy the ignominious and vile *Post*, purveyors of homophobia and yellow journalism. In the end, tackiness beat political correctness. I dashed out at five to the nearest newsstand. I picked up the *Post* and quickly flipped to the center photo. To my disappointment, in the later edition the caption had been changed to something along the lines of "Whatever you do, don't die on me, Richard." Luckily I was able to find a morning edition at the Hispanic candy store a few doors down from my charming apartment in scenic Hell's Kitchenette. Newspapers are of secondary interest at this store, which deals primarily in fluorescent two-foot crucifixes, Spanish editions of *Cosmopolitan*, *Selecciones* from *Reader's Digest*, and running numbers.

Well, when I first saw Allan at Jones Beach three years earlier, those were my sentiments exactly. His pecs would topple empires down before they withered. Allan's chest, two perfect mounds of flesh topped with exquisite nipples that served to evoke the painful memories of premature weaning, were well placed above a lean and hard stomach. His hair was the color of toffee, his mustache thick and blond. It was love at first sight.

Allan stood in the surf, wearing wrinkled red boxers that hid a multitude of possibilities. He was watching the gulls through soft, unfocused blue eyes. I think it was his eyes that did me in. Then he turned and saw me and smiled.

I dragged him to the dunes to have my way with him but then found myself oddly incapable of any act of lust; it would have been a desecration of our great love and we would lose respect for one another. Besides, the poppers were home in my freezer. So we did the mature thing and waited.

Allan came over to my charming apartment in Hell's Kitchenette the following night. It was well worth the wait.

He tasted every bit as delectable as he looked. He made love so tenderly. He said nothing but sweet nothings for the next night and day. He was absolutely perfect for me except for six tiny insignificant reasons:

1. He had a boyfriend named Ralph. This was not insurmountable.

2. He had another boyfriend whose name I could not recall. This was problematic at best.

3. He had a Doberman pinscher, and I was absolutely terrified of all dogs, especially Dobermans, because they turn against their masters.

4. He had another Doberman pinscher. Now I was quite intimidated.

5. He had a lover named Eric. I did my best to feign indifference, but I fear he saw through my facade.

and

6. He lived in San Francisco, whereas I lived in New York.

Two days after we met he flew back to San Francisco to his two boyfriends and two Dobermans and lover. In a frivolous delirium three weeks later I sent him the bathing suit I had worn the day we met. I had bought it on Mother's Day, the day I became a Jewish American Princess. I had gone to Macy's to buy my mom a last-minute present. The post office on Thirty-third and Eighth is open twenty-four hours a day, three hundred sixty-five days a year, and thus is extremely convenient for last-minute holiday shopping. Well, after I got my mom a present, I decided that I would get *myself* something for a change. I went upstairs and checked out the Speedos. That year's models were extremely appealing. I saw two that I particularly liked, and I just couldn't decide which I liked better, so I took out my plastic charge-card and purchased both of them.

But two weeks after I had met Allan while wearing the suit designed for a sleek and trim homo-on-the-go I returned to the scene of the crime for lyric reminiscing when to my *abject horror* I saw someone wearing *the exact same suit as mine*, only he was shameful and disgraceful and ignominious and grossly over-weight. Naturally I had to remove my suit *immediately,* and *of course* I could never wear it again. So I sent it to Allan, and he was just thrilled to pieces. I told my friend Rachel, who lives in a doorman building and has a full-length white mink coat and a mantle full of *tchotchkes* and is always complaining about how fat she is, even though sometimes I think she could give Karen Carpenter a good run for her money—in other words, she is the *genuine article* when it comes to Jewish American Princesses—and Rachel said, "That's gross," but she said "That's gross" when she dragged me to *Taxi zum Klo* (because her boyfriend said that she had to see it with me so I could explain it to her) during the famous golden-shower scene with the perfect arc of urine, and I would have seen it if I hadn't been inspecting my nails for cuticle damage at the time. I *do* have a weak heart; I ducked in *Alien* when John Hurt's stomach exploded, and I covered my eyes in *S.O.B.* when Julie Andrews bared her breasts I was so shocked.

Allan promised that he would be back to visit soon, but then it turned out that he couldn't make it in January after all. We kept in close touch by phone. I'd leave six or seven messages with his lover, and eventually Allan would call back. We had meaningful conversations like this:

"Hello."

"Yes."

"B.J., it's *Allan* from *San Francisco*." Allan stretched every other word for emphasis, adding a slight nasal whine. "How *are* you?"

"OK." My response was flat. I was still annoyed that he hadn't called back earlier or visited when he said he would or left his lover and moved in with me or bought me expensive presents or moved me to a deluxe apartment on Park Avenue that he could barely afford, making me a "kept woman," or sent me his jock strap or pretested marital aids of an extremely personal nature.

"Gee, it's *really good* to talk to *you*. You know, *I* really like *you*."

"What else is new?" I decided to file my nails.

"You know, B.J., I still have a *crush* on *you*."

"Oh, yeah?" I looked around. The knives needed sharpening immediately.

"Gee. It's probably *real late* out there. I don't want to keep *you* up. It was *great* talking to *you*. I'd better *go* now. Take care."

I decided that maybe I didn't like those green glass bowls that I had picked up at a junk shop secondhand and that maybe it would be nice to throw them against the wall, and so I did, and then I cleaned up the mess, and then I listened to Paul Simon for half an hour, and then I sucked in my stomach and slipped on some tight leather pants and went to a bar near the river called Degradation Alley.

On those rare times I got through to Allan, we'd have the same conversation, which was just so much white noise to me, only he would end it with, "Gee, B.J., this is probably costing you a *lot* of *money*. I'd better hang up now. You *take care* and *be good*."

For a month or so I toyed with the idea of moving to San Francisco and stealing Allan from Eric, but Eric had followed Allan to San Francisco ten years earlier, and I hated being unoriginal.

Once, I decided to inject a little content into the conversation: "How *are* you, B.J.?"

"Well, my herpes broke out again. My best friend, Richard, is back in the loony bin, suffering his nineteenth nervous break-down. My mother called me to tell me she is suffering from a degenerative bone disease. My sister is behind in her mortgage. My job is driving me bananas; some days I feel I've turned into a human memo-machine. And last night at two in the morning I got a jerk-off call from some sleazeball who had the nerve to hang up on me just as I was getting excited."

"*Gee*, I'm *really sorry*." His voice was full of concern. "Other than that, is everything OK?" asked Allan. "*Gee*, I *hope* it is."

I began to wonder whether Allan was a complete idiot.

Other times Allan would call and say, "Gee, I'm *sorry*, I've been acting *real creepy* lately. I'm sorry I didn't return any of your phone calls the past two weeks. I've been feeling *real de-pressed*. Things are tense here with me and Eric. He keeps wanting me to drop all of my boyfriends. Shit. I'm sorry. I didn't ask you how *you* werc. Are you feeling OK? I hope I'm not keeping you up. Gee, it's late in New York, and you have to get up early tomorrow. I'm sorry if I've kept you up." It was maddening.

Allan would send me art cards: photographs of empty rooms, a bed covered with rumpled sheets, shafts of sunlight illuminating the scene. Minimal designs of light blue on yellow. A black-and-white photograph of a limbless mannequin. A barbell on the floor of a deserted gym. All with the inscription "Thinking of you, Allan."

I decided not to collect deposits on the cans of Michelob I drank waiting for him to call me until he arrived in New York. Allan didn't make it in January, and then he couldn't come in March, and he'd tell me that he *still* had a crush on me, and then it became May, and when he finally arrived, it was August, practically a year later. By then I was pretty disgusted with the whole deal. I mean, if he was so much in love with me, *what took him so fucking long?* After twelve months of unreturned six-packs the apartment was a virtual shooting gallery in miniature, with a labyrinthine trail of beer cans winding through the rooms. I vowed never again to sleep with a married man. My resolve was strong. It lasted *at least* twelve hours. I broke it only twice during Allan's next two visits.

And now it was my turn to visit Allan.

Even though I had all but given up on Allan as a possible boyfriend or extramarital affair or transcontinental fuck-buddy or even a reliable phone-sex pal, I had developed a strong affection for him. Allan had some ineffable sweetness that made me love him against my better judgment, but I suppose all love involves the willful suspension of disbelief and rational thought. Anyway, New York was driving me crazy. I just had to get out of the city. I desperately missed Richard, who was currently undergoing detox at a halfway house in San Francisco. Allan graciously offered to put me up at his house. I thought it wouldn't be awkward because by then we hadn't slept with one another in at least a year and we were all adults and I always secretly wanted to pretend my life were the plot of some obscure Noël Coward play and if Eric was going to kill me in a fit of jealous rage, then I could always stay at the Y.

I had visited San Francisco once before, several years earlier. I hadn't known anyone in San Francisco then. I stayed at the YMCA in a tiny room where the wallpaper was singed at the edge near the bed as if someone had tried to set the bed on fire and failed. Above the desk was a rectangular spot where the wallpaper was less faded; I imagined someone had hung a portrait of Jesus on the cross there for six years and slowly gone mad. I was so depressed that when I returned to New York, I immediately dumped my membership to the West Side Y and switched to a sleazier homo exercise-palace.

I missed Allan at the airport. The flight had been a horror. "This plane appears to have Parkinson's disease," I said to no one in particular as we circled the bay endlessly, shaking violently. I cursed myself for being a tightwad and taking People's Express. I vowed never again to travel on that airline, with its shoddy surplus defective planes, and then deplaned to a fifty-mile-an-hour wind. The rain, which would plague me for the next week, was just beginning.

My mistake was to try the luggage area only once. I just had carry-on myself. For two hours I paced through the airport, from the gates to the ground-transportation area and back again. No Allan. I tried the irritatingly named yellow "courtesy" phone twice in order to page Allan, but it was busy both times. Meanwhile, Allan, an inert mass of confusion and growing annoyance, watched an unclaimed plaid suitcase make two hundred and seventy-nine trips around the luggage carousel.

I took a bus to the city and a cab from the depot while Allan drove his jeep back to his store. I stood at the doorstep of a Victorian house. I wasn't sure it was the right house: There were no nameplates by the doorbell or on the mailbox. I thought that maybe Allan had forgotten I was coming and gone with Eric to Tahoe for the weekend, or maybe he was still mad at me for not spending a few days of sin on Long Island with him last year, or maybe Eric had finally gotten fed up with Allan's New York boyfriends (I was one of many) and kidnapped him to Hawaii or in a jealous rage had murdered Allan and then committed suicide (but then I realized that was hardly possible, since Stephen Sondheim's *Follies* concert was scheduled for that week, and Eric wouldn't miss it for the world), or maybe I was at the wrong address, or maybe they had moved on me, and it was drizzling slightly, and I didn't know what to do; I didn't know how to get to the nearest YMCA or shelter for the homeless, and suddenly I found myself face to face with a Doberman pinscher that began to bark excitedly, and then, ten minutes and two quarts of profuse sweat later, Allan appeared at the stoop and rescued me.

"Gee, B.J., it's *great* to *see you*," said Allan. "I had *totally* given up on you at the airport: I called Eric and told him that you didn't show up and I was so pissed I didn't want to ever speak to you again, but here you are, and I'm *really glad* you've come. You'll have to come back and visit real soon. Next time we can go to Tahoe or Palm Springs or drive down the coast."

"Allan!" I shrieked. "I just *got* here. Cool down."

"Why, look, there's *Marie Antoinette* and *Josephine*," he said as the dogs tumbled down the stairs to greet him. Allan would italicize their names every time he spoke them for the next seven days. I shrunk to the corner of the entranceway. "Don't be afraid of my girls; they're *completely* harmless. Look, they like you already." One of them was sniffing my crotch. "Gee, I'm so glad you like them," he said as I cowered against the wall, holding my luggage up as protection. "I knew you would get along fine. I was honestly worried when you told me on the phone that you didn't like dogs."

We went upstairs and he showed me my room, a den with a TV and VCR on the cabinet and a Soloflex by the window. I was to use the Soloflex for drying out clothes in the coming week, the week of the floods.

"Well, anyway," said Allan, "I'm *really happy* to *see you*. We'll get to *spend* some *time* together."

For years Allan had called me on the phone and asked, "Gee, B.J., if it's not too much to ask, I'd really like to spend some time with you when I'm in New York." I'd say, "I'd much rather you spend money on me, but that's your prerogative." Then when he'd visit after the seventh or eighth cancellation, he'd hope that I'd have some free time blocked out for him, three to five days, and usually I'd be in the midst of a string of disastrous blind dates culled from the *Village Voice* personals or in the final stages of yet another dreadful nonaffair or dealing with another one of Richard's nervous breakdowns, and I'd be too irritable to cancel an entire weekend's worth of assignations to spend with Allan, who I was beginning to suspect was brain damaged, so typically I'd just meet him for cocktails if I could squeeze him in. Well, now that I was in San Francisco, it was a different story.

"Sunday," I said to Allan. "Sunday I'll be at your complete disposal. Do with me what you will."

"Don't be cheap and crude and vulgar," he countered.

LAYERS OF CLINICAL PSYCHOSES

Richard was staying at a halfway house nearby. I didn't think I needed an umbrella, because it was only drizzling when I left Allan's. By the time I reached the foot of the hill, it was pouring and I was soaked. An overweight man wearing bifocals showed me to Richard, who was upstairs, preparing a communal meal.

Richard looked the same as ever. He had put on a little weight. I was really happy to see him again. I had a lot of emotion invested in our friendship. In a way, we became closer after our tempestuous three-month relationship ended. I confided everything to Richard. Once we broke up, I was able to tell him about my many crushes and extramarital affairs without the threat of Tammy Wynette singing "D-I-V-O-R-C-E" to our respective attorneys-at-law. Richard was just a big softy beneath those pounds and pounds of muscle. Underneath the layers of clinical psychoses was a heart of gold.

Richard had left New York abruptly last fall. Like a boomerang, he returned to the city two weeks later. Another two weeks and he was back in San Francisco. He was hooked on Valium. He got into a detox program, then a halfway house for gay alcoholics, then a halfway house for the emotionally disturbed. If anyone knew how to take advantage of the social-service system, it was Richard.

Left to my own devices in New York, I tried calling Richard regularly. But he was usually at meetings or therapy or the gym; when I was able to reach him, it was just five minutes on the pay phone in the hall of the residence. There was a void in my life: I had no best friend. With no one to confide in, my exploits and adventures lacked substance and solidity; with no one to recount my tales to, they appeared to be inventions, fantasies, hallucinations.

This was the paradox: With Richard, I had subsumed my personality to some extent in his woes, losing some portion of my vague and ill-defined identity. Yet without Richard, my sense of self disappeared completely. And it seemed that this was an irrevocable loss.

Richard was sorry that I couldn't stay with him, but Tomorrow House was a therapeutic environment. I asked if I could stay for dinner. He went downstairs to get permission from the resident. "They have a lot of rules at Tomorrow House," he explained. "You get demerits if you miss a meeting or come late to dinner without calling beforehand. Ten demerits and you're out."

I was left holding a dish towel and facing his friend Maria, who was slicing tomatoes. She was concentrating intensely on making precise, even cuts. I thought of sending away for the incredible Vegomatic I had seen advertised on late night TV when I was a child, eons before the Cuisinart epoch, and offering it to her as a gift. Richard returned with the OK.

He was busy the next day. We decided to get together on Wednesday, the following day.

Dinner was awkward. I couldn't really talk to Richard in front of all of those strangers. We covered topics bland as the canned vegetables we ate. "You should probably get some rain-gear soon, B.J. I have a feeling we're in for quite a spell of rain," said Richard.

ACTS OF DEPRAVITY ILLEGAL IN AT LEAST SEVENTEEN STATES

Two days later I was lying in bed with Allan and his two flatulent but docile Doberman pinschers. They hadn't turned against me yet, but I knew it was only a matter of time. I was wearing a T-shirt from a college I had not attended in a city I had never visited, a pair of blue jeans, some Fruit-of-the-Loom underwear, and a pair of purple socks I had bought at Robbins (a tacky men's clothing store on Fourteenth Street in New York where everything is eight to eighty percent off) for a dollar. I had been taking Stresstabs constantly, since I was in foreign territory. Allan was wearing a gray Calvin Klein T-shirt that he *insisted* was a gift from one of his New York boyfriends (it wasn't me) and nothing else. Allan was buried under the covers, hiding from what should have been the sun but, since it was February and this was San Francisco, was deep cloud-cover; the sky was a vast expanse of gray.

It was the third day of my glorious rain-soaked vacation in fabulous San Francisco. I was having the very best time of my life, I kept on reminding myself. I didn't mind so long as Allan apologized for the weather each morning.

"Gee, I'm *really sorry* about the *weather*. It's been *raining cats* and *Marie Antoinettttes* since you arrived," said Allan from under the covers.

"OK. That takes care of today," I replied.

The reason that Allan and I were not performing acts of depravity illegal in at least seventeen states and immoral in another twelve, with or without the aid of the two docile but flatulent Dobermans, was downstairs making breakfast. His name was Eric, and Allan and he had been lovers for the past thirteen years. Although Eric was forty (Allan was thirty-five), he looked and acted at least ten years younger. Eric worked hard and played hard. He was a fast-talking dynamo in real estate. He loved the theater, discos, recreational drugs, dinner parties, sleaze, Allan, and Trivial Pursuit. Eric had a slight Brooklyn accent. Eric was around five-ten, with bright green eyes, brown hair, and considerable thickening around the middle. Eric was gulping his orange juice and two bowls of cereal and black coffee and a handful of vitamins because he had to be at the office by nine; he had a sales meeting scheduled for nine-thirty.

I was up at this ungodly hour because part of me was still on East Coast time. I had briefly toyed with keeping my watch on New York time but rejected this as too snobbish and impractical: I was on vacation, and there was no need to complicate matters unnecessarily. Then I thought I could play bicoastal with two Swatches (I had read this was fashionable for fifteen minutes about three years previously: I *always* try to be extremely fashionable and au courant three years after the fact. It's a harmless affectation. People are forever asking me insipid questions like "Oh, are skinny ties back in style again?"), but why should I stop at two? Why not have a watch for every significant city in the world? But I feared my bulging biceps would preclude such an action.

Allan stayed under the covers, huddling against his creatures of the night.

"Did you sleep well last night?" asked Allan.

"Sure."

"You know, your bed is better than ours. Yesterday Eric said that we would have joined you, but unfortunately the bed doesn't sleep five."

"What a disgusting thought. Were you planning on inviting two more lovers to torture me in my pitiful old-maidenhood?"

"No, he meant you and me and him and *Marie Antoinette* and *Josephine*."

"Tell me about Marie Antoinette's name again," I asked.

Allan paused and cleared his throat. "*Marie Antoinette* is named after the wife of King Louis XVI. *Marie Antoinette* is one of the very finest examples of the species known as the Jewish American Princess. She is royalty and should be treated as such. There is a votive candle burning on the table downstairs."

"To cover Marie Antoinette's farts?"

"Don't be crude, you unspeakable monster. Let me start again, pretending I didn't hear that insolent comment. There is a votive candle burning on the table downstairs. Do you know what scent it is?"

My brow furrowed in concentration. Sweat rolled down my forehead like the floods from the heavens. It was the $64,000 question, and time was running out. Right at the buzzer I ventured, "Could it be . . . could it be marigold?"

"Marie Antoinette Gold," said Allan. "Gee, I hope the weather clears up soon, or I will die of sheer depression."

HELIUM HEELS

"Have you ever autofellated?" I asked Allan, because I was bored.

"Have I ever *what*?"

"Have you ever autofellated?"

"What sort of a question is that how dare you what does it mean?" When Allan was excited, he tended to speak continuously, without the benefit of punctuation.

"I'll give you a clue: This has nothing to do with giving a blow job in the car."

"Have I ever autofellated? Have I ever sucked my own penis?

Is that what you're asking? Why I've never heard of such a thing it would never have occurred to me I don't think it's humanly possible do you?"

"I've seen it in the movies."

"Well I'm *not* that kind of person you *know* I don't go to *those* movies I wouldn't watch such *vile* pornography *not* in front of my girls do you want to rent one tonight for educational purposes only?"

"I can show you how to do it, roughly." I lifted my legs above my head and strained toward the nether regions. I was only a foot away.

"Don't you have to take off your pants first?" asked Allan.

"None of that now," I chided.

Allan and I talked about sex because it was much more fun than actually doing it. Safe sex was the operative. I suppose if I were ever able to actually stretch and reach myself, I would sheathe myself in a condom to prevent the possibility of transmitting some heinous disease to myself. Who knows? Maybe my lips would be cracked, or there'd be a canker sore. I'm so paranoid I masturbate with a water-based nonoxynol-9 lubricant. One can't be too careful.

I gave up on the demonstration. Allan promised he would try at every available opportunity. I lay down on the bed.

"Look," I said, "there they go again." My legs began to levitate. I would push them down, but then they would rise again, as if of their own power. "Are we weightless?"

"It's just those helium heels of yours," said Allan. "You're exposing your uterus. *Marie Antoinette* will get jealous." I stopped.

"Can I see your tan line?" I tried to lift the blankets off Allan.

"You most certainly cannot." He grabbed them tightly around his waist. "Modesty prohibits." I averted my eyes as he got out of bed, finally, to get dressed.

Marie Antoinette's Uterus Is Leaking

"Don't you dare take a photograph of me, seminude or otherwise." I had the camera hidden behind my back. The batteries were low, so by the time the flash was ready, Allan was already half-dressed. I got one nice shot of Allan protecting his left nipple from the onslaught of the paparazzi. Then he looked at the bed and said, "Shit. *Marie Antoinette's* uterus is leaking again." There was a stain on the sheet, and it wasn't from me or Allan or Eric.

Marie Antoinette had a bladder problem.

"The veterinarian *gave* me some *pills* to dry *up Marie Antoinette's* uterus but I asked him would he give his wife these pills to dry up her uterus? Or his daughters? I would *never* do such a thing to *Marie Antoinette*." Allan stripped the bed and went downstairs to toss the dirty sheets into the washer. "I'm going to take the girls out for a walk." The dogs were black and sleek and had floppy ears because Allan wouldn't let them be clipped. "Here we come down like a thundering herd," he said as they raced down the stairs.

Allan came back from his walk and made some coffee. I asked him to try to fellate himself when he was at work, and he said that I was keeping him against his will.

"I'm not going to wear any underwear today. I want some action. You know I'm just kidding, don't you?" I didn't.

Richard and I had a cryptic conversation at nine-thirty.

"I can't talk," he said in hushed tones.

"What do you mean? What's the matter?"

"Just give me the address, and I'll be over in half an hour," he whispered. I recited the address and he hung up.

Allan waited as long as he could to meet Richard. He left at ten-fifteen; he had to open the store.

Richard showed up ten minutes after Allan left. He explained that he wasn't supposed to be in the house during the day, but he had forgotten my number, so he had to wait for my call. He got two more demerits. "Jesus, are those Dobermans?" The dogs were sniffing his crotch.

I assured him that they meant no harm.

"Dobermans turn against their masters," he said in abject terror. "Let's get the hell out of here."

We took the train to the Castro for breakfast. Richard miscalculated the stop, so we had to walk seven blocks in the downpour. I groused about the weather. I got waffles; Richard got an omelet. We talked about Jessica, his cat. Richard complained about not having any friends in San Francisco. He wasn't sure whether or not he would return to New York. There were pluses and minuses; he hadn't fully weighed them.

We walked down Castro and ducked into Headlines. I bought three ties for five dollars; one of them was so atrocious I just *had* to have it. I figured I was bound to do something I would regret in San Francisco, and it might as well be this tie. At least that would be safe. The Castro wasn't the den of iniquity I had remembered five years earlier on my last visit, but then neither was Christopher Street. Cruising was almost obsolete. In bars men focused on their glasses, not each other. Allan told me that last year stuffing crotches with socks was all the rage, but I saw no evidence of the "padded look." This year the boys seemed chunkier. If anything, the pads had gravitated to the hips. Richard said that lean was out in San Francisco because it held that "sudden unexplained weight loss" aura about it, and that everyone had a good ten pounds to spare, as if ten pounds could protect one from death.

Richard took me to the Country Club, a nonalcoholic coffeehouse. We sat at a window table and watched a steady stream of people flow into the Blue Whale across the street. We talked about our health. Richard got tired occasionally; my herpes attacks were down to twice a year. I asked Richard why he moved to San Francisco: I figured I could get a straight answer because he wasn't hooked on any substances at the moment. I was half hoping he'd apologize for leaving me in the lurch, on two days' notice. Sometimes I wondered whether Richard was aware of anyone's feelings save his own. He gave me his stock response about being sick of New York, the crowds, the weather, the dog-eat-dog attitude. Then he thanked me for sticking with him through thick and thin. He realized that things had been difficult for us. He really cared. It meant a lot for me to hear this. We walked back to the subway stop. We hugged and parted.

Nights and Days in Seedy Homosexual Establishments in the Hopes of Finding True Bliss and Romance

Allan took me to a vegetarian Vietnamese restaurant on Thursday. He complained about his life nonstop, from the egg-roll appetizer to the dessert plum-wine. Allan tried to talk me into watching *Mildred Pierce* on the VCR, but I reminded him that he had promised to take me to the bare-chest contest at the Eagle that night. We ran into Richard on our way back to the Volvo. He was soaked. Rain poured off his rain-hat in rivulets. Richard was out for a walk. He was late for a meeting at the halfway house and decided to bag it. Richard was sick and tired of all of the rules and regulations. He was disgusted with the nonstop rain. He said he might come back to New York.

Allan decided that Richard was completely insane to refuse a ride. We arrived at the Eagle at around eleven. In front of the bar was a motorcade of Harley Davidsons. When we got inside, contestant number three was being examined by the crowd and the emcee, a drag queen named Naughty Nancy.

Bars generally depress me. Two nights before, I had gone to the Midnight Sun, a bar right off Castro. It was a nightmare. I felt like the star of *Gidget Goes to Clone Hell*. Everyone was six feet tall, and they were all watching these tiny video screens far above my head. I felt as if I still had several stages of evolutionary development left in order to catch up.

"Gee B.J. do you think it's too late to enter I'm sure you'd win first prize. I wish I had remembered to take *Marie Antoinette* along with me she would probably have gotten extra points because she has at least six breasts although I am far too discrete to count them individually myself."

"Shh, Allan," I said. "Pipe down for a moment so I can hear."

Naughty Nancy was asking the contestant what his favorite fantasy was. The answer was garbled in the noise of the crowd; I think it had something to do with three truckers, a deserted alleyway, and a crowbar. Allan became bored almost immediately. "I wanna go home," he whined. "How gross and repulsive this all is. I truly pity those of you unmarried bachelorettes. I don't have to spend nights and days in seedy homosexual establishments in the hopes of finding true bliss and romance. I have *Marie Antoinette* and *Josephine* to keep me company and Eric to buy me shirts and take me to Hawaii whenever I'm down in the dumps. How can you stand this? I've never understood why you're single, B.J. I'm going to have to go now."

"I want to stay for a while," I said.

"OK, see you tomorrow, I guess. Gee, thanks a lot for having me drive all the way across town to this unhealthy and unclean bar just to watch some depressing queens and a fifth-rate beauty pageant."

"Oh, and thanks for the ride, Allan, I really appreciate it."

"Oh, it was nothing. Bye. I have to get back soon so I can walk *Marie Antoinette* and *Josephine*." Allan left.

Contestant four was the best by far. Dubbed The Saucy Aussie by the emcee, Paul was a bartender from a rival bar. He knew all of the judges, one of them intimately. That was his downfall. Paul was from Melbourne and had a wit like a whip. Moreover, he was doomed to second place because he upstaged the judges. He accused one of his rivals of using mascara to outline his pecs, and the audience hooted.

I was standing by the bar. A few feet away stood the cutest man in the entire place. He was around six feet tall and had blond hair. Typically enough, not a single other man in the entire bar looked the slightest bit attractive to me. I was fully prepared to spend the next three hours staring at him in the futile hope that he would return my gaze. I always hate it when I don't have an alternative to fall back on.

I took a cab back home at around one.

A Harlot High and Low

The next morning I woke up and went to the kitchen. Allan was dressed, humming an old Rodgers and Hart tune.

"Allan, last night when I got back, you hadn't returned. Where were you?"

"Well I was outside of the bar talking just talking to this guy he was a truck driver I mean I guess I was a truck driver and so we were talking for about an hour he was very nice and then inside the cab of the truck he sucked my weenie I didn't ask him to do it he just did it oh no don't tell me you believed that I wasn't serious how *could* you and you're one to talk you haven't spent a single night here how dare you accuse me of such bad behavior I wouldn't dream of trashing the town not like you've been doing this past week you haven't spent a single night here. Every night you've slept out with strange men, you little trollop you, you shameless hussy; you're a harlot high and low, a vixen with heaving bosoms, shoving them into strange men's faces; you're just a bawdy barmaid with beer sloshing over your heaving bosoms."

"Did you try it?" I asked Allan.

"Did I try *what*?"

"You know, autofellation."

"Of course not, would I do a thing like that? Well, once or twice driving back from that seedy bar—what was it called, Suck My Meaty Weenie? But it was while the light was red I got real close to success but then the light changed and the three hundred and seventy-five cars behind me started honking their horns it was just like in New York City near the Lincoln Tunnel so I had to stop and zip up but very carefully because I didn't want to catch my foreskin and anyway I think I've been making some tremendous progress although I must admit it's an uphill battle. Tell you what: I'm going to practice every night, and as soon as I succeed, I'm going to *call* you immediately. I don't care if it's four in the morning New York time or what, I'm going to call you at once."

"Are you going to do it in front of Eric once you perfect it?" I asked.

"*Of course not!* Eric has never seen me naked what sort of a person do you think I am?" asked Allan incredulously.

"Tonight," I said to Allan, "I'm taking you and Eric out to dinner. We can go wherever you like, so long as it isn't *too* expensive and they take Visa."

"Gee, B.J., you don't have to do that," said Allan. "That's very sweet of you to offer. I'll ask Eric if it's OK with him."

They decided on a seafood restaurant near the Civic Center.

"Is it dressy?" I asked. "Oh, shit." I was going through my clothes and couldn't find a *thing* to wear because absolutely everything had gotten soaked from the rain. "I'd better go shopping today. I'm running out of clothes again."

"Let *me* do your laundry. I *insist*," said Allan, tugging at my socks and pants.

"I don't want to impose. You're sure it's not too much trouble?" I had completely forgotten how to run a washer myself. Back in Manhattan I spent all of the money I saved on rent with my cheap slumlord flat in charming Hell's Kitchenette on service laundry and sending out my shirts. Aeons ago, when I lived in Venice, California, I didn't mind doing laundry myself because they had unstaffed twenty-four-hour Laundromats on Lincoln Boulevard and you could go and drop off your laundry at two A.M. and then cruise down five miles to get some donuts at Arlene's in Santa Monica and then come back to transfer your clothes from the washer to the drier and you would never have to wait, like you do in New York, where there are only six washers and driers available for customers—the rest are for service—and the Laundromats are staffed by Spanish matrons who gossip all day long and there is usually a drug addict in front constantly rocking on the bench and the last wash is scheduled for half an hour after you get home from work. And in Venice, while your clothes were drying, you could pleasantly read a paperback because there would be only one or two other people there at 2:30 in the morning, maybe an evening-shift nurse with an interesting theory on how stress relates to cancer or an actor reading the works of Strindberg or a subdued housewife from Ocean Park with insomnia.

"Of course not you're the guest I'm the host it's my duty to make your stay here as pleasurable as I can here let me get you out of those creepy clothes they stink to high heaven."

"No, what I'm wearing is OK. It's *these* that are dirty." I handed Allan a plastic garbage-bag filled with dirty laundry. We went downstairs to the laundry room near the back porch. I watched as he transferred what was in the washer to the drier and threw my clothes into the washer.

We left for dinner at around seven. Eric said, "You look like a bar-mitzvah boy," and it was true; I looked quite innocent. People tend to forget I am capable of wearing nice clothes. I wear T-shirts and jeans all the time. It's a pleasant surprise to see me in a jacket and tie. I was wearing a gray-and-white striped linen hand-me-down jacket with an all-but-imperceptible tomato-soup stain on the lapel that I had found in the recesses of my closet back at my mom's in upstate New York. I was also wearing one of my three-for-five-dollar ties, but not the totally regrettable one.

We darted through the rain. The restaurant had singing waiters and waitresses. I winced. I figured if they had to distract you from the meal with Puccini arias, then the food would be mediocre at best. We ate in the sidewalk glassed-in extension, so the racket wasn't too bad. The bright incandescent spotlights were trained on the main dining area. I had my traditional Calistoga and lime. Eric had a double scotch; Allan ordered a Miller. Eric asked me, "I've been wondering about you. Don't you have any vices? I haven't seen you drink liquor yet. Who do you think you are, Little Lord Fauntleroy?"

I explained, "I have a very low capacity, and my vision isn't the best, and I'm afraid if I get tipsy, I may go home with the wrong person by mistake, and *that* would be tragic."

We had an overgenerous selection of mutant California fried vegetables for an appetizer: sequoia mushrooms, gargantuan zucchinis, and buttermilk dip. The main course was anticlimactic. I had seafood and pasta. Eric had stuffed flounder. Allan, whose tastes are rather limited, had a cheeseburger. To prove my sophistication, I asked, "Have you guys ever heard of a drug called Special K? I heard some people talking about it at the BeBop Club a few weeks ago in New York."

"That's a breakfast cereal gee don't you know any better?" said Allan.

"You only *just* heard about K? Where have you been, in seclusion?" Eric was lisping. "Special K has been around for years. I think it came out the same time as Extasy."

"Oh," I said. I didn't bother asking what that was.

Allan dropped me off at a bar on Market called Detour and wished me luck. "If it doesn't work out, you can call me any hour of the night and I'll come and pick you up," said Allan.

I entered the bar. I had to zigzag around a black curtain at the door. My eyes gradually adjusted to the dark decor. There were a few spotlit areas for the experienced poseurs; otherwise, it was murky with smoke. I went to the john because I was nervous. Inside, I saw a prophylactic dispenser that could have come from a gas station on Interstate 901. I got a beer and sat on a stack of empties in cartons against the wall. Two guys were playing pool seriously. I was the only one in the entire bar with a jacket and tie. Two beers later I hopped into a cab and went home.

THE NEGRESS LAUNDRESSES HAVE LOVINGLY
FOLDED YOUR LAUNDRY

I saw Allan on the couch in the living room, poring over the latest issue of *Metropolis.* "How are you?" I asked.

"I'm fine. Gee-thanks-a-lot. While you were out having a good time, I finished your laundry. The Negress laundresses have lovingly folded your laundry," he replied.

"Oh, great, that was really kind of you."

"*Marie Antoinette* and *Josephine* helped me. They watched as I slowly and laboriously folded those mounds and mounds of laundry you left me. I felt like a princess trapped in a tower, sentenced to fold laundry for the rest of my natural life. Mind you, I'm not complaining. I'm not trying to make you feel guilty. As though you were capable of such a feeling, you hedonistic piece of trash. I'm merely stating the facts."

"Oh, now I feel awful. Poor Marie Antoinette. I didn't know that dogs could fold laundry. How clever they are, those witches."

"Don't *ever* mention that word in front of my girls. They're *not* bitches. What a horrible thing to say."

"But I didn't—"

"*Marie Antoinette* and *Josephine* are shocked and most displeased at this display of ingratitude. They spent *hours* on your laundry. Actually," he admitted, "I must confess, they only watched and gave helpful hints. They told me whether I was doing a good job or not. In specific instances they instructed me to unfold a shirt or a pair of pants and then try again. My beautiful little angels are so talented that I don't think I've even begun to scratch the surface of their endless abilities."

"Well, anyway, thanks again. See you tomorrow." I kissed Allan and went to bed.

LARGER THAN LIFE

I wandered to the bathroom in the middle of the night. Eric was just leaving the bathroom and hadn't yet stuffed his penis back into his pj's. I was traumatized. "Can't sleep?" he asked.

"I just have to make a votive offering to the porcelain goddess," I replied, ignoring his penis.

"Catch you later," said Eric, still forgetting to stuff it back.

I dashed back to my room and shut the door. I considered moving the Soloflex to block the door and decided it would wake the dogs.

I went downstairs to the living room the next morning and there were Allan and Marie Antoinette. "Hi," he said. "Eric kicked us out last night. He said we were whining too much. All I did was ask him to take me to Palm Springs. The rain has worn my nerves down to a frazzle. *Marie Antoinette* and I are too depressed for words." Eric was already at work by then.

"Allan, I have something to tell you."

"How was last night? Did you have a nice time? I was so completely exhausted from the hours and hours of *lovingly* folding your laundry that I fell into a deep sleep the moment I lay down."

"It was great. Listen, Allan, is Eric trying to seduce me?"

"*Everyone* is trying to seduce you but that's beside the point why do you ask?"

"Last night, when I went to perform my nocturnal ablutions, I saw him briefly, and his penis was exposed to me."

"You mean he waved his throbbing manhood at you?" Allan asked incredulously.

"No, he had just come out from the bathroom, and there it was."

"—larger than life?" continued Allan.

"I don't know. I only saw it out of the corner of my eye."

"Gee, B.J., I don't know. I think he may have a crush on you too. Ever since he saw those pictures you sent me."

How Could You Possibly Do Such a Thing?

"You showed him those pictures?" In a weak moment, years ago, when I was still hopelessly infatuated with Allan, I had sent him some revealing photos of myself.

"Why yes of course he's my lover I show him everything I service him and sleep with him and let him see my wee-wee whenever he wants and let him buy me shirts and take me to Hawaii of course I let him see those pictures."

Those photographs have plagued me for years.

"Why didn't you tell me?" I asked.

"I just thought you knew it doesn't matter does it I mean if they were private and personal photographs then they wouldn't be in a magazine now would they I don't understand what you're making such a fuss over anyway."

"What magazine? Christ, Allan, sometimes you're impossible."

"If it's any solace to you, I didn't show them to *Marie Antoinette*. She's too delicate for that sort of thing. Her poor sensitive heart might burst if she were shown such shocking photographs. So at least there's *someone* in this house that doesn't know what you look like naked—that is, unless you've taken off your clothes in front of my daughter *Marie Antoinette*, and if you have, I'll have you arrested, you filthy pervert you, corrupting the morals of my little girl. How could you possibly do such a thing? How could anyone stoop so low? Some things are just beyond me."

Now I Can Bother You All Day

"Hurry up, Allan, come on, I don't have all day," said Eric. When he was annoyed, he lisped slightly. It was Sunday, and the three of us were going out for breakfast. Eric had to get some papers signed at ten A.M., so we had to be out of the house by nine. Allan was phlegmatic as usual.

I bounded into Allan's bedroom and jumped up and down on his bed. "Allan, guess what day it is?"

His eyes were bleary. "It's *early*. It's too early for it to be day. Try me in the afternoon."

"It's *Sunday*, and I'm all yours."

Allan perked up. "Good. Now I can bother you all day."

I went back to my room to put in my contacts. When I have my glasses on, it's just too horrible for words: I look as though I had single-handedly translated the entire Talmud. The dogs followed me into the room. Allan said that they were constantly cold because they had such sleek forms and light fur, and that was why they would huddle so close to you: for body heat. I sat on the edge of the bed, and Marie Antoinette nudged up next to me, and Josephine curled beside her. I was wedged between two Dobermans, and there was nothing I could do. I wondered whether Allan had any tranquilizers.

"I'm *so glad* you're getting along with my girls," said Allan from the other room. "You're *completely* comfortable with them, aren't you?"

The dogs readjusted themselves, closer, pushing me off the bed in the process. I went back into Allan's bedroom and asked, "Did you try it?"

"You mean the thing?"

"Yes."

"You mean, did I try to suck my own member?"

"Yes."

"I *completely* forgot. It *totally* escaped my mind. I must have driven it out subconsciously. I even forgot to tell *Eric* about it."

"You were probably too busy reading *Architectural Digest* last night to try it." I had peeked in to say goodnight. Allan had his reading glasses on and was seriously poring over the latest issue. Eric was studying some contracts.

"I don't read that trashy pornographic magazine how dare you it must have been a horrible dream," streamed Allan.

"Why don't you try now?"

"You mean like this?" Allan put his legs above his head. "No, it doesn't reach." This time he had his pj bottoms on. I restrained the temptation to unbutton the back flap. Even though Allan was an honorary Jewish American Princess, he still had his foreskin, which gave him a decided advantage over me in autofellation, or so I suspected.

"Allan, are you really in love with me more than anyone in the entire world?"

"*Of course I am,*" he protested, "except for *Marie Antoinette* and *Josephine* and Eric."

"You can move in with me to my fabulous New York apartment—"

"That dump? That hellhole in Hell's Kitchen?"

"—on one condition. You'll have to get circumsized. I don't want any smegma in my duplex."

"Don't be so crude and disgusting. I haven't even had my morning coffee yet. I won't stand for such behavior in my house. I'll sic *Marie Antoinette* and *Josephine* on you."

"Oh, and you'll have to leave the dogs with Eric."

"*How could you even suggest such a thing?* I don't *want* to live with anyone. I'm terribly crazy head-over-heels-in-love with Eric. Besides, when I move back to New York, I want to be left completely alone. I'm tired of having everyone look after my own best interest. I want to be alone except for my girls, of course, *Marie Antoinette* and *Josephine.* I would *never* go anywhere without them. You're in love with them too almost as much as I am, aren't you?"

"I'm coping," I said.

"You know, once I invited a trick over to the house. This was many years ago, back when I was still having boyfriends. I had been going to a therapist who told me I should stop having boyfriends. I realized she was right: I didn't have enough time to devote to them, let alone to Eric. So I dropped my therapist. That gave me an extra five hours a week, plus travel time. That was *plenty* of time for a boyfriend. Anyway, I brought someone home when Eric was on a trip, and the dogs got him unnerved." Marie Antoinette and Josephine had stealthily crept into the room and huddled next to Allan on the bed. Now they moved closer, if that was possible, when they heard they were being discussed. I didn't know why; I'm sure they had already heard this story a thousand times. "*Marie Antoinette* started to whine because she's a Jewish American Princess and wanted her walk. They're utterly harmless. My girls scare some people. I can't imagine why two gentle Doberman pinschers would upset anyone. They're so beautiful. Look, *Marie Antoinette* is showing you her heart-shaped vulva. She's a virgin, just like me."

George walked in. George was the cat. "Look, there's my son George. Now the whole family's here." George spent most of his time sleeping in the guest room in a big picnic basket that Eric had bought Allan in London. Sometimes George would play with the girls, but usually he just curled up in his basket and took naps. I petted George on the neck, and Allan finished his story.

"Anyway, this *person* that I took home takes one look at the dogs and asks me if I wouldn't mind keeping them in another room. I said, 'Yes, I *would* mind.' They were growling softly. They didn't like him one bit. I said, 'Well, if you don't feel comfortable, you can always leave, because I wouldn't do that to my girls. I wouldn't dream of locking them up in the attic.' Besides, we don't have an attic. And so he left."

The dogs started boxing on the bed. They playfully tapped one another with their paws and bared their teeth, pretending to look fierce. It got a little too physical for my comfort when I saw some froth at their mouths.

"It's just a little saliva, you little coward," said Allan as I leapt from the bed.

"Allan, you have exactly five minutes," shouted Eric from the kitchen downstairs. This had the desired effect. Ten minutes later we trundled into the BMW and drove to a delightful restaurant on the other side of town. It was only six or seven hills away.

Our attractive and attentive waiter was straight. Eric used to go there once a week, so he knew.

I lifted the plates and glasses to see who manufactured them.

"What a horribly tacky thing to do in public don't you have any manners at all?" said Allan.

"The crystal isn't Waterford. And the plates aren't Wedgwood china. I'm afraid we'll have to leave."

"Oh don't be such a poof and just order why don't you," said Allan. We all had six-egg breakfasts with hollandaise and béarnaise and mayonnaise sauces and deadly nitrite-spiked pork by-products. It was delicious.

"The wipers on the BMW have been giving me trouble," said Eric. "I went to the dealer last week, but they didn't fix it right."

"Let me do it," said Allan. "I know how to adjust them."

"OK. *Not now,*" said Eric. "We're eating. It's drizzling outside."

"It will only take a moment," said Allan, bolting from the table. "I'll go out right now and do it."

"He's very cute and eccentric," said Eric, "but after thirteen years it gets a bit tiring. Sometimes I think I deserve a medal for distinguished service and valor for putting up with him."

"He's very endearing," I said. "Especially the way he is totally devoted to Marie Antoinette and—what was the other one's name?"

"Don't tell me you believe that Marie Antoinette's her real name? He changes their names every few months to suit his fancy."

"You mean all of the Marie Antoinette shit is a complete fraud?"

"Her real name is Princess. She was Princess Grace of Monaco a few years back."

"Oh." I was stunned. Allan burst back into the room, filled with self-satisfaction.

"It's fixed now," he announced.

We finished breakfast, discussing old movies and Stephen Sondheim's *Follies* concert at Lincoln Center. At the end of the meal Eric said, "The current lending rate is 10.5 percent," and wrote "entertaining out-of-town investors" on the bill for tax purposes and asked me which honorific I would prefer preceding my name. Eric dropped Allan and me off back at the house and went to work. Allan immediately returned to bed.

"It's so rainy and depressing. I'm *really sorry* that the weather's been so creepy," moped Allan.

"That takes care of Sunday," I said, checking it off my list. "Don't forget to apologize for the weather tomorrow. It is totally your fault, and I don't want to have to remind you."

"What do you want to do today?"

"Maybe we can go to a museum."

"I wanted the weather to be nice for you when you came. I wanted to drive down the coast and take my monsters from Planet X along with me. My little Josettes could run along the beach. We could watch the fog rolling in. It's too cold and cloudy today. Shit."

Ralph, one of Allan's old boyfriends, called. "What am I doing? I'm in the bed with B.J. and *Marie Antoinette* and *Josephine*. No, we're not seminude at all. The weather is really getting me down. It's such a drag. Do you want to do something today? You do?" Ralph wanted to go out with Allan, but when he heard that I'd be coming along too, he changed his mind. He wasn't up to meeting someone new. They talked for about an hour. I went downstairs and picked up a book from Eric's office. They were arranged by subject: There was a movie section, a biography section, and a gay-fiction section. I started reading Renaud Camus's *Tricks*. Allan finally hung up.

"Eric told me during breakfast that Marie Antoinette isn't really Marie Antoinette, that that's just a name you made up for her." I looked accusingly at Allan.

"He did? That vicious pathological liar. How dare he! Of *course* her name is *Marie Antoinette*. He's just jealous of me and my devoted vampires from outer space. Try calling her anything but Her Royal Eminence and Imperial Majesty the Contessa *Marie Antoinette* and see if she responds. I am truly shocked that you believed him. How *could* you?"

I gave up. "So what are we going to do? I'm not going to sit at home all day and listen to you whining about the weather. You don't want to go to a museum?"

"*Marie Antoinette* hates museums; she finds them stultifying," complained Allan.

"Let's go to a gym." I told Allan of my plan to make a complete and utterly exhaustive study of San Francisco gyms during my visit. "We can go to the sleazy Body Center. It's free for me, since I belong to the New York branch."

"Why do you call it sleazy?"

"Because I'm a member, that's why." It's so much easier to pick up men at gyms than at bars. They're less likely to pass out on you, and you can inspect the merchandise in the shower.

"I have a lot of studying to do." Allan was taking a class in accounting, and he *had* to get an A. "I'm *so behind*. What with the store and our rental properties and *Marie Antoinette* and *Josephine*, I don't know how I'll get anything done."

"OK," I said sarcastically. "Thanks for *spending* all of this *time* with me like you promised. We can talk about it the next time I come to visit, which will be July 1997 at this rate. I'll just take a bus down to the gym by myself."

"No, you're right. Let's go to the gym." We rode in Allan's jeep. The rain hadn't let up. It took us a while to find a parking spot on the street. Allan forgot his baseball cap in the jeep and got soaked. "I want to have *enormous heaving breasts* like you," whined Allan. "I don't know why I don't already. I work out three times a week on the Soloflex."

"That's a wimpy machine."

"I used to go to the MidCity Gym by the Castro, but men kept on asking me to do nasty things with them, the sort of things that I had never heard of, so I just told them I was married and had two daughters (that's *Marie Antoinette* and *Josephine*) and a son (my son, George), but they still kept bothering me, so I just had to quit."

The gym was totally dilapidated, but the men weren't that bad. Outside it was raining buckets. I had borrowed Allan's yellow rain-slicker he had bought in the children's department at Brooks Brothers. I felt like an illustration from a Dick and Jane book.

Allan was slow and methodical on the Nautilus machines. I flitted rapidly from one to another. "I've never seen anyone work out as fast as you. Your arms were really flapping on the chest machine," said Allan.

"Yeah, I'm a regular human wind-machine. You'd better secure your hairpiece if you're working out next to me. I'm like a hummingbird, aren't I?" I rarely take kindly to criticism.

We sat in the steam room for a while, and I stared at a few naked bodies, trying to will their penises up (the famous Arabian snake-in-the-basket trick), and failed. Then we left and were completely soaked by the torrential downpour.

Allan wanted to study and catch up on his homework that night, so I went to a disco called the I-Beam alone. It was Sunday tea-dance, and it was really packed. The coat-check line took half an hour. Two huge video screens dominated the dance floor. I performed my spastic tribute to Buddy Holly on electroconvulsives and got ditched by two men. The first told me to wait while he went to the bathroom, and then he saw some friends on the way back and just expected me to wait another twenty minutes, and I was furious because he didn't even tell me, and it was so completely crowded that it took me *forever* to even find him. The second guy I danced with went back to look for his friend and was swallowed alive by the dance floor like the lava pit in the second *Indiana Jones* movie. I was exhausted after my deranged Ann-Margret–conquers–Las Vegas routine, which was just as well; by nine it was too crowded to dance anyway.

I returned to Allan's, and there were Allan and Ralph on the sofa. It was completely innocent; they were looking at photos from Allan and Eric's vacation in Hawaii. It turned out that five minutes after I left for the I-Beam Ralph called to see if Allan could go out to dinner, and he did. I was a little annoyed because it was supposed to be his day for me. We took Ralph (who was quite nice) home in the jeep. Eric was home when we returned. We played a game of Trivial Pursuit, and I came in last. Eric offered cocaine. I turned it down. I felt the occasion didn't warrant drugs.

I've Only Slept with Four People in My Entire Life and That Includes My Mother When I Was in Her Womb

"Gee it's great to see you I'm going to miss you a lot I think I already miss you B.J. you'll have to come back soon. Do you want some coffee?" asked Allan, even though he knew I didn't drink coffee. "We have a very busy day planned ahead of us. You know, I'm taking off the entire day from work so I can spend some time with *you*."

"I thought you had an important appointment this morning with a client to discuss the possibility of remodeling her home."

"*That* can wait. *You're* more important."

I yawned. "That's really quite nice of you. Do you think we have time for a nap?"

"B.J., I thought we had discussed this previously at great length. We are *not* to sleep together. That would be *sinful*. Eric doesn't allow it. What are you thinking of I've only slept with four people in my entire life and that includes my mother when I was in her womb which wasn't sexual at all how dare you," he said. "Are you ready yet?" he continued without losing a breath.

"Ready for what?"

"It's your last day in San Francisco, and we had better go to the Castro."

I had been to the Castro five out of the six previous days. I was a little sick of it but decided to keep my reservations to myself.

"We'll have a marvelous breakfast at the Patio," said Allan, "and then we get you a new bathing suit."

"Really?" I perked up a bit. I love shopping, almost as much as the telephone, and certainly more than any of my ex-boyfriends.

"Sure, I feel I owe you a suit for the one you sent me two years ago."

"It's a deal."

NINETEEN THOUSAND TERRIFIED HAIRDRESSERS FLEE VALLEY

I took a quick shower to wake up, and we were off. Breakfast was muffins and tea and juice at a pleasant little restaurant off the Castro. It was windy. I dashed into a store and picked up a sweater for next to nothing. Then we went to an extremely homosexual boutique and after much exhaustive consideration selected the precise suit that fit me to a T. On the way we saw the *Herald Examiner* in the racks on the sidewalk; the headline read "Nineteen Thousand Flee Valley." Nineteen thousand people had been evacuated from the nearby valley due to extensive flooding and mud-slides.

Allan said, "Nineteen thousand terrified hairdressers flee valley. Can you imagine?" I couldn't.

"I've always wanted to be a hairdresser," I mused, "ever since I saw *Shampoo* with Warren Beatty. Didn't you love it when Julie Christie said she wanted to suck him off at the restaurant?"

"Don't be shameful, you lecherous nymphomaniac."

"Have you ever thought of being a hairdresser? I have a friend who did Rosemary Clooney's hair for the Macy's Thanksgiving Day Parade."

"I've always wanted to go to the Wilfred Academy of Stylistics and Beautification," said Allan.

"Do you mean the Wilfred Academy of Beauty?" I asked.

"It *does* have the highest standards of any school, doesn't it? It's harder to get into than Harvard Law School, isn't it? If I went to the Wilfred Academy of Beauticians and Cosmology, I'd *definitely* get a job with Charles of the Ritz, wouldn't I?"

"Maybe even Maison Venus," I offered. Maison Venus, a Village fixture, with its potted palms in the window and silhouettes of Barbie Doll dos, is possibly the most tacky beauty salon in the known universe.

"I'm just sick and tired of the boring world of architecture and design."

"As for me, I've had it with the exciting world of data processing."

AT LEAST I DIDN'T MANIPULATE
MYSELF IN PUBLIC

"That salesman was really working you over," said Allan as we drove back to the house to pick up my suitcase. "He was licking his lips."

"He was licking his *labian* lips," I corrected.

"He was. That man was a serpent."

"But why did you have me try on so many suits?" I asked innocently.

"It was all for the salesman's benefit. Did you notice he had a semierection? Did you notice his semitumescent penis flailing away in his loose-fitting pleated pants?"

"Is that why he had his hands in the pockets?"

"I should think so," said Allan. "I myself had a similar condition, but at least I didn't manipulate myself in public, not like that serpent."

"And then you made me take off my sweater and shirt," I pouted.

"The way I remember, you were the one who kept on insisting on trying the black suit on. It barely covered your pendulous testicles. How could you have even considered it?"

"It was for comparison purposes only," I protested.

"Incidentally, I didn't want to mention this, but is your uterus leaking too? I noticed a tiny drop on one of the suits as you tried it on."

"You *most certainly did not*. It must have been something in your eye. It was probably your hay-fever acting up again." I was miffed.

"Well anyway that serpent wanted to eat you right then and there he was fondling his semierect excrescence in front of us I'm never going to shop there again. Gee, B.J., I'm going to miss you a whole lot. Would you mind if I took some photographs of you in that new suit that fits you so exquisitely?"

"Why not?" I must confess, I experience this helpless Pavlovian response: Whenever I see a bulb flash or hear a camera click, I immediately start doffing my clothes. This can be embarrassing if, say, I'm walking down Fifth Avenue and there happens to be a fashion shoot going on. Back in Allan's home I stripped in ten seconds flat. I stuffed myself into my brand-new bathing suit and lay down on the plastic lawn-chair out on the deck on the second floor by Allan's bedroom. The dogs looked at me curiously.

"Hurry up, Allan, I'm freezing," I said. Allan came out and took three photos, but then he was out of film.

"Damn," he said.

"That's it?" I asked. "There goes your last chance."

"You're sure?" He indicated a rather swollen area in the crotch of the suit.

"*Dammit, Allan, I'm HORNY!*" I said in my imitation of Lesley Ann Warren in *Victor/Victoria* (she played a floozy with a voice that was guaranteed to detumesce every male penis in a five-mile radius). "I've been here for an entire week and haven't had sex with a single man."

"That does it," spurted Allan. "Now go to bed immediately and take off that tacky and tawdry suit so I can sodomize and/ or lobotomize you totally and completely and repeatedly. I think it would be a crime against nature if someone with your enormous heaving breasts and washboard stomach were to leave San Francisco without being screwed at least once." Allan pulled me over to the bed and ripped off my suit and started violently kissing me. Marie Antoinette climbed on the bed, and so did Josephine. Marie Antoinette started to lick my foot, and Josephine was turning circles on the bed, chasing her stub of a tail.

"Allan, my flight!" I shrieked.

"OK, OK, but don't say I didn't offer you the best of my hospitality," said Allan. "I don't want you to go back home and complain to all of your fancy highfalutin society friends that I didn't offer you the most exquisite hospitality. Put your clothes on and get your bags. We're on our way."

We took the jeep. Allan switched to an oldies station. I left the city of San Francisco to the strains of the Weather Girls singing "It's Raining Men." As I stepped into the terminal I looked up. The clouds had begun to clear. The floods had ended.

How I Fucked Up

JULY 1987

All was not well in Mudville.

My boss, Maximilian Zeckendorf, a suave and stylish European who had only last year been given the title Associate Dictator for Life at Amalgamated, was in the process of being unceremoniously dumped. Complications arose from his status as a permanent employee. Zeckendorf had been working at Amalgamated since the age of puberty or the Age of Reason, whichever came first.

The powers that be were currently negotiating a settlement with Zeckendorf. Headquarters was overrun with lawyers, occupying spare offices, nooks, and crannies, poised for depositions and endless litigation. Normal activity had ceased at Amalgamated—the office was a morgue.

I was the last to be apprised of Zeckendorf's unfortunate situation, having been sent away for a five-day seminar on mismanagement at the height of the storm. Upon my return I sat at my typewriter, composing a twenty-page memorandum by rote, relying on my autonomic nervous system, unable to think independently of my fingers.

In 1987 I was bad news for those of gainful employ. My optometrist lost her job; my financial consultant at Citibank was replaced by a computer; even my regular checkout lady at the A&P was dumped from the payroll. That year, if you wanted a career change, all you had to do was conduct business with me.

So let me give you the full picture: My boss was on the way out. My social life was a shambles. I hadn't had a date since the Early Mesozoic era or the discovery of personal grooming, whichever came first. The paint on the walls of my apartment was peeling. My glasses were being repaired back at the Coke-bottle factory. My three-day shaving lapse looked less Italian fashion-model chic than Iranian terrorist. I had a loose filling. My phone was on the blink. The fridge needed defrosting. My gym membership had expired. I had run out of Stiff Stuff for my hair and was reduced to using Vaseline. I was a thirty-year-old male homosexual living at the epicenter of the worst epidemic of the century, and I still bit my nails and picked my nose on the sly, and I had yet to decide what I was going to do with my life if I grew up. In short, things were a mess.

And on top of this was the matter of Gordon.

My best friend, Gordon, was ill.

In 1987 it was unnecessary to specify of what.

It had only taken Gordon three months to tell me his diagnosis. He called me the week before Christmas to inform me that he had just been fired from his multinational conglomerate and that he was about to file an AIDS discrimination suit against them.

A rather roundabout way of telling the worst news in the world. But then Gordon was never known for straightforwardness.

Later, Gordon asked me if I could keep it under my hat for a while. "You know, it's sort of like coming out again," he said. "I guess you have to do it in stages."

"Sure, Gordon, no problem. I'm a great one with confidences. I've held some successfully for years."

"I think you're talking about grudges."

"Oh, right. Well, I'll do my best." Which was by no means enough.

Gordon began wearing makeup when he left the house. His face had swollen into a puffy mask. Gordon was taking some experimental drug through New York University Medical Center. He told me how difficult it was to get into an experimental protocol: You had to fit a certain physical profile and not be taking any other drugs at the same time. Doctors were lying about their patients' qualifications in order to get them drugs. Gordon had tried AZT, but the side effects were too much for him; it made him nauseous and depressed.

A week earlier I had dropped over at his apartment to loan him a paperback. He could see me only for a moment in the kitchen—he had to conserve his energy. The curtains were drawn. He sat there in the darkened room, wheezing asthmatically, staring at his glass of water. I averted my eyes. I hadn't seen him in several weeks. He wasn't wearing any makeup. I was embarrassed to see him: I felt my presence was an invasion of his privacy. We spoke briefly, and then I left.

So there I was, a woman on the verge of a nervous breakdown: My boss was being canned, after working at Amalgamated since the invention of rudimentary tools or the evolution of opposable thumbs, whichever came first, and Gordon was dying. I had spoken to Gordon that morning. His breathing was labored. The

KS may have spread to his lungs. The situation was not copacetic.

And then I blew it.

Joey Romano, a lecherous satyr and insatiable gossip, called me for his morning flirtation, insult, or whatever. He opened with the usual lascivious taunt, something to do with an Australian lifeguard and his disproportionate member and certain salacious acts he performed on Joey's person the previous night and how he wished I had also been present to observe or perhaps participate in the group activities.

I cut in. "I'm not really in the mood for that right now. I'm kind of depressed." I was worn down to the bone, without defenses. Typically a master of indirection, I was at that point incapable of fabricating the most elementary lie.

"What seems to be the problem, B.J.?" asked Joey.

"You know, I told you about the situation with my boss. And a friend of mine isn't doing too hot."

"Is it someone I know?" Question one of Twenty Questions. I didn't realize what was going on.

"I can't say." Gordon had sworn me to secrecy.

"It is," said Joey. "Oh, my God, it's not Gordon, is it?" Joey lived two blocks north of Gordon. He must have run into Gordon at the supermarket. I'm sure Joey noticed the change in Gordon's appearance, the slowness of his gait.

Feebly I replied, "I can't say." Shit. Two Judas denials and I was lost. Why couldn't I have done the right thing and simply lied?

"Oh, no, it is," said Joey.

"Don't tell anybody. He doesn't want anyone to know," I said, nailing the lid to the coffin.

"Of course not. Jesus. Gordon. I can't believe it. Although he has been keeping to himself for a while. Poor Gordon."

Loose lips sink ships. I knew that even though I'd asked Joey not to mention it to anyone, he would eventually spread the news, and it would get back to Gordon.

I hung up quickly and figured out my options. Should I tell Gordon? Should I just forget it? Should I immediately relocate to the Midwest?

Ironically, I had been the one to tell Gordon never to mention his illness to Joey, the biggest gossip this side of Sioux City, Iowa; give him some dirt and he'll fertilize the entire Napa Valley. I might as well have placed a notice in the back page of *The Village Voice:* "Gordon has AIDS. Don't tell anyone."

So, like a fool, I compounded the error. I called Gordon and told him I'd mistakenly spilled the beans to Joey. I figured it was time for Gordon to get out of the AIDS closet, whether he was ready or not. Glibly I asked permission to go public, reasoning that Gordon's condition was well known anyway by then, thinking that it would make things easier on Gordon and his lover. I was, of course, trying to justify my mistake, and I suppose I got what I deserved.

"You can say whatever you want," said Gordon. Then he hung up on me.

Rejection doesn't come easy from a best friend. You'd think that after all of the bars and gyms and bathhouses and parties I had been to, I would be able to handle rejection. Forget it.

I called Gordon the next two days. Same response. *Click.* I wrote a long and involved letter of apology to him. No response. I despised myself. He had asked so little of me—just one simple thing, to keep it under wraps. And I blew it. He told me in December, and I told Joey in April.

Later, Joey, figuring Gordon knew that he knew, called him up, offering help. Gordon thanked him and hung up. As time went by, Gordon's circle of friends grew smaller and smaller, until he was talking only to his lover and two lesbians.

I kept in contact with his lover and learned of Gordon's fevers, his depressions, his good days and bad. His lover told me that

Gordon still had angry outbursts about me, but Gordon was angry at everyone at times, including his own lover.

I saw Gordon once more, standing in the rain at the Gay Pride Run. His lover said by that time he had forgiven me. I'll never know for sure, though. Who can trust secondhand information? He told me not to call—instead, to send Gordon mail. I sent him another card. I got no answer, no indication that it had reached its destination.

So my boss departed and I remained, trapped in the bureaucracy of Amalgamated, unable to extricate myself from the morass of details and endless memos. Maybe I was fired a few months later; maybe I still work there; maybe I resigned. What does it matter in the scale of things? How does it compare to the origins of the universe, the moons of Saturn, or Gordon's final rejection of me?

Because no matter what, I'll have this hanging over my head until the sun runs out of hydrogen and implodes into a red dwarf, and the universe converts the final erg of energy into entropy and stops expanding and begins to contract, and time reverses or when I die, whichever comes first.

And of course now I don't talk to Joey anymore because of Gordon. It's stupid that I blame Joey; it wasn't his fault. (Why didn't he listen to me and stop prying?) And Joey feels guilty for ruining our relationship, and it wasn't anything he did. (Why didn't I just lie?) And Joey feels sad that Gordon rejected his offer of help. (Why did I tell Gordon about it?)

So, Gordon, if you're listening, I'm sorry, you goddamn shit, that I spilled the beans, opened my big trap, and let loose with a torrent of truths and betrayal, but did you have to drop me so completely, so absolutely? Can I be allowed to make a single mistake? Is my life just a long series of mistaken conversations? *Did you have to cut me out so completely?* What was this, some sort of object lesson? Why did you have to be so touchy? Why does dying make everyone so irritable? God damn it, I was your friend. Listen, I know you're somewhere else—heaven, hell, reincarnated as a paramecium, maybe just some dust and bones tossed into the Long Island Sound by Fire Island, living in an urn on someone's mantelpiece, or six feet under back in Buffalo, New York—but I know you can hear me. Well, fuck you, and I'm sorry, and I wish you well, and I won't do it again, and please forgive me, Gordon. Can we talk? Can we have just one more conversation? Because I'm so lonely without you.

·5·

Despair

My anxiety level was high, and it was time to do something about it. I had reached a particular level of anxiety that corresponded to the resonant frequency of my brain; one more day in this state and it would explode. I needed to either elevate it to a frequency that only dogs hear or decrease it to a reasonable level so I could focus my anxiety on things like nuclear war, famine, torture in Third World countries, Beirut, Afghanistan, Lebanon, the West Bank, crack, the homeless, and my relationship with my mother. In short, it was time to take the Test.

I decided to take the Test after I discovered by reading articles in *The New York Times* that two former sexual partners of mine had AIDS. The first article dealt with AIDS in the workplace.

"Why look! There's Morgan," I said to myself, coughing up breakfast and several unrelated meals from the past two weeks. The second was a human-interest story about AZT in action. "Gee, I didn't know Lloyd was on AZT these days," I commented from a supine position on the floor, having just fainted.

I decided to take the Test after reading an article in *The New York Times* in which the New York City health commissioner said that all those with the virus were doomed. The prevailing figures I had been reading stated that approximately fifteen percent of those exposed to the virus come down with AIDS within five years of infection. I figured I could wait it out: If I stayed well for five years, I'd be home free. I neglected to consider that at that time the epidemic had been tracked for only five years, and that the estimates stopped at five years simply because there were no further data. Now it turned out that after seven years' incubation of the virus, the incidence rose sharply.

I decided to take the Test after reading seventeen well-meaning liberal heterosexual columns in seventeen well-meaning liberal heterosexual periodicals where seventeen well-meaning liberal heterosexual people described how they each underwent their own personal well-meaning liberal heterosexual hell by taking the Test: their fear and trepidation, their casual doubts and anxieties, along with their awkward self-reassurances that it would be extremely unlikely to get a positive antibody result, although they may have had more than three sexual experiences with more than two partners in the past seventeen years, and it's conceivable that one of the partners was a hemophiliac bisexual who did intravenous drugs in between weekly blood transfusions, and it's conceivable that they were inoculated with a tetanus vaccine using a needle that had just been used on a hemophiliac bisexual who did intravenous drugs in between weekly blood transfusions when they were twelve and stepped on a rusty nail at Camp Mohonka in the Catskills, and it's conceivable that their mother could actually be Haitian and there could have been a mix-up at the hospital or the midwife's, and it's conceivable that the blood transfusion from the heart-lung-kidney-and-thyroid transplant by Dr. Christiaan Barnard had contained some tainted blood from a hemophiliac bisexual who did intravenous drugs in between weekly blood donations. I mean, I appreciated the first article where a well-meaning liberal heterosexual columnist described the trials and tribulations of taking the Test; and even five articles of well-meaning liberal heterosexual columnists would have been within the bounds of propriety and taste; but *seventeen* of those abominable articles just made me want to scream. I had it up to here with well-meaning liberal heterosexual ass-holes so far removed from the crisis that they could be living on Jupiter. You see, these well-meaning liberal heterosexual columns all ended exactly the same way, with the results sheepishly revealed in the final sentence, almost casually, nonchalantly: Oh, by the way, I was negative. What was this, I thought, some fucking dating service?

I decided to take the Test even though I had not had the mean amount of one thousand five hundred and twenty-three sexual partners in the past ten years that the papers reported from the initial group of AIDS patients (I was rather shy for my age), even though I had not undergone what was coyly referred to in the press as traumatic sex (although in some sense all sex is traumatic) in certain downtown clubs in the presence of a large audience, even though I had never been considered what was coyly referred to in the company of my friends as a slut (which is undeniably a relative term).

I decided to take the Test even though it wasn't necessarily the politically correct thing to do, and certain radical gay columnists in certain radical gay periodicals were predicting the most unbelievable repercussions: mandatory testing for HIV antibodies; discrimination in insurance, housing, and employment of those who tested positive; closing the borders to aliens who tested positive and at the same time other countries closing their borders to Americans who tested positive; internment camps for those who tested positive. As time passed, a significant portion of the above alarmist predictions became realities.

I decided to take the Test even though the local gay paper insisted, virulently, that HTLV-III was *not* the cause (although the virus had been renamed HIV two years earlier by an international committee in an effort to solve a dispute about who had discovered the virus first, an American scientist who discovered the virus in 1984 or a French scientist who discovered the virus in 1983), and the local gay paper was backing the African Swine Fever Virus Theory or the Tertiary Syphilis Theory or the Chronic Epstein-Barr Virus Theory or the Cytomegalovirus Theory or the Track Lighting and Industrial Gray Carpeting and Quiche Theory or the Immune-System Overload Theory or the Amyl and Butyl Nitrite Theory or a variation of the Legionnaire's Disease Theory in which some contaminant got into the air-conditioning system of the Saint discotheque, or perhaps a new noise virus at a certain frequency had gotten into the sound system, or the Government Germ-Warfare Theory, where some experimental poisonous gas had leaked, not to be confused with the Government Genocide Theory, where the government deliberately distributed contaminated K-Y lubricant at homosexual gatherings and contaminated needles at shooting galleries, or the Airborne Mosquito Theory or the Toilet-Seat Theory or the No Gag-Response Theory, where male homosexuals as a consequence swallow vast quantities of as-yet unidentified toxins. The local gay paper offered a new and improved conspiracy theory each and every month, and I suppose it was *just my problem* that I couldn't keep up with all of these new trends and fashions in disease consciousness; I mean, I guess I was being pigheaded and stupid to accept a parsimonious explanation that had been offered by our admittedly mendacious government, and maybe I was just too irritable and lazy not to make a concerted effort to keep track of each new crackpot theory (based on a somewhat-justifiable paranoia) that more or less ignored all scientific research to date and was generally so incredibly stupid that were the theory to be rated on the Stanford-Binet test of general intelligence, I doubt it would be able to tie its own shoelaces unassisted or balance a check book or cross the street without being run over by a Mack truck.

I decided to take the Test because I was from a rational background, and I decided that it wouldn't kill me to know, even though a friend who had AIDS told me that if I found out I was positive, this would create additional stress, which would in turn weaken my immune system, thus allowing the virus to replicate, a sort of Heisenberg effect where the knowledge of a situation affects that situation, so in fact it *could* kill me, a little faster than otherwise, and what would the benefits be of finding out if I were positive because there wasn't a cure, and why would it help to know my status if it wouldn't change my behavior because I would continue having safe sex and getting enough rest and eating right and exercising and taking Geritol either way? I told him that if I turned out positive, I would brood and contemplate suicide and lose perspective and quit my job and go to Italy and finally learn how to deal with my mother and stop transferring money to my Individual Retirement Account and move it into an insurance policy and only renew magazines by the year and would insist on being paid in a lump sum if I won a lottery as opposed to a twenty-year payment scheme because I would probably be dead in twenty years and the tax benefits would be outweighed by the worldwide cruise through whatever countries still allowed HIV-positives to travel, and maybe I would take one of those fancy new placebos that everyone is talking about, like active lipids or naltrexone or dextran sulfate or wheat-grass juice, or maybe I would see a nutritionist and stop eating sugar and become macrobiotic and then die a lot faster from not eating enough protein, or maybe I would start meditating, or maybe I would finally achieve a sense of spirituality and meaning in my life as it neared the end and drop this worn cloak of cynicism for crystals or Gurdjieff or reincarnation or God or free parking, or maybe I would start writing like Anthony Burgess, who, when misdiagnosed with a brain tumor, wrote four novels in a year, or maybe I would have some mystical cosmic revelation because I was ready for it, or maybe I would join a bowling league, or maybe I would just give up. I mean, I operated under the basic premise that ignorance is *not* bliss, and why should I stick my head in the sand when I should perfectly well be able to stick the gun in my mouth instead? And then, of course, there was the extremely slim chance that I was, in fact, HIV-antibody negative. Maybe—who knows?—I could actually relax for a few minutes. I mean, Rome wasn't built in a day.

I decided to take the Test because although I generally don't believe in predestination as opposed to free will, from a logical standpoint we are all born with certain finite constraints: None of us is immortal; hence, none of us has an unlimited number of heartbeats left. Women are born with a finite number of ova, ready to plop down the fallopian tubes at the rate of one every four weeks, from puberty to menopause; similarly, we are each born with a finite number of orgasms to experience, cigarettes to smoke, and lovers to betray. Knowing whether I tested positive or negative could help me determine more precisely what those numbers were. I was just moderately curious to find out what would be a reasonable number of cocktails, nightmares, Lean Cuisines, boyfriends, vacations, apartments, breaths, jobs, and bowel movements to expect in this lifetime. Perhaps if I knew I had only a few sexual encounters left, I would avoid intercourse in order to stretch things out.

I decided to take the Test because I had reached the point where I believed that it was a fundamentally irrational act *not* to take the HIV-antibody test, and after all, I *did* graduate from Northeastern University several aeons ago, majoring in mathematics and minoring in philosophy, and consequently I still felt a responsibility to behave rationally.

So, nervous like when I was seventeen and in college and still a virgin and went to a drugstore and spent hours studying de-

pilatories and decongestants and diuretics before finally asking
the kindly pharmacist for condoms in a cracked voice, I picked
up the phone and dialed the city AIDS hotline and made an
appointment to take the test at the earliest available time slot,
six weeks later. Like a secret agent, I was identified by a numeric
code only.

During the next six weeks I did the usual things: made a will,
sold my co-op, changed my job, upped my insurance, reconciled
with my family, worked out at the gym seven times a day, had
sixteen failed romances, volunteered as an astronaut at NASA so
I could experience the relativistic effects of traveling at high speeds
(time contracts when approaching the speed of light, thus the six
weeks' wait would seem less interminable).

The six weeks' wait was an eternity.

That morning ("There's still time to chicken out," said my friend
Dennis) I woke up early and took the bus. I had scheduled my
appointment for 8:30, when the clinic opened, so I could take
the test, vomit, and then casually waltz into work fashionably
late, as usual.

There was no time for breakfast; I didn't want to be late. I
took the bus down Ninth Avenue. I had to stand until Forty-
second Street. I couldn't concentrate on the *Times*. The bus let
me off right in front of the Chelsea clinic. I hadn't been there
since 1980 to get treated for a venereal disease.

Outside, several homeless people were sleeping on benches. A
man swept debris from the concrete with a broom. The clinic
was next to an elementary school, with a jungle gym outside. It
was 8:15. The building was closed.

I circled the block. On the sidewalk several sexually responsible
individuals had thoughtfully left their used condoms. I recalled
the first time I ever set foot in a gay bar, back when I was nineteen,
in Pasadena, California. I had circled the street seventy-two times
before gathering enough courage to enter. I was shy; I wasn't
ready to make a life-style commitment at that point in time, and

I thought entering a gay bar would be an irrevocable step. I mean, they'd all assume I was a homosexual.

I had a quick bite to eat at an awful deli on Tenth, surrounded by the harsh accents of the outer boroughs: the snide voices, the know-it-alls, the wisecrackers. "How could they joke at a time like this?" I wondered. I returned to the clinic, ten minutes late for my 8:30 appointment. Two people were already in front of me. I was given a brief and informative booklet to read. Why did the print fade the harder I tried to concentrate? The woman at the desk asked for my number and then asked me to make up a new one, tossing the first away. I signed a release form by copying a statement instead of signing; with no signature, I remained anonymous. Then I had a brief counseling session with a therapist, a woman with dark hair cut butch, a warm and sympathetic lesbian.

"How do you think you were exposed?" she asked.

"I may have forgotten to use a condom five or six thousand times back in 1982, before there were rules and regulations to follow."

"Why are you taking the test? What will this knowledge do for you?"

"I thought"—I thought that this was a test, and the right answer would be judicious and thoughtful and beneficial to humanity—"that I might be able to help further the cause of science and medical research by becoming an experimental subject should I test positive."

"I wouldn't if I were you," she counseled. "They have double-blind experiments. For all you know, you could be eating sugar pills. And what's worse, you may be on some toxic drug. Suppose you're in a study and they find out another more promising drug. You can't switch." Then she told me about stress reduction and homemade AL 721 and macrobiotic diets.

"That's a bit drastic for me. I mean, should I give up meat just to live another six months?" There was this trade-off between sex and life, between red meat and a few more years. Why should I have to be making these choices?

"For the next two weeks, I want you to act as if you have already tested positive," she advised. "Prepare yourself." Did she know something that I didn't know? Why couldn't I enjoy my last few possibly blissful weeks relatively stress-free (although by this time my anxiety meter-reading was off the scale)? I made an appointment for two weeks later to get my results.

A Pakistani medical assistant looked up from his textbook and put on two pairs of red plastic gloves. "Give me your arm," he instructed. Carefully, he stuck me with the needle and filled a test tube with my blood, then wrapped the gloves around the sample for safety. I wondered how he could do this all day. How could he stand it?

That night I found out that Gordon had died in the afternoon. My first reaction was "See what you get for taking the test?" Although I eventually convinced myself there was no cause-and-effect relationship between the two events, still, I felt it was not a good sign.

"You can always just take it and not bother getting the results," said Dennis. "You can back out at any time."

The next day I called Richard in California.

"If it turns out I'm positive, I'm going to take the next plane out of here and get a cab to your apartment and knock on your door, and you'll answer, and I'll say, 'Thanks,' and pull out my pearl-handled revolver from my purse and shoot you dead."

"Come on, Benjamin, I didn't necessarily infect you. It could be any one of thousands."

"I know it was you. Who else fucked me with such relish and regularity? Who else do I know who had lymphadenopathy in 1982? Besides, it's easier for me to deal with when I can pinpoint the blame on someone else."

"You should be here in San Francisco. There are so many twelve-step and self-help groups out here, we even have groups for people who are waiting to find out whether they tested positive or negative."

"Two-week groups?"

"That's right."

"If only they came out with the safe-sex regulations two months earlier, I'd still be alive."

"You *are* alive, Benjamin."

"You know what I mean." Was it better to have loved and gotten infected than never to have loved at all? Was I even capable of love? Who knew?

Instead of San Francisco I went to Provincetown, the only gay mecca to which I hadn't yet made a pilgrimage (I had already been to Key West and West Hollywood). I had another disastrous safe-sex romance, and then I got too much sun and not enough sleep, because there was sand in my weekend lover's bed, and being the Jewish American Princess that I am, it felt just like a pea; the pullout mattress hadn't been turned since the War Between the States, so I tossed and turned and created my own force field of anxiety, and my face decided to punish me with a minor outbreak of herpes, which, in turn, got infected with impetigo, which, in turn, increased my level of anxiety, so the herpes got worse and worse, and by the time it had reached its nadir I looked more or less like Jeff Goldblum in the remake of *The Fly*, and this was not during the first half-hour of the picture; this was *serious* skin disorder. So I went to my doctor, who had fled the city that January because of burnout from the AIDS crisis, and saw his cruel replacement, a cold and inefficient reptile who misdiagnosed me with shingles, a disease that typically affects only half of the face, whereas my face was a *complete* disaster area. And then this lizard had the tact to tell me that I should definitely take the HIV-antibody test because shingles was one of those opportunistic infections that tends to strike people with lowered immunities, and he said that he felt there was a ninety percent chance that I would be positive. At which point I told my own personal nominee for Mr. Compassion and Tact of 1987 that I had already taken the test and as a matter of fact was expecting my results the following day.

I went back to the clinic for my results, looking like the Creature from the Black Lagoon. Guess what? Unlike the seventeen well-meaning liberal heterosexual columnists in the seventeen well-meaning liberal heterosexual periodicals, I turned out to be positive. Hold the presses! This had to be front-page news. If I wrote a column, I'd make *The Guinness Book of World Records* and the covers of *Time, Esquire,* and *Women's Wear Daily* as the first columnist to turn out positive in the history of civilization and parlay this into immediate financial gain, a guest spot on *Hollywood Squares,* a bit part in *Miami Vice.* Then I realized I would be dead before the residuals came because my life expectancy wasn't quite so long as it was even a week ago; there I was thinking like an actuary. I decided it was time to get a television set, something I had been struggling successfully against acquiring for the past ten years, along with a VCR, so when my apartment was converted into a sanatorium, I'd be able to amuse myself. Although I didn't go whole-hog: Cable would have to wait.

And oddly enough I fell into this deep funk.

I had a friend who was nice and supportive, and after I took the test and got the results, he got really mad at me because I was depressed because what did I expect? and didn't I realize the likelihood of being positive? and what difference did it make anyway? and I told him it was the doom, the absolute doom, that got to me, and he said didn't you know about that before, you imbecile? and I said this is the sort of thing you can't really figure out what your reaction will be until you do it, and I tried to explain to him about the Heisenberg principle, but he had math anxiety in a bad way, so he stuffed his fingers into his ears and said I don't want to listen. And of course a couple of months later he took the test anyway, on the advice of his doctor, who told him that if he had high blood pressure, wouldn't he want to know if he was at risk of a heart attack, even if it was only a ten percent chance? And he was negative. And another friend who had moved to Japan three years ago to evade the AIDS crisis and the Reagan administration and also because something snapped in his brain when he turned thirty and he—with no prior warning—became a deeply depraved rice queen who had to move nine thousand miles just to get laid; well, he took the test and was negative too. And then another friend who had according to conservative estimates sucked every Negro penis in the tri-state area in such venues as subway tearooms, trucks, changing rooms, and in the back seats of cars; well, he took the test, and he was negative too. And part of me, since misery loves company, wanted just one close friend to be positive too, but the sensible part of me, the part that still has occasional communication with my cerebral cortex, said, "Thank God they're negative," using the expletive for effect, since thank god my experience had not changed me so profoundly that I was no longer an atheist.

So this is what I do: I go on with my life. I go to ACT UP meetings, never saying a word, and end up more stressed-out than I was before; I go to demonstrations and scream myself hoarse and then visit my new primary health-care practitioner who, unlike the lizard, gives me hugs and prescribes medication for my sore throat and my various and sundry female disorders; I get my T-cell count taken every three months; I go to a few Body Positive meetings and attend a group rap-session that is headed by a psychopath and shortly thereafter drop out because once again my stress-level has tripled; and I want to end the AIDS crisis and stop the government logjam of red tape and paperwork, and there should be some sort of cure in the near future, and the only thing is whether I will still be alive to use it; and I'm wary of the macrobiotic diets and crystals and lipids and other untested and unverified treatments, but at the same time I'm afraid to do absolutely nothing—maybe I'm paralyzed by inertia and fear, I don't know—and I don't want to take AZT when the T-cell count drops below 200 because it's highly toxic, but at the same time I know it can't be all bad because some more insane people at the local gay paper want to sue all doctors for malpractice for prescribing it. And I take acyclovir for my herpes twice daily to prevent recurrences because herpes is particularly bad for the immune system, and I'm avoiding the sun: This summer I'm going to be an alabaster nymph, a pale creature of the night. And sex: What about sex? When I see a guy I've been flirting with for the past four years, what do I say? What are the rules? Should this be broadcast? Are there any tactful ways of telling the relatives? How can I have sex with someone without telling? Does it matter if the sex is absolutely safe? What do I say when I meet someone new: Would you like to have sex with someone who may or may not have a fatal disease?

And now I never sleep through the night; I always wake up at three or four, tense, filled with anxiety. Like Dorothy in *The Wizard of Oz,* I sit, watching helplessly as my T-cell count drops every three months, the sands of time running out.

Once I awoke from a wet dream, swimming in a sea of infected sperm; I leapt out of the bed to wipe it all up quickly (how does one stem the tide, the flow?). And one day I was sitting at a coffee shop, and my nose began to bleed spontaneously. I hadn't had a nosebleed in years. The blood dripped bright red onto the plate, onto the napkin. All I could think of was infection and disease. All I could think of was the virus that was coursing through my blood. I blotted it out with the napkin and sat there ashamed, frightened, in despair.

·6·

Inevitable Love

AUGUST 1988

I suppose it was inevitable that I would fall for my doctor, Wendall Harrington Browne, M.D. (certified for general family practice in three states), of the firm demeanor, icy countenance, steel-gray eyes, Armani suits, bear-trap grip, tiny lips forever pursed in concentration, deep Southern drawl, and incalculably large penis.

I grew up in Blandville, U.S.A., with an eternal crush on Richard Chamberlain as Dr. Kildare. While all of the other children were playing kick-the-can in the street, I was conducting extensive physical examinations on my sister Sheila's dolls in my mini-laboratory office, billing them upon completion. The founder of our local chapter of Future Entrepreneurs of America, I took Visa, Mastercard, and American Express, along with Medicare. I practiced my lines carefully, aiming for a firm yet benevolent demeanor. "Turn to your side and cough," I would urge Ken. "Another test can't hurt; I'm sure your insurance will cover it," I assured Barbie. I performed several illegal abortions on Midge. With plastic dolls there was never blood.

In my youth I would undress at the drop of a hat: for orthodontists (I had quite an overbite due to an uncontrollable oral fixation), ophthalmologists (my vision grew worse and worse each year; this I blamed on excessive self-abuse), psychoanalysts (for reasons that should be obvious by now, I was in intensive therapy for years), and even for my bar-mitzvah lessons (the cantor took it all in stride, regarding me with cynical pleasure, one eye raised, as I took him over the altar).

Everyone has an ideal lover. Aficionados of substances that require prescriptions for licit use frequently find themselves involved with pharmacists, anesthesiologists, and dental hygienists. Muscle worshipers have been known to frequent personal trainers, a different gymnasium every night, in a futile attempt to find the ideal. Those of a sartorial bent spend endless Saturdays trying to woo salesmen at Barneys in the hopes of obtaining employee discounts. Camp-seekers and pseudointellectuals flock after Susan Sontag en masse. Those with flawed cheekbones, supernumerary nipples, or Picasso visages are on the prowl for plastic surgeons. Writers slink through the aisles at the American Booksellers Association convention in provocative garb, seeking to snare editors. Actors and actresses in full décolletage hand out canapés and pastry puffs, discreetly slipping in their phone numbers, at parties peopled with agents, producers, and backers.

As for me, a helpless hypochondriac, a doctor, M.D., was my dream. I was the one with the 102 fever achieved purely from friction, constantly sliding the thermometer in and out of my mouth. I read the *Physician's Desk Reference* into the night with the avidness of a detective-novel junkie, psychosomatically coming down with at least seven unrelated symptoms a day, helplessly popping multicolored breath-mint candies I pretended were pills. I sterilized my dishes by running them through the dishwasher three times before using them; I washed my fresh fruit with pHisoHex; I shaved with a new disposable razor every day; I made my bed once a week with seven sets of sheets, alternated with rubber ones, discarding three layers every morning.

But perhaps this was understandable considering the circumstances. I was HIV antibody-positive, and my T-cells were plummeting: I was desperate.

I had fled my evil former doctor, a man with all of the humanity of a Nazi experimenter and all of the charm of Leona Helmsley on crack, clutching my chart in hand. As one last indignity, my evil former doctor made me Xerox my medical records at my own expense, as he needed the originals on hand should I ever decide to sue for malpractice. My chart, a thick tome more swollen than an engorged penis, charted the weekly ebb and flow of my anal warts, replete with countless illustrations of my anus. That was the bulk of it, although on alternate pages were diagnoses of strep throat, pharyngitis, tonsillitis, gonococcus, seborrhea, psoriasis, tinea versicolor, ringworm, rashes bacterial and fungal, and a host of other minor complaints. I had had so many varieties of penicillin in the past few years that for a time I considered culturing my own moldy bread in the Frigidaire to save money.

I suppose my affair with Wendall Harrington Browne, M.D., could be completely imaginary, yet another unrequited love. Yet during the initial prostate examination I clocked him at twenty-three minutes. My head was swimming.

"Lah down," he told me. My folded shirt sat on the chair, patiently; my pants hung limply over the back of the chair; my shoes and socks lined up at attention at the foot of the examination table. He had pulled a fresh length of butcher paper for me to sit on. He placed the icy-cold stethoscope on my chest and exhorted me to breathe deeply. "Again. Again. Again." I did my best to obey. "Nahce stummach," he appraised, smoothing his calloused hands down my chest, my stomach, my pelvis, and beyond. His clinical manner only served to increase my excitement. "Drop y' sho'ts," he commanded. To my embarrassment, I had a hard-on. This is not an infrequent occurrence with me, although it does tend to happen at inopportune occasions: when my boss is dressing me down (do I secretly crave humiliation?); when one of the six thousand interchangeable Italian barbers at Astor Place Hair is razoring the back of my head (is it the vibrations or the olive eyes?); or when I am within a five-foot radius of a naked penis (at the showers at the gym—occasionally a sympathetic response will evidence itself).

Dr. Browne held my penis like a specimen, an object for classroom discussion, a pointer for indicating important agricultural centers on the Mercator map of the world on the flip-chart next to the blackboard. "There's nothing wrong with getting an erection during an examination," he said as he inspected the shaft of the item in question for irregularities. "It's quaht common. Are you mastuhbatin' enough?"

"Not more than twice a day, usually. Does that suffice?"

"It's very important to mastuhbate regularly," he continued as he probed my testicles for unnatural growths. "You don't want to have prostate problems, do you?" Casually, he discarded my penis, having concluded his business for the moment. "Now please bend over."

Sheathed with rubber glove, Dr. Browne cautiously entered the sanctum sanctorum. Twenty-three rapturous minutes later he withdrew. I was reduced to insensate amorphism, guttural monosyllables.

"Do y' have any questions?"

Must I wait another year before another physical? Would you like to meet for cocktails? Can I have my next appointment at 6:30, after your secretary has left for the day? But of course I was incapable of expressing even the most rudimentary wishes orally. Dr. Browne had rendered me speechless.

"No? You may put your clothes back on now."

I went to the receptionist's desk to pay my bill, receive my insurance receipt, and dream of future appointments.

I invented mysterious ills, minor ailments: the funny pimple at the base of the cock (an artificial mole intended for the dimpled cheek, affixed with glue); the weird rash near the anus (drawn in with lipstick); the infection at the nipple due to a purportedly botched piercing (swollen by leaving a clothespin on it overnight and gently shaded with tincture of iodine for the appropriate color). "Hmm," said Dr. Browne. "Let's take a closa look. Remove your clothes."

Eagerly I doffed my clothes in a matter of seconds.

"Workin' out at the gym, ah see." His voice was calm, dispassionate. Did I detect a hint of prurient interest? I could not tell for certain.

I spent hours deciding what underwear to wear on an appointment: the Swedish mesh-net? the scanty item from the Undergear catalog? the Japanese thong? the yellow jockstrap? or nothing at all? Then one appointment he seemed to notice the burgundy Calvin Klein underwear. I immediately went to Bloomingdale's and bought six more pairs.

I sat in the waiting room, nervously thumbing through last month's magazines, as Dr. Browne's deranged receptionist, Zelda, hummed some obscure film score from the thirties and ordered tongue depressors by the gross. In the background I heard the steady mechanical wheeze of two or three patients in for their biweekly intakes of aerosol pentamidine.

"The doctor is ready to see you now." I wilted.

Having all but forgotten about the pleasures of anal sex, I told my doctor that I had a new boyfriend, and consequently, we should resume the treatments for anal warts. There was, of course, no boyfriend: I only had eyes for Dr. Browne. The warts had been with me for the last seven years and seemed to have no intention of ever leaving. They posed virtually no problems to me; I was blissfully unaware of them most of the time.

Not once did he suggest simple laser surgery to eliminate them completely once and for all. That would mean forgoing our monthly visits. A tiny voice in my head said, "And those monthly payments."

After the seven hundredth treatment for anal warts, he fastidiously wiped the K-Y jelly from my ass. Oh, Dr. Browne, you're the only person who has touched me there in three years or more. As in industrial factories in the Midwest, there was a sign above my bed, updated nightly, which currently read: "1,043 DAYS SINCE THE LAST SEXUAL INCIDENT."

Mes billets doux. Dear Diary. He sent me one today.

I know, only someone with the rarest of intelligence would possibly recognize the simple announcement on an engraved card that Dr. Wendall Harrington Browne was pleased to announce that Dr. Gerry Clayton would be joining his practice as a love note. I wrapped a pink ribbon with a bow around it and placed it gingerly into my hope chest. A few weeks later, another card arrived. "It's time for your annual checkup." I lay languorously on my divan, fanning myself with this note, tears staining my face. A full-scale examination. I must plan on a new pair of unmentionables posthaste!

I didn't care about the rumors, the gossip: that he voted Republican; that he had been divorced three times and had children in Tallahassee, Florida, and Tucson, Arizona; that his lover was a model for Yves Saint Laurent; that he went to private sex-clubs in the meat-packing district once a month; that he hired male prostitutes for rough sex; that he had a closet filled with whips and harnesses. His outside life didn't concern me.

His life outside of the office was immaterial.

Dr. Browne was strong, tall, and handsome, with blond hair,

blue eyes, and a body of death. Dr. Browne was my WASP ideal, my personal American tragedy: It was painful to be in his presence, so great was my desire, so cool and professional his demeanor. I was sure that underneath his glacial facade lay a man of unbounded sensuality.

Dr. Browne spoke so deeply you had to lean forward to hear him. He spoke in the voice of unmodulated reliability. Dr. Browne spoke the language of love. "Strip!" he ordered. "Strip," I heard him gently cooing into my mind's ear. I followed his instructions to the letter, without reservation. As if I could ever say no.

"You're fahn," he assured me. "Most people who are HIV-positive are doing fahn. You seem to be in good shape. Judging from your T-cells, there's a ninety percent chance you won't get ill this year."

My heart sank. What about next year?

"We'll run them again in six months. Any questions?"

After six months, he advised rerunning the tests in three months. Hmmm. Somehow I didn't feel quite as confident as last week. How could I get my doctor to sleep with me? Emotional blackmail, telling him that this would be the only way to reassure me?

His thigh was wedged into my side as he took blood from my arm. I imagined I was on the subway at rush hour, the twilight hour, the hour of lust, the hour of musk.

If I ever actually became ill, I feared I'd be too confused to digest his information, so enraptured was I by his physical presence.

The night before my second physical, I dreamed of Dr. Browne. He tweaked my nipple, testing the erectile tissue there. "It's a standa'd percedure," he commented. "Now open your mouth." First his tongue explored the alveolar ridge and oral cavity. "It's easier to do this examination without instruments. Now close your eyes. Ah'm gonna probe your throat." I lay down on the examination table naked. I opened my eyes to darkness. The lights had been turned off. Gently Dr. Browne placed his fingers on my lids and closed them. Slowly he entered me. I woke up gagging.

That morning I tried to masturbate. I couldn't even achieve an erection. Work was worse than useless; the insurmountable problems, the myriad brushfires I was presented with to put out, did not even serve as a distraction. I thought only of my 12:30 appointment.

I arrived promptly. In record time I was lying on my stomach, nude. Dr. Browne seemed distracted; he performed his proctal probe without enthusiasm.

"Is there something wrong?"

"No, everything seems to be in order," he told me, at the volume of a muted harpsichord.

"I mean, are you OK?"

"Of course."

I turned over slowly, shyly revealing the results of his probe. "You're sure there's nothing I can do?"

"You'd better put your clothes back on," he said.

"Have *you* been masturbating regularly?" I asked.

"Please put those back on," he remarked, seated, hiding behind his clipboard.

"Are you sure?"

"It would be extremely unprofessional to continue in this manner."

"All right." Begrudgingly, I dressed, stuffing my erection into my shorts. How much longer could I fight this? I couldn't keep it inside any longer. I had to speak. "I know you have a lover, and I know you're a professional. Still, I have to tell you that I think I've fallen in love with you. I should probably change doctors. I doubt I'm even your type. We have so many differences. And there's the health issue, my antibody status. Yet somehow, I feel I know you better than you'd think. And maybe, just maybe, there's the chance that sometime in the future, we just might—"

"Benjamin," he said to me, looking me straight in the eye, "where did you get these ideas? Don't you know ah'm straight?"

I suppose the whole thing could be explained as a simple case of transference.

A few months later, I sat in the dentist's chair, with its fifteen axes of rotation, listening to that all-commercial station they pipe into dentists' offices, staring at the poster-sized reconstruction of Cro-Magnon man's teeth, something out of a Hollywood special-effects lab for some horror movie. This is what happens when we *don't* floss. The hygienist had left me momentarily; the dentist was currently monitoring six or seven patients. The doctor would be with me shortly. Tense, I awaited the verdict on my X rays.

Suddenly, I had an inspiration. The door was closed. Quickly, I moved into action.

Soon the dentist would come with news. Naked beneath my robe, I waited expectantly.

Breaking Up with Roger

JUNE 1989

HOW WE BROKE UP I

We broke up over omelets in a rather inexpensive restaurant in the East Village. I was dipping his French fries in ketchup. "Smoking is very glamorous," I said, putting two French fries in my nose à la Brooke Shields, pretending they were cigarettes.

"Maybe you should stop that?" Roger Taylor suggested softly. Still, his voice was twelve octaves beneath my own harridan's shriek.

I had ordered an exotic omelet, which arrived with a mound of creamy green pesto that resembled avian cloaca from a rare and possibly extinct specimen. "Should I be eating garlic? Are we going to be kissing later tonight?" I asked, smearing my Italian bread with gobs and gobs of sauce.

"I don't think so," said Roger.

He cleared his throat.

"You'll probably hate me after I tell you what's on my mind."

"Oh, are you going to drop me?" I inquired, disingenuously. "Don't bother me with last week's news. I was *just* about to drop you. *Thanks for saving me the trouble.*"

"Shouldn't *I* be telling *you* this?" he asked, moderately relieved.

"Or do you mean that maybe we should sort of cool down for a while, maybe we shouldn't be talking to one another for a while—you know, try to be apart and think about things and maybe dump one another in a few weeks or so? Is that what you're trying to say?" I questioned.

"Something along those lines," he admitted. "I guess you're not as upset as I'd imagined."

"Why should I be upset, you cad, you hypocrite, you imbecile, you hateful scourge of society, you insect, you Precambrian layer of igneous material, you spineless creature, you jerk, you simpleton, you heartbreaker, you infidel, you bore, you know-nothing, you atheist, you Pet Shop Boys fanatic?" I said, as I tossed a glass of Mondavi Cabernet Sauvignon 1987 (a fruity, subtle, full-bodied varietal) at Roger, who was wearing a lesbian-identified lumberjack shirt.

He ducked. The slim and elegant waitperson ("Hi, my name is Gregory, and I'll be your server this evening"), who wore enough mousse in his neatly coifed hair to style seventeen Farrah Fawcetts, managed to catch the entire volume of liquid in a flask that he carried for such occasions.

WHY DID WE BREAK UP?

1. We had absolutely nothing in common, aside from HIV-antibody status.

2. Roger was deeply committed to a long-term till-death-do-us-part-or-at-least-till-I-run-out-of-conditioner relationship, and I, a novice at deep, meaningful, fulfilling relationships, had read only fifty pages of *The Male Couple's Guide to Living Together* in preparation.

3. I was a closet radical who went to demonstrations and shouted in protest and even once got arrested in the hopes of being strip-searched by the policeman of my dreams; Roger was so apolitical he didn't even *vote* in the last election (and if he *had* voted, he would have voted for *Bush,* but only because the name Dukakis didn't sound "presidential").

4. I was a proabortion atheistic knee-jerk pinko faggot; Roger was a Catholic who had spent several years unsuccessfully trying to cure himself of homosexuality because of the obvious religious conflict. Moreover, Roger was deeply offended by Madonna's video "Like a Prayer," whereas I worshiped her and secretly yearned to lick her stigmata.

5. Roger liked to have fun, and I preferred to suffer. Roger liked going out to bars and dancing on tabletops and smoking unfiltered cigarettes and eating brunch with other homosexuals of his ilk, whereas I preferred to stay home in my wreck of an apartment to the point of agoraphobia, reading the works of Schopenhauer, drinking bitters. Roger was extremely loyal to a highly selective group of friends numbering three, whereas in all of my relationships I was fundamentally promiscuous, and my acquaintances numbered in the hundreds. I'm sure he eventually smelled the rancid stench of my constant infidelity, which I was able to conceal so ingeniously that even I wasn't aware of it.

6. Roger was a virgin, and I was a whore. I would rush away a moment after ejaculation to wash off the *deadly* spermatozoa,

and Roger would happily lie in puddles of spunk for days. I masturbated constantly—I'm masturbating this very second!— and Roger would rarely, if ever, perform an act of self-pollution, possibly because subconsciously the voice of God was telling him that it was a sin and he would go straight to hell if he did it, but more likely because he found it boring.

7. I was a pseudointellectual and a poseur and snob, and Roger was not particularly interested in printed matter when it didn't concern the internal mechanisms of automobiles: Whereas I read Kafka, Roger read car manuals.

8. I had complained that I didn't have enough time for a job, gym, reading, movies, plays, therapy, doctor's appointments, the beach, running, AIDS activism, museums, galleries, endless phone calls, visiting friends in the hospital, cleaning the apartment, doing the dishes, the laundry, ironing shirts, making dinner, eight hours of sleep each night, and a relationship; Roger responded sympathetically by casually eliminating the final item of my list.

9. Roger fell instantly, profoundly, completely, and eternally in love with me the moment we met: He told me he was experiencing deeper feelings for me than he had experienced for anyone else in the past eight years since his first cocaine-addicted lover named Larry, the first of three cocaine-addicted lovers named Larry (funny how we all have a "type"). And of course, two months later, after I returned from a ten-day separate vacation, he fell instantly, profoundly, completely, and eternally out of love with me. That was, of course, the point when I was gradually realizing that my feelings for him were growing to the point that separation would be unthinkable and I was actually considering releasing the floodgates of my frozen and stultifying emotions for a moment and admitting that maybe, just maybe, I might be in love with Roger; although, as one would expect, I only really fell in love with Roger two weeks after our tragic breakup.

How We Broke Up II

We broke up over dinner at the Heartbreak Restaurant, down in Soho.

The walls of the Heartbreak Restaurant were covered with repulsive art that changed every month: One month photorealistic canvases of grossly enlarged contorted faces blanketed the scene; this month, nonrepresentational splotches of violent shades of red. Our table, raised and centrally located, had two spotlights focused on it. The sound system played dramatic music from some unspecified *film noir* of the forties. On a videoscreen above the bar I could see Barbara Stanwyck with tears running down her black-and-white profile.

Roger was prompt and sweating slightly. I staggered to our table, having subsisted on vodka and cranberry juice during the past few weeks. The waiter left us separate checks when we ordered and informed us that tips were requested in advance of service, since very few meals were completed at the Heartbreak Restaurant.

"I have something to tell you," Roger began gently.

"Oh, are you going to drop me?" I inquired, disingenuously. "Don't bother me with last week's news. I was *just* about to drop you. *Thanks for saving me the trouble.*"

"There's no need to be nasty," he chided.

"What can I say? We laughed, we cried, we had good times, we had bad times. If you don't get on that plane, you'll regret it: maybe not today, maybe not tomorrow, but some day. Laszlo needs you more than I do. When you remember me," I said, arm poised with a glass of pink champagne, "and you will, you will, think of me kindly," I continued, tossing the contents at my white alligator shirt and stalking angrily out of the restaurant, to thunderous applause.

How Did We Meet?

We met in typical approaching-the-fin-de-siècle manner: at a People With AIDS Coalition Singles Tea. We had both come with friends who didn't want to go alone, hardly expecting to meet anyone ourselves, merely as support. My friend Jim said I would be Rhoda to his Mary. Our friends had both developed full-blown AIDS; at the time Roger and I were asymptomatic antibody-positive.

The official *yenta,* a nice Jewish boy with aspirations in the profession of musical theater, asked exceedingly embarrassing questions of the gathered group to help narrow down our choices. Audience members raised their hands, indicating answers in the affirmative. "Who has more than twenty-seven T-cells? Who has less than fifteen hundred T-cells? Who is currently in a relationship with a member of the clergy and willing to have six to ten additional relationships on the side? Who has never had a relationship that lasted longer than the Broadway run of *Moose Murders?* Who owns an apartment in Zeckendorf Towers? Who lives in a Salvation Army shelter? Who bites their nails? Who has a two-thousand-watt blow-dryer? Who has a penis that is ten inches or larger? (Please see me later in the back.) Who will have oral sex with a condom? Who will have oral sex with a condom only if the condom has a penis inside? Who is on aerosol pentamidine? Who owns their own nebulizer? Who rents? Who won more than ten thousand dollars in the New York lottery? Who goes to the gym more than five times a week? Who goes to twelve-step meetings more than twice a day? Who uses deodorant on a regular basis? Who shaves more than his facial hair? Who shaves more than his facial hair daily in the Chelsea Gym shower? Who has been in therapy for longer than ten years? Who hasn't been north of Fourteenth Street in ten years? Who has appeared as a model in *Mandate* magazine? Who used to hustle? Who is allergic to pubic hair? Who has slept with more than one thousand men in the past ten years? In the past five years? In the past ten weeks? Who has been disowned by his family? Who has disowned his family? Who likes to wear lace occasionally? Who is currently wearing frilly underwear? Who wouldn't mind displaying them to the group?" And so on.

By the time all of the questions were asked, the only remaining question would be "Your place or mine?"

How We Broke Up III

One day it just happened. It was over. It ended. After a while I lost interest. We just let it fade away and die. I went home quietly and took an overdose of sleeping pills and turned on *Carson*. I went home quietly and called up the phone-sex line and had a lovely time. I went home quietly and baked a dozen hash brownies and sat there, eating them, watching a rerun of the final episode of *Berlin Alexanderplatz* on Arts and Entertainment. I went home quietly and rented a masseur and had a lovely time; he stole my stereo, my CD player, my VCR, and my personal computer, along with most of my software. I didn't care. Life was meaningless. I made a conscious effort to at least appear upset to the outer world. I failed. It was over. I didn't even notice his absence. I looked in my little black book and easily found a substitute. It ended quietly. There were no harsh words. We both agreed that we had relatively little in common, and although we did have a pleasurable experience, it was best to part. It was enough to just go home and cry into my Laura Ashley designer pillows and play Billie Holiday CDs and drink absinthe and smoke opium from a hookah and try to forget.

My old flame. I can't even remember his name.

What Did Roger Look Like?

Roger had deep, bright, sensitive brown eyes; thick, full, sensuous lips; a short, neatly cropped brown beard; and well-groomed brown hair thinning along the temples, indicating a high production of testosterone. He was extremely tall, at least for me: six foot one or two. He looked to be in his mid-to-late thirties. He was bundled in a plaid overshirt and jacket, possibly concealing several defects, for we met in the dead of winter. His clothing was rather unremarkable, leading me to the mistaken impression that he wasn't overly interested in fashion. His voice was deep and satisfying.

Later I would discover he had a not inconsiderable member, henceforth to be referred to in a voice several octaves lower than my normal range as his "tool."

How We Broke Up IV

We broke up in a civilized manner. Afterward we returned to our respective apartments and shot ourselves with a single silver bullet in the head, between the eyes. Moments before, we had neatly laid newspaper around to catch spills and notified our menservants. We left our wills in plain sight. Unfortunately, we had named one another as executors and had, in fact, left the bulk of our estates to one another. The wills were in probate for years.

Why Did I Approach Roger?

I kept my eye on Roger throughout the question-and-answer period. He'd occasionally look in my direction. Jim and I came to the singles tea expecting the usual emergency-room overflow crowd, the kind of congregation one might find at Lourdes or at one of Louise Hays's evangelical lectures, ready to throw away their crutches and dance onstage with tambourines and ethyl rags. It wasn't quite that awful; still, it was like a bad night at the Barbary Coast: The pickings were pretty slim. Early on during the mass interrogation Jim and I decided that Roger was the only appealing prospect. Jim threw in the towel early, complaining that Roger hadn't noticed him. I then announced my intention to secure him.

So afterward I walked up, introducing myself. "Even though we're completely incompatible, since you are homeless and I am a complete slob, I would like to give you my phone number."

"I'm not homeless," said Roger, in a deep baritone that reverberated at the base of my spine.

"You didn't raise your hand at any of the questions regarding place of residence," I pointed out.

"I live on Long Island. It wasn't on the list."

In former years this would have been an automatic cause of disqualification—the red light, the buzzer, the seat-eject, the trapdoor, the shepherd's hook, you name it. However, in the approaching-the-fin-de-siècle manner, one uses a less exacting set of criteria in selecting possible dates. In other words, we've lowered our standards. There was a time when I didn't date men who smoked cigarettes, were in any of the design professions, wore leather pants, had tit rings, appreciated the opera, drank to excess, danced in the gym, or had been in therapy for more than ten years. Now, however, I'm just looking for a warm body to cuddle, hopefully with a life expectancy longer than that of my five-day deodorant. The rest is immaterial.

How We Broke Up V

Roger and I broke up every week, on Friday. After considerable experimentation we had decided that Friday would be optimal, giving us the rest of the weekend for a Harlequin "second chance at romance." We were doomed to repeat our breakup scenes endlessly, with only minor variations, in our version of Boyfriend Hell. One week I would break up with Roger; the following week, he would break up with me. One week I would toss a glass of chablis at Roger; the following week, he would retaliate with a glass of Mogen David wine, kosher for Passover. Yet, inextricably linked, powerless to resist, we remained faithful to our Friday-night assignations.

How Did Our First Date End in a Rather Typical Manner?

We promised not to start too fast and ended up having sex on the first date anyway.

"You seduced me!" he accused. "It was that look you gave me, with those big brown eyes of yours."

"They're hazel. If only you were paying attention."

"Whatever. It must have been what you whispered in my ear."

At every step Roger hesitated, from the door to the chair to the couch to the bed. Ever the disinterested participant, I was willing to offer no advice, either pro or con. I neither encouraged nor discouraged his advances; of this, I am certain he will dispute me. "I would rather get to know you better," he said on the couch, enveloping me in his brawny arms and kissing me on the cheek, "before we continue."

I offered the suggestion that we contain ourselves to necking and petting above the waist, with at least one foot on the floor at all times. Roger consented. All too soon, we went the way of all flesh. "Would you hate me if I stopped here?" asked Roger.

"Of course not," I murmured, circling his sensitive nipples with my tongue.

Perhaps we were both too passive to stop.

Was it my fault? I mentioned the possibility of a change of venue to the bed, in the interest of basic human comfort. Roger *was* six foot two, and my farcical couch was tiny, a suburban sleeper suitable for Japanese apartments and preadolescents. I had bought this midget divan for the express purpose of avoiding sleeping with a siren from the Midwest who had visited me roughly nine years earlier intent on converting me to the wonderful world of bisexuality—she who, like Marilyn Chambers, was "insatiable."

Of necessity, shoes were removed. At that point it only made sense to continue disrobing. Socks, pants, and expandable watchbands were sporadically tossed in the direction of the couch. I hid under the sheets, burrowing deep down under like a gopher, curling up into a fetal position. Roger soon followed.

We were down to our underwear. "Would you feel foolish if we stopped here?" asked Roger.

Answering neither yes nor no, I went to the kitchen for twin glasses of water. When I returned, Roger lay flat on the bed, arms outstretched, legs spread, a pillow replacing his white Jockey shorts. His eyes were closed. Following the most primitive of all categorical imperatives, I doffed my shorts and dove in.

Was it a momentary lapse of reason, a convenient case of temporary amnesia, or merely situational ethics of the most abhorrent and venal kind? For some reason, in the heat of passion I invariably forget the logic behind not sleeping with someone on the first date. I vowed to spray-paint the elusive reasons in day-glo block letters on the ceiling for precisely these occasions.

We all have our own personal scales of intimacy. Perhaps mine was skewed? It ranged from such relatively impersonal contact like shaking someone's hands, greeting them on the street, having violent and profound sex with them, exchanging first names, sharing recreational drugs with them, pointing out unseemly semen stains in public to avoid undue embarrassment, to exchanging last names, adding phone numbers to the quick-dial feature of auto-memory, naming one another as correspondents in divorce cases, exchanging house keys, and so on.

Sleeping with someone was rather low on my scale of familiarity. "Don't take it personally," I rushed to reassure Roger, who feared we had gone too far and was consequently banging his head against the plaster. "What happened to you could have happened to anyone."

How We Broke Up VI

I was coming home from work late one evening. I decided to take the shortcut through Great Jones Alley. I patted my wallet self-consciously. I heard footsteps behind me. I started to pick up my pace. Soon, we were both running. I made a quick left into a blind alley. I was stuck. There was no way out.

He had a flashlight shining on me. I couldn't see his face. And then he spoke, that deep familiar voice of gravel. "This is for the emotional scars you've given me these past six months."

"But, Roger," I began, "I didn't mean to hurt you—" That was when I felt something harsh splashing on my eyes. I screamed. Battery acid. I was blinded for life.

Why Doesn't Anyone Go Slow Anymore?

Because there just isn't enough time.

How We Broke Up VII

Once we broke up, we severed all contact. I believe Roger moved to Baltimore the following autumn, with an insurance broker. I remained firmly ensconced in my venomous flat in Hell's Kitchenette. Christmas cards were not exchanged. Birthdays were forgotten. A few years later, it was as if I had never known Roger at all.

How Long Were Our First Three Dates?

Roger wanted to stay over. I acceded to his wishes, although my omnipresent infinite list of things to do weighed heavily on my mind.

It was a very long first date.

A few weeks later, I realized that each of our first three dates extended longer than twelve hours. Perhaps we were getting serious? I consulted my horoscope for clues. The enigmatic forecast was immediately covered with the wet quicksand of my failing memory.

When Did Roger Learn My Phone Number?

Roger learned my phone number by heart after our first date; I always referred to the yellow stickum on the bulletin board, next to the laundry ticket and the film-festival schedule. I ultimately didn't memorize his number until about two weeks *after* we broke up.

How Did Roger Kiss?

Every kiss was an event. Roger's kisses were gentle morning dew on my cheeks, teasing passes of a butterfly's wings at my lips, mad B-52 bombing runs on my mouth, kamikaze attacks on my throat, atomic-bomb explosions on my nipples, urgent stingray bites on my pelvis, laconic feathers slowly wafting their way earthbound on my stomach.

"Look!" he would say, pointing his finger toward the ceiling.

"What is it?"

"No, the other way," he'd continue, veiling his approach with subterfuge, throwing me off the track with false promises of Halley's comet. I would turn my head, following the imaginary trajectory of his fingertip to the sky.

He would bring his finger to my lips. "Shhh."

If I turned to look at him, he would warn, "Don't watch."

Shy and secretive, he would make his gentle approach, with all of the stealth of an invisible jet-bomber. "Don't move!"

I pretended I was in Bermuda, merely hallucinating Roger. I felt Roger wanted to protect me, rejuvenate me to the point of being too young to realize I was naked. "You don't want to spoil it, do you?" said Roger with his eyes.

Every kiss was magic. I can only fail in my attempts to describe the unbearable lightness of Roger's lips. Thus inclined, he would make his gradual approach. "Excuse me, what's that?" he would say. A piece of lint? A freckle? An invisible spot?

I would feel a gentle, sweet, soft contact on the cheek as Roger kissed the locus of our deception. "Got it!" he'd announce successfully. "It's gone now."

Who wouldn't swoon?

What Were We Afraid Of?

I was afraid of dying.

Roger was afraid of getting sick.

He said he didn't mind dying; it was just the getting sick that he hated.

I said, "Are you crazy? Nobody wants to die."

How Did We Get Along with One Another's Friends?

I hated all of his friends, and he couldn't stand any of mine; every chance meeting was fraught with peril. It was safest when we stuck to our apartments and ordered out Chinese, rented old horror flicks, and had copious amounts of sexual intercourse.

The snideness of his friends' responses was unparalleled in the history of queendom. Roger's friends discussed accessories constantly, along with fashion utensils, sexual appliances, household demographics, makeup secrets, interior deconstructionism, and skin-care secrets. They all worked in the madcap world of design: remixing music videos, deranging window displays, bending hair, slinging hash, filing teeth, and so on.

My friend Cameron didn't fare any better with Roger. The three of us met in a Mexican restaurant. Cameron chose that moment to inform Roger that Madonna's latest blasphemous video had changed his life. Cameron then made us move to another table because the lighting was rather unflattering. For some reason that escapes me, Cameron grated on Roger's nerves, although Roger was kind enough not to bring it to my immediate attention.

Did Roger Sleep Naked at Night?

Of course he did.

What Kind of Underwear Did Roger Wear?

Roger wore plain full-cut white underwear, and I wore gray Calvin Kleins because I took vitamin B, and pee stains were rather unattractive.

How Does Roger Drop Men?

"I try to drop men as soon as I know that it won't work out," explained Roger to me on one of our twenty-three-minute post-breakup phone calls. "I don't believe in dragging out an affair. I try to be as gentle as possible in my approach. I usually hint around. I never break up over the telephone. It's always in person—usually over a chef salad."

"All I wanted was to better my personal record of three months for a relationship," I whined in reply. "I was hoping to break one hundred days. Maybe *Time* magazine would do an article on our relationship, like a recently inaugurated president. 'Roger and Me: The First Hundred Days.' "

"Everything was wrong from the start with us. The first time I saw you, sort of goofy looking, slouched down in that chair, an admitted slob, hair all over the place, painter's overalls with one suspender—not the height of fashion in my book, if you ask me."

"I don't recall posing the question," I replied, stung. "At least I've never been involved with cocaine addicts."

"Maybe it was a blind spot on my part."

"It's not as if I had any fantasies of sex with a grease monkey either."

"You were weird from the beginning. I should never have even dated you. Yet for some reason I was drawn to you. I don't know why."

What Did I Always Want to Do with Roger?

I always wanted to go for a drive on his motorcycle, with my long blond hair blowing in the wind, hugging him tight around the waist of his leather jacket, holding on for dear life as he sped around a curve. Unfortunately, at the time I was a brunette with a crew cut. And when I finally found the appropriate wig, Roger had already sold his Harley Davidson.

Roger had wanted a motorcycle for years, but when he finally got one, he was too nervous to drive it with any regularity.

Who Called the Other First
after Our Tragic Breakup?

I suppose it was me.

DOES SIZE MATTER?

"And suppose I had a two-inch penis," asked Roger during one of our twenty-three-minute post-breakup phone calls. "If after you looked into my big brown eyes and boyishly sat next to me on the couch and then seduced me with your lips and took me over to the bed, leading me like the blind leading the blind, and then as we tussled on the bed and you caressed my legs, my thighs, my loins, feeling around, very casually, for some hardened *tool,* and then licking my bountiful chest, suppose after you had finally undressed me, taken off my shirt, my pants, then my underwear, you found that I had a two-inch penis. Would you have still loved me the same?"

"I probably would have pressed the bed-eject mechanism and sent you out flying through the window onto the hard sidewalk."

"You wouldn't have loved me for my charm, my wit, my sweet, loving kindness?"

"Of course not."

"I can't believe how shallow you are. You never loved me for what I am, just for a *thing.*"

"What about me? What about if I had a two-inch penis?"

"That's beside the point," responded Roger, in the sullen voice of a child refused. He paused for dramatic effect, long enough to let the dark and heavy cloud of guilt envelop me. "I was just playing with you," said Roger. "I was just teasing. You can tell, can't you?"

"How long is it, anyway?" I asked, wanting to quantify my lust once and for all.

"I never actually measured it. I think maybe eight and a half or nine inches. The last time I measured was when I was twelve. I don't know. It may have grown since then."

How Did I Fall in Love with Roger?

I fell in love with Roger over the phone approximately two weeks after our tragic breakup. Let me describe the progress of love: It is a slow and fitful process, fraught with complications; it follows a narrow and tortuous path; it is accomplished through a series of almost imperceptible gradual shifts and the accretion of idiosyncracies and minute details of personality. My love, the love of a callous and jaded cynic from the island of Manhattan, was like a snowball in hell surreptitiously gathering frost from the freezer of a poorly maintained Kelvinator in the devil's locker room. And as I gradually fell in love with Roger, he became more and more remote from me: He was firmly resolved to uproot our geminate lust and render asunder the tendrils of our mutual affection. He became impermeable to my entreaties. My methods were inappropriate, my directives invalid, my tactics incoherent, as he remained inaccessible.

Love is Lucy van Pelt, Charlie Brown, and that goddamned football. Every autumn, Lucy convinces Charlie Brown that she won't pull it away at the last minute. Stupidly, he makes his approach, gathers speed, focuses all of his kinetic energy onto his right foot, lifts, and Lucy removes the ball as he is almost upon it; he kicks the air and falls flat on his back. Charlie Brown is in traction for months; he is psychologically paralyzed for life. Yet he persists in learning nothing from the experience, repeating it the following fall.

What Do I Plan on Doing?

I plan on seducing Roger back, so *I* can drop *him* properly.

Why Wouldn't It Have Lasted Anyway?

"Guess what I have?" asked Roger one day during one of our twenty-three-minute phone calls, about two months after our tragic breakup.

"Thrush."

"How'd you know?"

"I assumed it was something bad," I answered. "I assumed it wasn't something *that* bad, or you would have been more alarmed. Thrush is the least serious thing that you could have. Don't worry; it goes away. It's no big deal."

"I guess I should expect something like thrush with my T-cells."

"How low are they?"

"I dunno. They were around one hundred sixty in January," he replied.

"One hundred sixty! Why didn't you tell me? If I had known your count was that low, I wouldn't have even bothered attempting a relationship with you," I lied. "I was looking for a long-term relationship. Two, three, maybe even four weeks! And you obviously couldn't sustain that. You might as well have worn an egg-timer in place of your heart."

Why Didn't I Just Let Go Once and for All like Every Other Eligible Homosexual in Manhattan and Quite a Few Ineligible Ones and Go to the Spike on Saturday Night at One a.m.?

Because I didn't want to meet all of my six thousand ex-boyfriends at once. Every Saturday night there's a meeting of the Benjamin Rosenthal Ex–Fan Club. They convene at the Spike at midnight, at the wall by the pool table, to dish me.

WHY???

Roger, sweet Roger. When I found out about the lymphoma, I wanted it to be anyone but you. I was already stuck with survivor's guilt, and neither of us was dead. Yet. But what do you expect from someone who wrote the book on the power of negative thinking (*How to Lose Friends and Irritate People*)? I always wanted to know why tumors were constantly compared to fruits, generally of the citrus variety. Roger had a tumor the size of a navel orange in his liver. As the famous Chinese philosopher Lao-tzu once said, "This sucks the big one."

Why did it have to be you, Roger? Why not me? This was the tragic knife in the side, the dagger at one's heart. I'm the personification of evil, whereas you were never anything but good, except, of course, when you callously dropped me, three cocaine addicts, and countless others.

So our eventual reconciliation, the first time we actually saw one another since our tragic breakup, which I have magnified into legend, into history, into melodrama, into an archetypal primal scene, took place at a Jewish hospital on the East Side. Were there strains of music in the hallways as I entered, men in somber rented tuxedos playing violins in the airshaft that his room looked out on? No, only silence, soundless television in the background. All three of Roger's hideous friends were there, in solidarity against me. And inevitably, I found myself falling in love with Roger for one last time.

We made out on the hospital bed after his friends left. Roger threatened to hang me from the ceiling, using the curtain tracks, and then to grease up his arm. He was just kidding, which was a good sign. In a few days he'd start chemo. "I guess my hair will fall out," he said, sorrowfully.

"It was bound to happen sooner or later."

"But I'm only twenty-six," he said.

"I know. I know."

I don't know why, but I almost cried when he told me over the phone, and I stopped myself. Does this make any sense? Does anything make any sense anymore? My friend Seymour Goldfarb died during the weekend we waited for Roger's liver biopsy. I went out to the hospital on Long Island to say good-bye to him on Saturday. He was breathing roughly, eyes closed. By Sunday he was gone.

WHAT DOES ROGER DREAM OF?

Roger dreams of a lover to take care of him the way he took care of his best friend, Bill, a few years ago. He still keeps Bill's photo in his wallet. Bill was one of the first to come down with AIDS, back in the early eighties.

Now Bill's mother comes to visit Roger at his home. A nervous nicotine addict with a three-pack-a-day habit, she invariably blows smoke into his face. Although she annoys him, he is too polite to tell her. Even when Roger chain-smoked around me, he was always careful to notice in which direction the wind blew. Since Roger got sick, he lost the taste for cigarettes.

THE FUTURE OF OUR RELATIONSHIP

We talk on the phone every other day. Sometimes he calls me, but usually I call him.

I tell Roger that he's my pal. He likes the sound of the word "pal." I tell Roger that we'll be pals forever.

·8·

The Very Last Seymour

JUNE 1989

There are no more Seymours. Seymour Goldfarb, of Massapequa, Long Island, was the very last one. He died on the tenth day of April in a year delineated by far too many hospital visits and memorial services.

In my brief, sad life I have, as yet, met only one other Seymour, Seymour Schlumberger. Active in drama society and other like extracurricular activities at Boswell High, deft and fey, popular with the fast set of the posh suburbs of Rochester, yet saddled with a name given to second-generation immigrants of middle-European heritage, he changed his name to Sandy as soon as he reached sixteen, the age of attorney.

A couple of summers ago Philip and I were driving back from Jones Beach in his lime-green '85 Pontiac. Philip and I, the sob sisters of Sigma Chi, had been pals for almost seven years. We still retained a sharp rhythmic edge of amicable discord. I had persuaded him to drop me off in midtown, although he preferred the lower Manhattan route, since traffic was better downtown en route to Jersey City.

Midtown was then bursting with socially responsible activity on the real-estate front: Donald Trump was building a Grand Hyatt for the homeless in the Fifties, and Zeckendorf was building a sixty-story AIDS hospice on Broadway. Tru-Value and Rite Aid pharmacies were distributing free needles in an attempt to curb transmission of HIV. And I was Mamie Eisenhower.

In actuality, we were stuck in the single lane left open due to construction of yet another luxury rental on Fifty-third. Philip suddenly pulled over in front of the Museum of Modern Art and motioned for me to unroll my window, the a/c now turned off. "Seymour!" he shouted.

There on the sidewalk stood Seymour and his sister, Miriam. Now, if Philip was a size-sixteen juvenile at the age of thirty-seven, Seymour at twenty-five was a slightly reduced Philip. He couldn't have been much taller than my mother, who stands five feet in stocking feet. Accountants both, they shared the same small frame. Philip had lupine brown eyes; Seymour's eyes were the bluest of blues. Seymour was covered with hair: A few tufts peeked through the V of his unbuttoned blue polo. Between two thick eyebrows I could see soft stubble. Miriam had on a pair of thick tortoiseshell glasses and a simple peasant blouse.

"Did somebody forget to turn off the radio?" asked Seymour. A teenager was sitting across the street, his boom box blasting away at peak volume. A car siren went off.

Brief introductions were exchanged. Seymour and Miriam had just seen the Ansel Adams photo exhibit. They were on their way to Brooklyn for dinner. Seymour looked a little peaked. We said good-bye and drove on.

"He has AIDS," explained Philip. "It's such a shame. He was just in the hospital for a few weeks with pneumonia. He's so young. It's a tragedy. I really like him a lot."

"Where'd you meet him?"

"In the neighborhood. Ron was having a party. So we started talking. I told him I really liked the music, and he said that he had made up the tape. It was a professional job: The cuts were clean, the segues smooth. It was a mix of the Supremes, George Michael, and the Eurythmics."

Philip was more than ten years older than Seymour, yet they were frequently mistaken for one another. Maybe it was their size; maybe it was the brightness of their eyes. Even Tom, Seymour's ex, confused the two that summer on Gay Pride Day. Philip was trying to sneak into the Gay Italians. They immediately booted him out when they heard Tom shout, "Seymour!" Philip had to stand on the sidelines and wait for the Black Cops on Motorcycles.

"It kind of bothers Seymour," said Phil. "I don't know why."

"Maybe it's the age difference?" I suggested. "Or perhaps the resemblance is so uncanny that he fears dating you would be the height of homosexual narcissism, one step away from kissing yourself in the mirror."

The following winter I went along with Philip to visit Seymour in the hospital. Seymour's entire family was in attendance. Miriam was his size, his mother even shorter, his father a tad taller. They all belonged in some fairy-tale pop-up book, neatly folded when closed, asleep in the mystical land of nod.

Miriam sat in the corner, chewed gum, and read Tolstoy.

His mother offered me a miniature chocolate.

His father leaned against the window ledge, eyes closed.

I half-imagined seeing animated birds chirping sweetly above, painted in bright cartoon pastels. Honey, I shrunk the Goldfarbs.

Of the entire family, only his grandmother was larger than lifesize. Correction: Only his grandmother's *mouth* was larger than life-size. Nadine Goldfarb, a native of Brighton Beach, interrupted every exchange with querulous questions and inane commentary. Nadine was totally out of control: She never stopped to think before speaking.

And Tom, Seymour's ex, was there. I laid eyes on Tom and immediately tumbled into lust. Tom, a caterer by day (no doubt a playboy by night), had brought trays and trays of petits fours to the room, left over from a wedding he was working. Tom wore a white starched shirt. His green eyes sparkled. He smiled with a set of choppers that could have easily been the centerpiece of an Ultra Brite commercial on TV. His thick brown hair was artfully combed, a few bangs on his forehead.

Tom called Seymour's parents by their first names, as if we were all adults. By romantic coincidence they were both named Leslie. To avoid confusion, Dad was referred to as Les, and Mom as Lee. Tom even called Seymour's grandmother by her given name, Nadine. Nadine was knitting a quilt. She didn't look up from her work as she interjected her two kopeks at every available opportunity.

Seymour was telling Miriam a story about his ex-roommate Will. Seymour wasn't afraid to tell lurid tales in front of his parents. I myself shrank from such frankness, although I didn't feel at all uncomfortable discussing my sexual habits aloud on all modes of public transport, including the train to the plane, the bus from Newark, and the IRT Number 2 subway. I was never embarrassed, only my companion would be, yet *he* was invariably the one wearing the golden earring I had always coveted but was far too shy to wear myself.

Les picked up a *People* magazine and thumbed through it, engrossed. He sat by the window. Les ignored us with benign neglect. Lee was drinking a Diet Coke and working on a crossword puzzle. She offered fruit from a basket delivered by mistake to the wrong room.

"Once it's inside, they can't take it out. It's contaminated," muttered Nadine. The trash cans were lined with pink plastic disposal bags, marked for special handling: "CAUTION: INFECTIOUS DISEASE." Nobody bothered with gloves or gowns. They weren't necessary.

"So Will picked up this trick at Port Authority who ended up stealing his boyfriend's camera and watch while Will was in the bathroom cleaning up afterwards. Needless to say, his boyfriend was none too pleased when he heard about it."

"I'm going for a walk. I can't stand this talk. It's disgusting." Nadine got up and left.

"That Will is always getting into messes. I suppose they ended up in divorce court over the incident," said Tom. I stared at him. He didn't seem to know I was watching him.

"How are you feeling?" asked Philip.

"All right. A little tired," said Seymour. "Entertaining guests can be exhausting. I need a maid to clean up after all of my visitors."

"Does your grandmother ever shut up?" I asked.

"She talks in her sleep," said Seymour.

"I think I remember a lull in the conversation on December 7, 1946," said Lee.

"Are you sure it wasn't dinner and her mouth wasn't full?" asked Seymour.

"She's really broken up over this thing with Seymour," said Lee.

"Seymour and Nadine are the same person," commented Tom.

"What?" I didn't understand.

"I beg to differ," said Seymour.

"The two of you always say exactly what's on your minds. That's why she gets on your nerves," Tom replied.

That spring, Philip and Seymour took a noncredit architecture-appreciation class through the New School. They roamed the streets on Sunday afternoons, stopping to stare at gargoyled arches atop Art Deco buildings in midtown. Seymour took notes.

Seymour was doing fine; he didn't mind walking. He took long naps in the afternoon.

Afterward they went out together for dinner. Philip didn't want to insult Seymour by paying. Seymour was collecting disability. He hardly had any money. I told Philip he should treat.

"I invited Seymour over one night," Philip told me. "We didn't do anything. Well, we didn't do much. You know, it was safe and all. Anyway, he slept over in my bed. He got really sweaty that night, and I must admit I felt a little uncomfortable sleeping in the same bed with him."

Seymour held a Mickey Mouse theme party in July in his parents' backyard. He had given up the share in Brooklyn and moved back to Long Island a few months earlier. His friends Louise and Gregory, who are related by the sacrament of marriage, gave me a lift outside an evangelical church in Times Square. Seymour used to work with Louise in an accounting firm in New Jersey. Louise and Gregory recognized me by my Sapphic T-shirt of a large-breasted woman staring at the mirror, fixing her hair, with the thought bubble "If they can put one man on the moon, why not ALL of them?"

Nadine was lying on a lawn chair, guzzling iced tea and swatting mosquitoes. Les poured some more lighter fluid on the charcoal grill, preparing for hot dogs and burgers. Seymour wore a Disneyland T-shirt with Mickey and Minnie, along with an eponymous watch. He had a buzz cut. He looked too cute for words. Seymour popped another tape into the portable tape-player on the cement steps leading into the kitchen. "Glad you could make it," he said to me and Louise and Gregory.

"I remember you from the hospital. Was it Barry?" shouted Nadine unnecessarily, as I was standing right in front of her.

"Benjamin," I corrected.

"Good to see you again. Too bad it's so hot. At least it's not likely to rain today."

Tom was sitting at one of the picnic tables, talking to a guy with a diamond-stud earring. Again, I felt that sinking feeling at the pit of my stomach that could only be chronic lust or severe indigestion. I wondered how I could subtly position myself next to Tom without getting Seymour piqued. Tom worked the backyard like a professional.

"You look even better than last time," I said.

"That's because I'm wearing less clothes." He smiled. He was wearing Ocean Pacific shorts and a green tank-top.

"I wonder if I'll get the chance to see more of you," I suggested, rubbing his ankle with my big left toe under the table.

"I'm sure you'll manage. If you'll excuse me, I have to talk to Lee." He got up and went over to Seymour's mom and started chatting with her.

I kicked my own shins in frustration.

"So I figured since hardly anybody was coming out to see me, I'd have a big party," Seymour explained to Louise and Gregory.

"Oh, don't say that." Louise was a little red from the sun.

"I didn't mean you two," said Seymour.

"Philip really wanted to come. He just had this trip to California planned," I mentioned.

"He'd rather go to L.A. than Massapequa? What's wrong with his priorities?"

"Who wants a burger?" asked Les. "The first batch is done."

"Get me one that's well done but not burnt," Nadine advised Lee. "And could you put some ketchup on it too?"

"I did the potato salad," announced Seymour. "You should really try it. Wendall loved it!" Wendall was his dog.

"How's my little monkey?" asked Tom, ruffling Seymour's hair.

"Stop it! You know I hate it when you call me that," said Seymour.

"Just teasing," replied Tom. Why couldn't he tease me?

Louise and Greg had to leave at 3:30. I managed to get a ride with Morgan, a hair stylist, who was also driving Tom back to

New York. We said our good-byes at five. Morgan and Tom, sitting in front, discussed the perils of business and notoriously fussy clients as I, in back, rubbed Tom's neck. Morgan dropped us off at a Brooklyn subway. Tom gave me his number. "Things are pretty chaotic with me now. Give me a call and maybe we can get together. I can't promise when, though. I'm really busy with work. I'm going on vacation in a few weeks. Try me," he said, and then he took the infinite escalator down to the IND line. I waved good-bye.

I tried calling Tom six or seventeen thousand times. He was evidently inhabiting some other astral plane: We didn't connect. Philip had a chalkboard next to his phone so he never called the same person twice by mistake without receiving appropriate encouragement in the interim. I threw myself back into the hapless affairs of the heart and loins with which I invariably entangled myself. The sheets fell in slow-motion sequence from the forties movie-calendar, accompanied by Technicolored leaves: July, August, September, October.

"Seymour's back at Beth Israel, with an infection," said Philip. It was November.

"I'll try to see him soon."

I carefully redistributed the piles of papers on my desk at the office. In between, I called the hospital. "Busy this afternoon?" I asked Seymour. "I thought I might drop by for lunch."

"Let me check my appointment book. Lunch with Jackie O. Shopping with Diana Vreeland at Saks. Late-night supper with Madonna and Sean. I think I can squeeze you in. I'll cancel Jackie; she'd understand."

On my way to the hospital I picked up a bunch of flowers at a Korean deli.

"Flowers. How nice. Did you bring tulips? Could you close your eyes and place your two lips on mine?"

I kissed Seymour on the cheek.

Seymour played with his peaches. "I'd offer you some lunch,

but I'm not sure whether you like gray meat. I'm so glad this isn't a goyish hospital. I get spooked by those suffering martyrs on every wall," said Seymour.

"If you want, I can bring in my neon Jesus," I offered.

Seymour was in a semiprivate room. His roommate was Cuban. "They always put me with someone who doesn't speak English. It's like the United Nations here," complained Seymour. "These things always happen to me. Don't you get annoyed when you buy the Sunday *Times* and the only section that's missing is 'Men's Fashion'? Don't you get irritated when you walk five blocks in search of a working pay-phone and when you finally find one, you get a wrong number with your only quarter?" asked Seymour.

A few days later, I ran into Tom at the hospital. Seymour, propped up on pillows, stared out the window, sighing. Tom was in the middle of another sob story.

"So I get back to the loft and find out that we've been robbed. I figure it was bad karma. I was late for a party. I had lost my watch. I must have left the window open, but who would think someone would crawl in a window on the eighteenth story of a building? It looks like they broke in next door and climbed through the window. But you know, what goes around, comes around. Larry, my partner in the loft, he bought a hot stereo a few weeks ago, and he knew at those prices that it must have fallen off the truck, if you know what I mean. So I guess cosmically it makes sense, although I don't know why I have to be the one to get ripped off."

"Get off with this karma crap, Tom. I suppose this is because of something I did in a previous life?" Seymour objected, referring to his own unjustified health status.

"I didn't mean that."

"It isn't fair."

"You're right," said Tom. "I'm sorry, I'm so sorry," he said, running his fingers through Seymour's thinning hair. "It just isn't fair."

"We have to stop meeting like this," Tom told me at the Greek diner across the street from the hospital. Seymour's parents had just arrived for the evening shift, so we went out for dinner.

I wanted him so bad it hurt.

Tom's green eyes were flecked with gold; he had a black mole on his forehead. His teeth were ivory-white; his skin soft as satin. Half-Irish, half-Indian, half-French, half-Moroccan, Tom was a self-described mutt, a self-contained melting pot, a conglomeration of only the choicest portions of each of his many ethnicities. His body was smooth, honed like a knife, a tight frame lined with lean muscle.

"I'm free tomorrow, the next day, the following day, and likewise for the next ten years. Perhaps you would like to make plans?" I offered.

"Let's try Saturday. Could you do me a favor? Try not to mention it to Seymour," cautioned Tom. "He's still a little jealous, even though we broke up over a year ago."

Our relationship was doomed from the start. Tom's timing was off; his internal mood-clock was solar-powered, and maybe it was perpetually cloudy, maybe there was an eclipse, maybe the batteries were dead? Tom was forever late for dates and appointments. He existed in his own personal time-zone.

Tom was constantly getting robbed and forgetting engagements. There was some cosmic jinx on him. At the airport he would frequently end up in Elmira when intending to fly to Sarasota. I had a few New Age friends whom I tolerated so long as they didn't mention Shirley MacLaine in my presence; however, Tom was *beyond* crystals. He flew to Florida to swim with dolphins; he went whale-watching in Nantucket. He visited the Healing Circle on Tuesdays. Once a week, he would practice rebirthing, lying submerged in the bathtub, breathing through a straw.

Tom was an aesthete, and gorgeous beyond words. Yet he was aware of flaws no one else could detect: He had skinny ankles; he stopped working on his chest because he felt it was getting too large for his frame; he couldn't get rid of the muscles at the side of his waist which interfered with the V torso.

I saw Tom several times. He vanished periodically into thin air, like an FM radio station from New Jersey with weak reception, swallowed by noise. Tom was like mercury: intangible. He retreated whenever anyone got too close to him.

"When we were together, he kept on saying that we should see other people," said Seymour. "Whenever I felt we were getting close, you know, really making a commitment, he would mention going out with other people. I would think things were going really wonderful. We'd have an incredibly intimate weekend together, and then, out of the blue, he'd mention seeing other people."

Consider the complicated dynamics of the four of us: Draw a diagram. Model it with a mobile by Alexander Calder, chimes blowing in the wind, pieces crisscrossing, touching, and then eliding—every combination a potential disaster.

Philip despised Tom because Tom couldn't answer a single question from the Silver Screen edition of Trivial Pursuit. Tom was none too fond of Philip after Philip mistakenly knocked over a tray of canapés Tom had carefully arranged on the table next to Seymour's hospital bed. Seymour became annoyed at Philip's cautious attentions for reasons completely unrelated to Philip himself. Philip was unsure whether Seymour was mad at Philip or just mad at the world. Tom visited Seymour almost daily, with a couple of the latest cassettes, spending hours rubbing his feet. Seymour always perked up when Tom came; he had never really gotten over Tom. It wasn't that I was in love with Tom; it was more that I was under his spell. Tom responded in kind on those rare occasions when our astrological charts and biorhythms were compatible. Seymour and I shared a rare (for me) platonic relationship. I had slept with almost all of my gay friends, generally within twenty-four hours of meeting them, although it took a nine-month gestation period for me and Tom to get together.

For a while, we represented four points on the HIV spectrum. Philip had determined through exhaustive and prodigious personal research that would have been accepted at most medical journals as statistically significant that it was next to impossible to contract HIV through oral sex: He was a neggie. Completely at odds with my gloom-and-doom personality, I was positive and had been for up to ten years, ever since an unlucky incursion by some nameless and Trojan-less horse-hung stud I had undoubtedly met at St. Mark's Baths or maybe by Richard, my disastrous affair from 1980. Seymour had made it into the CDC charts with a bullet twenty-four months earlier, and I was not privy to further data. Tom, of course, was a question mark in our survey: He was in the nebulous region of the untested.

That December I was walking down Ninth, exhausted, bundled in muddied sweats and a nylon jacket, recovering from my five miles of hell with the Front Runners on their Saturday morning "fun" run. I ran into Seymour, in a surprisingly good mood, and his friend Annette, from Washington. They were wearing identical wire-rimmed sunglasses. Annette must have been exactly the same height as Seymour. I had to stop them, snatch the camera from Annette's neck, and take a photo. "I'd like one three-by-five, one five-by-eight, and several wallet-sized photos to give out to strangers," Seymour said.

I called him from work and asked if I could visit him after five. It was February, and he was back in the hospital.

"I'll be here," he said in that small, sad, ironic voice of his.

I brought presents: a plastic tube with a spiral path and oil bubbles that fell down the spiral when it was upended, a key chain that made pinball noises (death rays, sirens, and so on), a hologram of an eye.

I went to visit Seymour on Valentine's Day. No valentines for me. Two years before, I had had a blind date, a personal ad. I had sent him my photo. He was predictably late. I was predictably furious. I started off on the wrong foot. I made some comment about his bald spot. It wasn't working out well. We went to the Little Mushroom, sharing a table with a pair of Koreans. We left and parted. The next day, I read an article about a woman who had swallowed cyanide because she was dateless on Valentine's Day. I clipped the story and glued it to a postcard of the Parisian catacombs (*mucho* grisly skulls piled up in a decorative fashion), sending it to my would-be amour with thanks for saving me from such a fate. For some reason he never returned my photo, although I had asked him to.

I picked up a box of twenty-eight valentines, including one for Teacher (that went to my mother). I gave Seymour a teddy-bear card. His mother got another one. I skipped the grandma; she was off wandering the hallways of the hospital.

Seymour was in the hospital to get a Hickman catheter implanted because he had developed CMV retinitis, and he was trying an experimental drug, ganciclovir, known in the trades as DHPG. How was he expected to remember it? I told him a story: Cher, nominated for an Academy Award, went to her favorite hairdresser for a styling. She was three hours late for her appointment; it was, of course, the busiest day in Hollywood for hair-benders, rag-hawkers, makeup geniuses, and personal trainers. M. Maurice (né Morris Kaminsky, of Teaneck, New Jersey) was justifiably furious at the delay; moreover, Arnold Malicious, a hustler who had been staying in his swank Silverlake digs, had left him that morning, handcuffed naked to the toilet, taking six credit cards, one VCR, and three ounces of coke. M. Maurice went crazy and shaved Cher completely bald. Naturally, she sued.

The headlines in *Daily Variety* from the court: "Deranged Hair-dresser Pleads Guilty" (or DHPG).

"Can we still go to the beach with my hickey?" asked Seymour, using his nickname for the Hickman catheter implanted in his chest. DHPG is administered daily with an IV drip; without a catheter, you usually run out of veins.

"I'm not sure I'm going to the beach anyway," I replied. "You know, deadly rays and all."

"What's so bad about going to the beach? The sea air should do you a little good," said his grandmother.

"I guess it's bad for the immune system."

"So what isn't?"

That winter I sent Seymour three coupons. One was for a movie of his choice, another for a play of his choice, and the third for dinner at the restaurant of his choice. These coupons had no expiration date. The only condition was that he accompany me on these occasions.

He never redeemed any of the coupons.

Philip and I were slowly drifting apart, on ice floes in the Arctic Ocean.

Seymour was losing his hair.

Tom was flaky and I was cynical: This was the crux of our incompatibility. Tom reminded me that I had told him this during our final post-relationship orgasm, although it didn't seem to bother him particularly.

Yet, long after the demise of our affair, I continued to call Tom, concerned about Seymour. Did Tom think Seymour wanted to talk to me? He didn't know. Should I send Seymour a card? Perhaps. I was afraid of fucking up again. I've always dragged out friendships long past the point of diminishing returns.

Once, I took the train out to visit Seymour on Long Island. I took him and his mother out to the movies: *Crossing Delancy*. He was effectively blind in one eye. His mother drove. He had been having chills that week. We went back to their storybook home, with the chocolate shingles on the roof and the perfect ovals of smoke from the chimney. We ordered out pizza for dinner, a feast on paper plates. Seymour drove me back to the station, and I kissed him good-bye in the car.

I felt guilty. I should have been doing more for Seymour. Tom went out to see him one day a week. Tom was a saint. Life should have been suspended in order to help Seymour, to cheer him up, but it couldn't be. There were other friends to attend to. Sadly, he wasn't the only one who was ill.

"His lung has collapsed," Tom told me. "He's hooked up to a respirator. It's because he had PCP. You get these sores on the lungs. The blisters popped, and the lung deflated. They're waiting for the sores to heal. They're hoping it will reinflate by itself. Another friend of mine had the same thing happen. They had to staple his lungs to his chest. It was very painful."

I was trapped in a Kafkaesque maze at the hospital, trying to find Seymour's room. Was this a nightmare? They had moved him to the AIDS ward, next to the hospice for cancer patients, many of whom would never leave. I didn't want Seymour to be there, but he was. I circled and circled, and finally I stumbled onto his room.

Seymour had grown a beard in the hospital, because it was difficult to shave. His hair was matted flat, dull with grease.

"It's nicer in the AIDS unit than in the general section. The nurses are here because they want to help. But still, I can't stand it here. It's the small things that get to me. When I feel I'm getting a fever, it takes half an hour to get a nurse to give me some aspirin. And they keep on trying to get me to see a social worker. I played along and saw the first one they sent. She was a complete waste of time. She kept on stressing the spiritual comfort of God. Why aren't there any Unitarian hospitals? I want to get out of here," said Seymour. "I'm so tired."

"Frankly, I didn't think he'd make it off the respirator," said Tom.

I went to visit Seymour a few weeks later during lunch, laden with a Pepperidge Farm special assortment. He was on drugs for PCP and having a bad reaction. They hadn't actually determined that he had PCP; they decided not to bother with the painful bronchoscopy and treat him for it anyway. I was in the middle of a sentence, and he threw up, and I just sat there, numb with stupidity, waiting for the adults to tell me what to do next.

I called Tom that night and started to tell him about what happened. He told me that Seymour's friend Marie was there when he threw up, and she didn't do anything, and then I told him that that's what I did too, and he said it was OK, but I knew I blew it.

That's when everything began to go downhill.

I had screwed up before with Gordon, and I didn't want to screw up again. I felt like I was stuck in a bad *Twilight Zone* flashback, doomed to repeat it until I got it right. Was this an object lesson in maturity? Whatever it was, I hated it.

The course of the illness left one raw. The protective coatings were stripped, and nothing was left but tension and anger. Seymour got irritable, and I didn't know what to say. What do you talk about to someone at the hospital? Do you aim for the trivial or stick with complex philosophical dilemmas, like what ten albums would you pick if you were stuck on a desert island, knowing you were limited to one Streisand and one Garland? How much money would they have to pay you to get rights to photograph you for those subway ads for the New York State Lottery with your hair askew, and what would your outrageous dream be if you won? Politics was irrelevant. Likewise with religion and last week's fashion trends. I was down to two topics for discussion: the truly irrelevant and the totally inane. Yet somehow every topic led inexorably to the same thing, which was Seymour's present condition.

Seymour lost his taste for eggs.

Seymour told the rabbi that he wasn't particularly interested in speaking with him.

Seymour left the hospital and went home.

Seymour slowed down like a clock unwinding, like a mechanical doll whose batteries were running out. He gradually stopped talking. Tom told me that even listening was an effort for Seymour now.

Philip was very polite, perhaps too polite. He didn't know whether Seymour liked him anymore or was just putting up with him at that point. Philip called Seymour's parents to ask them permission to speak to Seymour. He was usually sleeping. Philip didn't want to go out to see Seymour if Seymour was too tired for human interaction. Philip didn't want to annoy Seymour with his presence, wasn't sure whether he was helping or harming or merely excusing himself from a painful task, didn't know if he should hold on or let go.

Tom faithfully visited Seymour once a week. He tried physical therapy on Seymour as Seymour lost his strength. Seymour was weak; he barely walked; he stayed upstairs in his room and played old 45s. His ankles hurt when he walked. Everything was an effort.

"If you want to see Seymour, you had better do it soon," said Tom. "There's not too much quality time left." He started crying. "Les and Lee can't see what's happening. He's fading, Benjamin."

"I hope he dies in his sleep," said his grandmother. "He's been suffering for so long. I hope he dies soon."

"He's been sick for three years," said Philip. "Three years. That's a long time."

"Seymour is gone," said Tom. "That's not Seymour. That's what's left of him. Seymour went away weeks ago."

Two of Tom's exes were dead, and the third, Seymour, lay sleeping in Long Island Jewish Medical Center in intensive care. The chart at his feet was marked "DNR": Do not resuscitate.

I had to convince Philip to visit Seymour with me. Philip had a car. I couldn't face it alone, the L.I.R.R. and a taxi to the hospital. Philip didn't really want to go, but he said he'd go if I insisted. "What's the point?" said Philip. "Will he recognize us? Will he even know we're there?"

Seymour was in a coma.

Tom cried on the phone. "What do you mean, you're not sure whether you'll visit? Can't you see, there may not be another time? But you have to do what you have to do. I understand," he lied.

Was I going only to impress Tom? To assuage future guilt? Because I wanted to say good-bye? Because I could never forgive myself if I didn't go? I didn't know.

I called Philip back a few hours later. "Let's go."

"The thing is, I want to remember Seymour as one of the cutest guys I ever met," said Philip. First impressions count, yet how lasting are final impressions? "I don't want it to be years before I can see the Seymour that once was."

"We should make the effort," I insisted.

"OK," said Philip, reluctantly.

Seymour was sleeping softly, rhythmically, at the hospital. He looked at peace. There was a moment when his breathing stopped. Philip and I froze. What should we do? There was the fear: Suppose he dies, and we're there alone? Death was private and personal, for lovers and family. But wouldn't we be intruding as friends?

He started breathing again.

Les and Miriam came in.

"Should we wait and see if he's going to wake up?" asked Philip.

"He isn't going to wake up," said Miriam.

We said good-bye.

On the ride back, we finished a one-pound bag of peanut M&Ms.

Seymour died the next day.

I skipped the funeral and went out to visit his family that afternoon. I took the train to Massapequa and then a cab to Seymour's house. Tom was there with Rodney, Seymour's old Brooklyn roommate. The family seemed to be holding up well. Miriam said it was the longest day of her life. Nadine said, "Of course it was; you were up at five." Les remarked on the weather. Lee offered bagels. In the kitchen was a three-foot basket of fruit, wrapped in a sheet of colored cellophane.

We sat and talked about Seymour. Tom told us that just last week he had unearthed some old 45s of the Supremes. His face lit up as he played "Baby Love." I couldn't believe Seymour was gone.

I got a ride back with Rodney and Tom.

———

"Don't you think it was tacky of Rodney to have us help him move his computer today?" Tom asked me over margaritas at Benny's Burritos. Rodney had rented a car for the day, and he thought as long as he had the car for a few more hours, he might as well transfer his PC from his apartment to his office in Manhattan. Tom and I had three margaritas apiece. I don't remember whether or not we had sex that night or whether we just staggered back to my place to sleep together.

A few months later Philip was driving back from an antique show in Pennsylvania. "I put on a tape that Seymour had made for me. He had played me this tape when we met, and then about a year later, he gave me a copy. It was very sweet of him. And I thought, how sad, it's such a shame, all of the music that Seymour will never hear."

·9·
———

Snap Out of It!

NOVEMBER 1989

A ZILLION TRICKS

At eight P.M. on Monday, August 28, 1989, I, Benjamin Joseph Rosenthal—a hapless, neurotic, asymptomatic antibody-positive homosexual, aged thirty-two and perpetually single, given to shameless fits of self-indulgence that lasted weeks if not years— took my very first capsule of a nucleoside analogue (whose initials, in a curious confusion of cause-and-effect, spelled "A Zillion Tricks") in full public view at a meeting of the AIDS Coalition to Unleash Power at the Lesbian and Gay Community Services Center on Thirteenth Street in New York City.

If possible, I would have chosen an even more public venue for my first pill, complete with an announcement over the mike system, a spotlight, and a drum roll, provoking tumultuous applause from the audience, as if by overexaggerating the importance of the moment I could paradoxically diminish its effect on my fragile psyche. Instead, I settled for relative anonymity, sitting amidst the crowd of several hundred rabid activists and sardonic wits. A glass of Perrier would have helped. For me, however, it was easy enough to swallow a pill without the inducement of liquids. Enough had gone down my throat in the past with little or no coaxing.

The pills came in a bottle with an extremely effective child-guard cap. This was about as apt as a warning posted on a bathhouse wall for pregnant women to eschew alcohol. Attached to each bottle was a highly technical five-hundred-page pamphlet too depressing for words, listing warnings, precautions, contraindications, adverse reactions, dosage and administration instructions, and approximately 16,457 side effects, of which my favorite was "taste perversion," which I interpreted as a strong predilection for chintz and black velvet paintings of nude large-breasted women.

Like any other certified professional hypochondriac, I, who had achieved intimate knowledge verging on the biblical with my copy of the *Physician's Desk Reference,* was able to perceive in myself up to eighty-five percent of the side effects listed, even those symptoms that were more prevalent for the placebo comparison. But mostly it was the standard side effects: headaches and nausea. Although my doctor assured me that there was a minimal likelihood of any side effects with the initial low dosage given my relatively robust blood counts (robust compared to what? anorectic ballerinas? autopsy reports?), my head pounded, primarily at the sinuses, for the next 168 hours while I envisioned the drug crossing the blood-brain barrier. I stared at the *Interview* photo taped to my wall of Joan Didion experiencing an extreme migraine. Concurrently, I felt a slight nausea: Although it was not significant, I was left with the uneasy sensation that I might cough up my cookies at any given moment.

Now my life was divided into discreet four-hour intervals between medication; I was reduced to waiting for my next fix. I spent the next four days transfixed by the clock. Against advice from an ex-boyfriend and fellow pill-popper, I purchased a battery-operated pillbox-timer to remind myself automatically with a gentle beep.

This brought yet another complication into my life. Suppose the beeper went off, unattended, in the gym locker while I was upstairs pumping iron or downstairs in the steam room pumping a more malleable construct? Would the health-club attendants assume that a terrorist time bomb was about to explode and break open the locker with an axe? What if it went off as I undressed? What would the bevy of half-naked beauties dishing in my aisle think? Conversely, when the bicycles at the gym had been pedaled for their due course of set time, they would peal the identical tone as my alarm, and how was I to tell the difference? What was to stop me from automatically reaching into my pocket? Confused by identical stimuli, I always reached for the phone when it rang on the 8:14 A.M. dog-food commercial on WNEW-FM.

And what of the endless fumbling if the timer signaled during the first act of a Broadway show? Should I smuggle a small flask of some carbonated beverage in the inside pocket of my jacket or stumble over sixteen irritated theater patrons on my way to the lobby to purchase an orange-colored elixir composed of sugar, water, and food coloring? Should I stick to my own saliva?

Further, it was now imperative to schedule seductions around these force-feedings of pharmaceuticals. It was one thing to interrupt intimate behavior with a discreet visit to the powder room; another to temporarily stay the proceedings with a frantic search for what one might call the tools of the trade (oil, powder, grease, water-based nonoxynol-9 spermicidal lubricant, rubbers, prosthetic devices, marital aids, adult art videos, cock rings, leather harnesses, rubber sheets, and/or Fieldcrest towels); but to pause in the midst of carnal desire for a poison pill put a rather harsh chill on events, not unlike when an unsuspecting trucker realized all too late the actual genital status of the hooker he picked up at the West Side Highway. I could always defuse the beeper and rely on my watch, much as I took down the smoke detector and removed its batteries whenever I made burgers, but my memory, like some bad Sinatra song, was unreliable, undependable, and irresponsible.

I tried to be honest and forthright about my antibody status before entering into close encounters of the primary kind; I had had two years to practice this and seen enough erections melt not to take it personally. Sometimes I wondered whether an informal system of sexual apartheid was arising, strictly separating positives from negatives.

Were seductions even possible anymore? Ever the persistent failed libertine, wanting to mark the occasion of my last drug-free evening with something momentous, I had attempted the night previous to get fucked by one Oliver Wolinsky, former Mormon and current twelve-step addict. There remained between the two of us a few kindling embers of a brief misalliance from 1982, along with considerable psychological trauma. Oliver was quite the stud: tall, dark, handsome, and emotionally disturbed to a remarkable degree. Oliver had many annoying habits, perhaps the worst being the mercantile reflex of transcribing all conversation he overheard and participated in, in the hopes of incorporating the dialogue into one of the six television pilots he was penning. Oliver, unfortunately, was unwilling to get involved with someone who had not been in continuous therapy for at least five years, which neatly eliminated me. But then again, Oliver was the classic top, and I, game for anything that evening, had convinced myself that there might be a fit between the two of us, like in the proverbial aptitude test of blocks and holes; however, to my chagrin, I discovered that I was virtually impenetrable, as if my sphincter muscle had been fed a steady diet of anaerobic steroids for the past decade and swollen tight, stubborn with inertia—as if concrete had set in the several years of desuetude of my anus, not allowing anything past. To clear passage, depth charges were unfeasible; butyl nitrite, out of the question.

I wanted desperately to sleep with someone, anyone. Oddly enough, I wasn't referring to the euphemism; I just wanted to spend the night in slumber next to a man of appropriate dimensions and gender.

My New Line

"I'm taking A Zillion Tricks," I practiced to the mirror. "Care to be a zillion and one?"

Several Failed Seductions

I was walking up the street, headed toward the local A&P. A blond approached in bicycle shorts, the eighties male equivalent of the push-up bra of the fifties: They made a nice ass look dynamite and a great ass look fabulous. I turned, swiveled. Our eyes locked. Pheromones were exchanged, crotches indicated with a downward glance.

I was concerned about etiquette and proper behavior at all times. In this case protocol involved negotiating safer sex. But was this possible right on Ninth Avenue, in front of the video-rental store specializing in Spanish movies? Somehow, I knew I was destined for another heartbreak tango. What was this, the Paris peace talks? Would we spend months arguing before eventually deciding on a circular bed? Should legal counsel be present?

At that moment the blond said, abruptly, "I only like big dicks."

I was taken aback. Ah, sweet mystery of life, where hast thou gone to? Once again, the fundamental questions of the universe loomed large before me: What was quality, and how does it compare with quantity? Was there any meaning in life? Was there life after death? How big was big? "Would an average-sized one do?" I offered.

The blond abruptly took his leave, and I was left to ponder.

Should I have lied or exaggerated? Then, having finally drawn the gentleman in question to my boudoir, perhaps something could have been done with magnifying glasses and mirrors. It was all a matter of perspective, wasn't it? For me, there was a size above which additional length and girth were meaningless, even verging on the absurd. I'm sure such a size existed somewhere; I just hadn't come across it yet.

One fine summer day I saw a man with a salt-and-pepper beard and eyes like coals on my way back from the doctor. Once again I found myself performing some ancient ritual dance: the dance of the sugar-plum fairies? the mating ritual of the black-widow spider?

"Do you live around here?" I asked.

"Yes. I was just doing some errands."

"I'm on my endless lunch hour. Another one of my biweekly doctor's visits."

"Once every two weeks?"

"No, it's more like twice a week. I suppose you might call me a hypochondriac. Thank God for group health-insurance. Who's your doctor?" I inquired, as casually as in the past I might have asked which gym do you go to, or did you get to the Mapplethorpe exhibit at the Whitney, or are you fond of blow jobs and is your apartment within three minutes' walk and do you mind if I don't come, because I have a meeting with my boss at three P.M. this afternoon and can't possibly stay longer.

"I guess you could say I'm between doctors," said the dark stranger. "I don't have one at the moment."

"That's odd," I commented.

"Well, my last two doctors kept on telling me to stop smoking, cut down on the cholesterol, watch my alcohol intake, exercise, the whole routine. And you know what? One died last year, the other six months ago."

"That is not very encouraging."

Two weeks later I went to a smoke-filled benefit for a gay-rights advocacy group. Part one was a cocktail party at a chichi doorman apartment-building on the seventeenth floor, with a view of the Con Edison building. The living room was littered with Oriental sculptures, half-empty glasses of single-malt whiskey, and investment bankers. Later, downtown, there was a dance and an endless awards ceremony. I would have slunk home after my customary three glasses of club soda and lime had I not been intrigued by a tall man in a plaid shirt open to the fifth button. Counter to my usual AA honorary-mascot stance, I quaffed several low-calorie beers, engulfed in conversation with Salvatore, a former therapist who had gone back to school to study sociology. When Salvatore indicated that he was going to the dance, I reluctantly followed, hoping my electronic reminder wouldn't go off in the cab.

At the dance space I immediately excused myself and went to the bathroom, cupping my hands under the faucet for water to help the pill go down. I lost Salvatore in the crowd for about an hour. I was ready to drop. Finally, the music stopped. I found Salvatore standing against the curtains as the awards ceremony started. By then it was maybe 1:30 A.M. An androgynous actor who had just copped a Tony for his portrayal of a transvestite started singing volumes 1, 2, and 3 of the Cole Porter song book into an electronic mike. I prayed for a power outage. It was then, after three hours of leading me down the primrose path of vice, that Salvatore decided it was time to give his "It's been fifteen years since I last had carnal knowledge of another man" speech.

"Even though I taught seminars on safe sex at GMHC," he said, "somehow I just can't get myself to do it. I always want to do the bad things, the things that aren't permitted."

"You could have told me earlier," I said. "Why did you have to wait until past my bedtime to tell me this? I'm just thankful it's not a school night."

"So how are you coping with the crisis?" Salvatore asked me.

SELF-DELUSION

As long as it was a pill or a sort of liquid, an elixir, I could convince myself that it wasn't medicine, that it was just vitamins. However, plasmapheresis, intravenous drug infusions lasting up to ninety minutes daily, and overnight blood transfusions weren't as likely candidates for the willful suspension of disbelief.

ORAL SEX

"Don't go to the beach," advised my new doctor, who had a share at the Pines and the dark brown skin of a sabra. "Sun isn't good for you. And avoid putting the head of the penis into your mouth during oral sex."

Former beach bunny and sun worshiper, I was crushed. What did that leave? Parcheesi? Miniature golf? The rapid consumption of massive amounts of calories, followed by systematic purges? On my top-ten list of favorite things to do, nine of them involved oral sex. Reading movie magazines, scarfing down chocolate bonbons, and taking two-hour bubble baths seemed masturbatory in comparison.

The generally approved alternative involved anal sex with rubbers. I suppose that if I hadn't gotten those worrisome warts, which I was told would magically disappear the day I turned thirty (a cruel, cruel lie), and if I hadn't contracted the deadly Human Immunodeficiency Virus that way, I might have thought differently about my ass. And the converse, being the "active" partner, retaining an erection for however long it took, gently pumping away in someone's precious gentle sweet rosebud, was about as stimulating to me as sawing a board.

"Maybe," I thought to myself, "if I avoided the sun and just sucked dick *occasionally?* . . . I guess this is what they call bargaining."

But hadn't the safer-sex guidelines changed? According to Boston's *Gay Community News,* condoms were necessary only if he came in your mouth. In Montreal oral sex had been downgraded to minimal risk. (O Canada, my Canada!) In San Francisco there were suck-off parties. Fellatio was fine in Philadelphia. New York remained the only hard-liner. Even lesbians there were encouraged to wear wet-suits during sex.

How was it possible that cultural relativism affected something as objective as safer sex? Perhaps this was a corollary of the Supreme Court decision to base obscenity on community standards. Why weren't scientists performing experiments to determine whether gastric acid annihilated the virus? Was saliva effective in neutralizing it? In October 1989 *The New York Times* reported a one-line item about two cases of oral-sex-induced AIDS in San Francisco. But did they swallow? Did they brush their teeth vigorously beforehand? Exactly how many men had they blown? Whatever happened to investigative reporting? *Youth wants to know!* Later, I picked up a *Bay Area Reporter,* a gay rag from San Francisco that had information additional to "all the news that's fit to print." One man had severe gum disease; the other had performed more than three hundred blow jobs in the previous year.

Was it OK to gargle beforehand? And what about breath mints? Were there rules similar to the kosher dietary laws that specified how many hours one had to wait between dairy products and meat? Did one have to wait until the following day to floss?

"If you keep jerking off, you'll go blind," the voices of authority warned me as a child. "I'll only do it until I need glasses," I replied. Needless to say, my glasses were very thick indeed. "Perhaps," I wondered, "there was a similar compromise, a middle ground, for fellatio, too. Maybe just one a month or no more than ten different ones a year."

I personally believed oral sex without ejaculation was risky only when one was recovering from oral surgery and one's partner was having his or her period. There was risk in everything. How did it compare to crossing the street? Or using a can of Aunt Millie's spaghetti sauce that didn't make that satisfying *pop* sound when opened? Given the choice between botulism, being run down by a yellow cab, or death by oral sex, I would invariably choose the third option.

WHY MY SEPTEMBER PHONE BILL WAS IN THREE DIGITS

"Hi."

"Hello."

"Who is this?"

"This is Rick. Who's this?"

"This is Tom."

"Hi, Tom. What are you doing?"

"Just hanging out. What about you?"

"Same."

"I'm real horny."

"Me too."

"What do you look like?"

"I'm five eleven, one eighty, brown hair, green eyes, work out, eight inches, thick."

"I'm six two, two hundred, blond hair, mustache, brown eyes, seven and a half, cut."

"Does anyone want a foot slave?"

"What are you wearing?"

"A jockstrap."

"A pair of Jockey shorts."

"A Calvin Klein ensemble from the spring collection."

"Wrong number. This isn't Chicks with Dicks line."

"Any tops out there?"

"Tom, you still there?"

"Yeah."

"This is Rick. What are you into?"

"I'm pretty versatile. Depends on how hot the guy is."

"I'm versatile too. Can I give you a call?"

"Sorry, I can't give out the number."

"Does anyone want a foot slave?"

"I can't either."

"Hello?"

"_____"

"Who's out there?"

"John."

"Where are you calling from?"

"Westchester."

"Oh."

"_____"

"Anyone from the Upper West Side?"

"Yeah."

"Hey, it sounds like someone's taking a piss."

"Anyone into phone sex?"

"Anyone from the Bronx or upper Manhattan?"

"Hi, who's this?"

"This is John. Who's this?"

"This is John, too. What do you look like?"

"Six two, good build, work out, smooth body, black hair, blue eyes."

"Sounds hot."

"What about you?"

"Who's this?"

"This is John."

"Five nine, one eighty, blond hair, blue eyes, good build."

"What are you into?"

"I'm looking for a top."

"Me too."

"Sorry."

"Good luck."

"Does anyone want a foot slave?"

"Hi, this is Rafael."

"_____"

"Is anybody there?"

"_____"

"I'm really horny tonight."

"Hey, who's pressing the buttons on the Touch-tone?"

"Stop it!"

"I'm beating my meat."

"Is everyone a bottom tonight?"

"Who's this?"

"This is Bill."

"Where are you?"

"I'm on the Lower East Side."

"Can't hear you. Bad connection."

"Is Chelsea Dave still on?"

"I can't give out my number."

"_____"

"Any masters out there?"

"Yeah, boy. Are you obedient?"

"Yes, completely."

"Give me your phone number, boy."

"No."

"_____"

"_____"

"Does anyone want a foot slave?"

For a brief period, a matter of weeks, I was hooked on the phone-sex lines. Late at night, with the lights out, I would lay my head down and try to sleep, but the chorus of disembodied electronic sirens was constantly luring me with a sweet song of seduction. The problem was, my phone was too close to the bed. Maybe I should rewire? It was too convenient: I need only dial a universal prefix and a suggestive mnemonic to hear voices hot with desire, thick with naked need. But all the while the meter was running. The pile of chits grew larger and larger as I fell deeper and deeper into debt.

Eventually, I recognized some of the voices. I had a series of desultory meetings, all disastrous. It was safer to stay home and want. There was something perversely satisfying about this detached, dislocated gratification.

I had thought that the top-bottom dichotomy was over. But I did know at least three unrepentant clones who wore key chains in their back pockets. On those evenings when seven voices would fruitlessly plead for tops, I took a sip of the glass of iced tea on the night table and imagined rows upon rows of buns, as far as the eye could see, tanning alongside some California pool painted by David Hockney.

I committed the indiscretion of giving out my number on the lines ten or twenty times. Moments after I hung up, my phone would usually ring, although there were a few disappointments when no one called. Occasionally I would call others; shrewd verbalists with call-waiting would play the field and not hesitate to use their hold buttons. With only voices to go on, I would invent the best possible physique and face, given the somewhat sketchy clues in personals-ad shorthand. Although there was ample opportunity to lie, I generally stuck to the truth in describing myself. I did my best to merge my own fantasies with my caller's, in the spirit of compromise. If I committed the indiscretion of an almost instantaneous silent orgasm, I was quite willing to fake a vocal one later after coaxing my partner to the brink. Yet nine times out of ten, the line would suddenly go dead in the midst of the heated conversation as exchanges shortened to telegram length. I resented being hung up on. I preferred empty promises of future call-backs and possible meetings to the bleak metallic finality of the dial tone.

A TRIP TO THE DOCTOR

On alternate Tuesdays I took a two-hour lunch to visit the office of my primary health-care practitioner for the purpose of inhalation of aerosolized pentamidine.

"It's no big deal," I said. If I could pretend that the AZT and the acyclovir were just "vitamins" that I took with the blind allegiance and regularity of a health-food addict, well, the pentamidine was a rare form of dope smoked through a smokeless hookah. I took a deep breath, inhaling the mist into the deepest recesses of my lungs, and tried to keep it there for as long as possible, just like a toke of hashish. Instead of getting high, I ended up slightly dizzy fifteen minutes later, with a bitter taste in my mouth. There were debates in the medical literature on the optimal posture for inhaling: sitting, reclining, or lying down. Was prone better than supine? Had anyone tried it hanging from inversion boots? Would circulation be increased with a Jeff Stryker dildo up your butt? If not, would fingers do? It was only a matter of time before *Consumer Reports* rated nebulizers.

Occasionally, while I was inhaling, my doctor would emerge from the office with a patient to weigh him. I smiled the automatic smile I used for attractive men, unless I had the plastic tube in my mouth at the time. After I finished the biweekly dose, I'd close the issue of *Life* magazine celebrating the eighties that I was rereading, take a sour-cherry ball wrapped in cellophane from the candy jar on the counter, and go to exchange a check for an insurance receipt.

I DON'T THINK

One day as I left, I saw my friend Jim in the waiting room. Jim had survived two bouts of pneumonia; he had been diagnosed with AIDS three years earlier. I had had dinner with Jim a month ago at a Chinese restaurant. Jim had said, "I don't think I'll stay well forever. Up until a few months ago, I thought I would go on indefinitely. But after that last bout of pneumonia I got weak. And now I don't think that I'll stay well forever anymore."

THE PHOTOS ON THE WALL

I was somewhere in the middle of a five-year anxiety attack that showed no signs of abating. I was also in the middle of a six-month sore throat. Every three weeks my doctor prescribed yet another variety of penicillin. My fever would abate, my tonsils would deflate from the size of zeppelins to the size of anteater's testicles, for a period lasting up to three days after the course of the medication was completed.

Back in my apartment my wall was covered with posters, post-cards, advertisements, and photographs from magazines. It was the usual combination of underwear ads, gym promotions, Saint invitations, Chicago Film Festival posters, and pages torn from *Advocate Men*. The level of homoeroticism was high enough to deny me a grant from the National Endowment for the Arts. Somehow this pleased me.

I stared at the photo from *Details* magazine from the AmFAR benefit at the Javits Center. A dead Perry Ellis was on the right. Ryan White—the world-renowned hemophiliac, high-school student, *Life*-magazine cover, and innocent victim—was on the left. Liz Taylor beamed in the center.

I turned to the closet, pulled out my collapsible suitcase, and began packing.

DON'T TELL MAMA

I went home for a long weekend for some dread Hebrew holiday, determined to break the news to the folks.

"Why tell them?" asked my friend Dennis, former priest and perennial *mensh*.

"Don't you think it will be obvious—what with me taking a pill every four hours, every time the pillbox beeps—that something is awry?"

"Why not just pretend it's allergy medicine?" he continued. "I myself have frequently used that ruse. You'd be amazed at the alcohol content in nighttime cold remedies." Dennis demonstrated with his hip flask and a straw.

"Why shouldn't I tell the truth?"

"You don't have to share everything with your family. I am impelled by the sanctity of the confessional to keep my lips sealed. I suggest you do the same."

"I made up my mind a few years ago: When I started taking AZT, I'd tell. Not before, because why scare them unnecessarily? I'm perfectly capable of creating enough anxiety on my own; I don't need to enlist help from the family."

At the time of my visit I was on several antibiotics for the sore throat, with varying schedules: One was to be taken every six hours on an empty stomach for ten days; another, with milk, every four hours for twenty days; and a third, twice daily, while reading the *Encyclopaedia Brittanica*. I had taken the liberty of signing out a Toshiba portable computer from work to aid in my dosage calculations. This was all in addition to the dread zidovudine. Every fifteen minutes (the greatest common divisor of the least common multiple), I would dash off to my room for another dose of snake oil.

I spent the weekend in a state of avoidance. I didn't tell them when I arrived or the following morning at breakfast, when my mother had thoughtfully defrosted two Lender's bagels and a tiny tub of lox flakes. I didn't tell them on the drive over to Aunt Maude's in the suburbs. I didn't tell them during the opening credits of Bette Midler in *Outrageous Fortune*, a rental I had seen a lifetime ago with Gordon. I didn't tell them during the evening news, which droned in the background as we ate a supper of eggplant Parmesean and iceberg-lettuce salad in the kitchen.

Finally, three days into my visit, I told my sister over margaritas at a Mexican restaurant.

"You couldn't have picked a better time to tell me," said Sheila. "This is what I've dreaded for seven years. Here I am, completely bummed out. My therapist calls it postpartum depression; I call it the dumps. I've never felt this blue before in my life. What I mean is, if I was in a good mood, this would pull me down, but as it is, you might as well dump on me now. It makes no difference."

"Sorry, Sheila."

"Oh, it's not your fault. Don't get me wrong! I'm not blaming you. Jesus, this is coming out backwards. It's just that I was so happy when I was pregnant. And I love my baby. But sometimes it feels like my whole life is going down the drain. The baby takes up all of my attention. Alexander is jealous of the baby. Can you imagine it? So I had to quit my job; I just couldn't hack it with the baby. But now I'm bored, staying at home all of the time. And we're behind in the mortgage, and my Chevy is falling apart. I've got to work part-time, but doing what? And don't suggest day care if you don't want to see my picture on the cover of the *Rochester Republic,* beneath the headline 'Bloodbath at the Nursery: Woman Scalds Twenty Children; Blames PMS.' But how could you keep quiet about this for two years?"

"Don't you understand? All my life I've been lying. My entire life is premised on lies."

"Oh, yeah, like you were in the closet for twenty-two years."

"So, I guess Mom's next." I cleared my throat.

"Why tell Mom? She'd only freak out. She wouldn't understand."

"What about you? Should I have told you?"

"Of course you should have. You know I'm on your side one hundred percent. If you ever need anything, you can come to me. I'll help you. But Mom, I don't know. She'd get really depressed."

"You don't think honesty is the best policy?"

"Grow up. That is one of the silliest clichés ever invented. Don't you read Ann Landers?"

"Every day. OK, what about this? She always gets jealous if she finds out that I'm sharing something with you and not her. Besides, don't you need someone to confide in? Doesn't misery love company?"

"I've got my husband."

"A lot of good that's been."

"I think you should wait on Mom."

"Whatever you say."

But I was still conflicted. Wasn't there something dishonest about keeping this secret? Wasn't I just hiding in the closet? Wouldn't I be breaking down a barrier between myself and my mother? Wouldn't we get closer? Did I *want* to get closer to my mother? As it was, I called her up twice a month, on an irregular basis. The last time she called me was April 1983, at the instigation of Sheila, who had broken her ankle while rock climbing and asked our mother to notify me. Even then, I swore I could hear the sands of time running down through the egg timer, a foot away from the phone.

So I finally screwed up enough courage to tell my mother on Sunday, the day I was leaving.

I don't know why, but everything was more difficult with Mom. How many times did I have to come out? Twelve years before, when I bought my first condom, I thought that that was the last time in my life that I would be embarrassed. Fat chance.

I remembered an old joke about coming out. A guy tells his mother that he has an inoperable malignant brain tumor and he has only six months to live. Then he tells her he was kidding, he was only gay. But somehow, I couldn't conjure up something worse to tell so that being HIV-positive would be a relief in comparison.

I wasn't the only one with the nuclear family. Oliver's sister, who was three months pregnant at the time, leapt out of a moving car when she found out that her only brother was gay. Gordon's father disowned him. Richard's mother tried to seduce him—does it count as incest when you're adopted? I braced myself for the worst. I walked into the living room. The Sunday paper was spread in seventeen sections on the floor. "Mom?" No answer. In the kitchen a half-empty cup of black coffee sat, already cold, in a saucer on the counter. "Mom?" The cat breezed by my legs, bounding for the dining room. The remnants of a half-eaten can of Purina cat food lay in his dish on the floor on top of an old newspaper. I heard the soft padding of slippered feet from my mother's bedroom. I turned and stood in the arch at the hallway. My mother had gone to the bathroom and was making quiet, retching sounds.

"I think it's a twenty-four-hour virus," she said weakly a few moments later.

I hadn't even told her, and already she was puking her guts out. It was like that scene in *An Unmarried Woman*, where Jill Clayburgh gets sick on the street after hearing her husband is leaving her. How could I make things even worse? So I decided to sit on it for another few months. In other words, I chickened out.

A VOICE FROM THE PAST

I returned to my disaster of an apartment none the worse for the wear. Nothing had changed, except there were seventeen more bills to pay, thirty-three pleas from various and sundry charities, and three thick monthlies stuffed in the mailbox. I tossed the fifty-odd envelopes into the trash, under the watchful gaze of Joan Didion on the wall, and turned on my answering machine. Ten hang-ups in a row. Probably from the phone-sex lines. "What was the point?" I wondered. "They could at least breathe heavy." And a message from Lonnie's mom, wondering how I was doing.

LONNIE

In a way, I did not fully accept the constant tide of deaths. Maybe some things were beyond the powers of human comprehension, like quantum mechanics, love, infinity, and the process by which consciousness arises from matter. I had heard that it takes two years to complete the healing process and fully recover from the death of a close friend. Yet everyone was dying. There was no time left to cope. Were the two-year sentences of grief run concurrently or consecutively? Was there time off for good behavior?

Whenever I got hopeful, whenever I emerged from the blanket of despair, whenever I was about to leave my funk, whenever I was about to regain my mental balance, someone died; someone stuck a pin into my shiny balloon and popped it.

Lonnie died the previous April. His mother had given me the news.

Lonnie had found out that he was positive the day the space shuttle exploded. Lonnie had the double whammy: Not only was he gay, but he was also a hemophiliac.

Lonnie had volunteered to be in a hemophiliac research study. Blood tests were performed every six months, and Lonnie elected to find out the results. This was back when everyone except the U.S. government advised against taking the test; even I told him not to bother learning his status.

He did fine for about a year.

I had met Lonnie on the beach a few years earlier. He stood in the dramatically crashing surf, with a George Hamilton tan and a body of death. The sun glinted at his nipples. I was smitten. As he approached, I realized they were pierced. I suppressed a horror-stricken scream. Later, after determining that Lonnie too was a son of Abraham and Moses, I told him, "With pierced nipples, they'll never bury you in a Jewish cemetery." I couldn't figure how he could have had his body voluntarily mutilated, since he was a bleeder, complete with a Medic Alert bracelet.

Lonnie explained that as a hemophiliac he had to worry only about internal bleeding, and piercing was barely subcutaneous. "For some strange reason, when they see the tit rings, men think I'm into S and M," complained Lonnie. "It's purely decorative." That was the clue I ignored: Lonnie, a fashion victim if ever there was one, was himself purely decorative.

Lonnie was another also-ran in the prospective lover department. He and I had great sex, and he was nice and sweet, but he lacked a certain—shall we say ironic?—sensibility. Lonnie's favorite book was *The Red Balloon,* and he was the type that would go to Great Adventure in New Jersey on a date and ride the rides. Lonnie went dancing at the Monster and was a great fan of Spielberg's *An American Tail.* I was too busy contemplating Kierkegaard to reread the Curious George stories, and *my* nightlife consisted of watching Susan Sontag declaim and expostulate at the 92nd Street Y and going to the Eric Rohmer movie that Pauline Kael said was like watching paint dry. Like most Americans, Lonnie's primary ambition was to become marginally famous in some as-yet unspecified capacity: perhaps as a backup dancer in an MTV video or as an award-winning belt designer who starred in his own obsessive advertisements. My own dreams were more modest: eternal notoriety as an arcane footnote to an unread microfilmed doctoral thesis on sexual hysteria sequestered in a locked vault in Ann Arbor, Michigan. So by autumn we separated, with "irreconcilable differences" writ large on our divorce decree. Yet, as was my habit, we remained friends.

After I got my positive antibody-test results, I figured that I would give Lonnie a call, to see how he was doing. I basically wanted some reassurance. I figured that since Lonnie had had a year to get used to the idea of being positive, he would be able to help me adjust.

Lonnie was a mess.

There was a tumor in his stomach; maybe it was lymphoma. He had bad headaches. He had been in the hospital once a few months earlier, which was when they diagnosed him. He told me how he had been delirious on morphine for a week. He was living on the south shore of Long Island with his mother, the one with the voice like a foghorn.

A few weeks later Lonnie's mother called me, after midnight. "Lonnie's back in the hospital," she boomed. "He won't eat." She warned me that his personality had changed. "Please call him, Benjamin." So I gave him a ring. Lonnie responded to my inquiries quite listlessly, without enthusiasm. I recounted my usual litany of one-minute movie reviews, minor character defamations of mutual friends, and endless complaints. Lonnie closed with that ultimate in conversation stoppers, "I'll see you at my funeral." I was so impressed with Lonnie's statement (was it the phrasing, the cadences, or the delivery?) that I was momentarily speechless. But then I suddenly felt very weak and useless. I told Lonnie that I would call him back when I had something positive to say, and Lonnie said OK as if he were indulging me, as if he really couldn't care less, as if it made no difference if he ever heard from me again.

Somehow I screwed up the courage to call Lonnie a few weeks later. Lonnie completely disregarded our previous conversation. He was still depressed, but he didn't mention the deep six or the pearly gates or the floral plans for the funeral. We chatted. I gave Lonnie the latest dish on several inconsequential topics of moderate sociological interest to urban male homosexuals: Pia Zadora, Zsa Zsa Gabor, and Liza Minelli. I truly felt at that moment that it was the digressions that counted in life, the nonessential items, the vestigial organs, the filler, the inert ingredients. And then, at the end of our rambling conversation, Lonnie told me that I was his best friend. I, rarely at a loss for words, was once again silent. Had Lonnie scared away all of his other friends with talk of death and despair? Was it his ferocious mother, with the lungs of Ethel Merman? Maybe he, like most New Yorkers, had a very large set of easily shed acquaintances and only a few close friends.

I thought, "This is pathetic. He thinks I'm his best friend, when all I've been to him is humanly decent."

So I called Lonnie periodically. When I spoke to Lonnie's mother, she would ask, "When are you planning on coming out to visit again?" I went once for some Hebrew holidays, and another time to go bowling, but that was about it. Sometimes Lonnie was busy eating when I called; Lonnie would say he'd call me right back, but he'd forget for a week or two. I would call again, and we'd chat, and I would tell Lonnie what was going on in my life, and Lonnie would say that nothing was going on in his life.

On the third day of April, Lonnie's mother called me at work, ten minutes to five. "He died this afternoon. He was in a lot of pain. It was terrible, but now it's over."

Then, fifteen minutes later, I heard that Seymour was dead. "Fuck," I thought. "Two deaths in a half hour. Life sucks. It truly does."

That night I called up Richard in San Francisco to see if he was still alive.

"Hi, Richard. Are you alive?"

"Yes," he said, in a reassuring voice. This wasn't the first time we had had this conversation. "How about you?"

"Still breathing."

"You're sure?"

"Wait. Let me check my pulse. Damn, I can't find it. I'm not getting a goddamn thing."

"Take your hand off your wrist and try your neck," suggested Richard.

"Thanks. Yeah, that's much better. It's fairly steady."

"What's wrong?"

"Somebody died. Actually, two people. I might as well buy condolence cards wholesale."

I called Walter, the photographer who had taken those suggestive poses of me ten years earlier when Walter's lover was away in France. Walter started going to Bible-study classes after his lover died of toxo six months before a treatment was discovered. He was diagnosed two weeks after his lover's funeral. Walter once told me that I was his dirty little secret. Walter's machine played the same message as last year; I assumed there was no change.

I checked the phone directory and called up Lloyd, whom I hadn't spoken with in years, just to hear his voice on the machine. Lloyd had been extremely abusive to me when he taught me that I was a size queen the hard way, at the tender age of twenty-six. Lloyd's best friend volunteered to be a GMHC buddy and ended up dying of AIDS two years before his client eventually did. Lloyd never answered the phone directly, preferring to monitor incoming calls on his answering machine. A feeble voice answered. I hung up immediately.

Lonnie's was a typical Jewish funeral service, complete with networking at the funeral home. A woman gave me her husband the headhunter's business card. The relatives were tearful, with sweet reminiscences. Lonnie's last lover, Mark, hid in the wings. They had broken up during the period when Lonnie was telling all his friends that he'd see them at his funeral; not too many of them showed up.

I hitched a ride with Mark from the funeral home to the Jewish cemetery, which was covered with shrubs: A shrub grew on each grave. Older grave sites had taller shrubs. It reminded me of radioactive carbon dating. Afterward, Mark and I discussed the existence of God over ham sandwiches at a local diner. He dropped me off at the train station. I waited half an hour on the platform, alone save for a pair of high-school students skipping school to go into the city for the afternoon.

Him with His Feet in His Mouth

I met Cameron, guest lecturer in fashion at the New School for Singles Recreation and all-around snob, for lunch the following Tuesday.

"I bet he'll ask me how I am at least three times in the first ten minutes, and really mean it," I said to Dennis. "It used to be just a simple colloquialism, with zero content. And now, it bugs the hell out of me."

"Who would think that those three words would carry such loaded meaning?"

"Sometimes I think it was a mistake to tell him when I started naltrexone. Sure, I was upset then. I sort of figured if I told everyone in a ten-mile radius of my apartment, it would somehow diffuse the news. But now, whenever he sees me, he just reeks with concern. His eyes get big like some Keane painting and I can practically see a single Plasticine tear glued to his cheek. I hate it!"

"He only means well."

"I know, but it still unnerves me. If there was something wrong, and I wanted to tell him, you know me, I'd blurt it out. He's treating me with kid gloves. I don't know; maybe they're plastic sterile gloves. I mean, I'm not dead yet."

"I'm sure you're exaggerating."

"Girl friend!"

"Girl friend!"

Cameron and I planted fake Hollywood kisses in the air, in the general vicinity of each other's cheeks.

"Benjamin, you really look great," said Cameron.

"Oh, come off it."

"No, I mean it. You really look good." The lady doth protest too much. I wondered whether I had mustard on my mustache or egg salad on my beard. Then I remembered we hadn't started eating yet. "So, how are you?" asked Cameron, right on schedule.

"I'm OK," I replied.

"I mean, how *are* you?"

"I *am* OK. Hey, do you mind if we do this in three stages? I'd like to drop off a prescription before lunch."

"No problem. Where do you want to go?"

"Let's try Pizza Piazza. The food sucks, the waiters have attitude, the design is post-modern pastel, and they have a luncheon special."

"I really don't want to go to a place with lousy food."

"Let me upgrade that to mediocre."

"Are you sure?"

"OK. The food's fine; it's passable."

"Why not?"

"And it's only a block away from the drugstore. Cameron, I've got a confession to make."

"Shoot."

"I've become a drug addict. I need a fix every four hours. Tell me; you'd know. Is there a twelve-step program for AZT?"

"I heard through the grapevine you were on it."

"I thought you saw it on 'Page Six.' That's where I read about your mad doomed romance with a married man from Weehawken."

"Who told you that trash? And not a word of it is true."

"You did last week."

"Oh, yeah."

"But you left out some pertinent details. Such as name, rank, serial number, and key-chain position."

"My lips are sealed."

"Not *all* of the time. Not from what I heard from an unnamed source," I bluffed, hoping to get more dish.

"You can call her Deep Throat."

"She's not the *only* one."

"If I ever have to give your eulogy, I'll be sure to mention your wicked tongue, you vicious gossip."

"Don't bother. I've already written one."

Cameron paused, embarrassed. He had just slipped in the muck. "But I hope I won't have to," he said, digging himself deeper into the mire.

"I told you. No problem. The deed has been done. Change subject?"

"Seriously, Benjamin, are you suffering from any side effects?"

"Oh, the usual. My dick grew a couple inches, but I don't think it's permanent. Which reminds me, you busy this weekend? I don't think we have much time. I mean, this stuff may wear off in a few weeks." We walked into the Leroy Pharmacy together and fought our way through the crowded aisles, back to the prescription desk.

"I'm sorry, girl friend, my dance card is quite full this weekend, thank you."

I handed the prescription to the woman at the counter. "It will be ready in fifteen minutes," she said.

"I'll be back in around an hour, OK?" I replied. "So, how's *your* health?" I sneered.

"I'm doing fine. I had a scare this summer. I came down with herpes in August. I have no idea how I could have gotten it. It makes me wonder about my immune system."

"But you're a neggie, aren't you?"

"I tested negative three times, but what does that mean? I've known people who died testing negative."

"Oh, give it a rest. Your T-cells are faboo. You've got nothing to worry about."

"I guess you're right." We seated ourselves at a window table. "Let's order serious carbs. We've got to keep our bountiful figures up. Benjamin, are you getting thin? I think it's time to binge."

HAVE YOU LOST WEIGHT?

"Have you lost weight?" was the way of asking people if they had AIDS. There was a precarious balance between slim and sick. One *could* be too thin. I was constantly monitoring my calories. I was terrified of obesity, in myself and others. I would never be fat. Then again, some men blimped out to become sexually unattractive, so no one would want them except for the anomalous chubby-chaser.

And I thought fat was a feminist issue.

OVERHEARD AT MY GYM

"What's the point of making new friends when they end up dying anyway?"

SPONTANEOUS COMBUSTION

It was enough to make me wonder if one day I would explode. My friend Mason from college, who wanted to be president but knew he couldn't because he was shorter than five foot ten and from the South and half-Jewish to boot (Mason said that Jimmy Carter made it only because he was a born-again Christian, it was a fluke, and they were never going to elect another Southerner president), was a schizophrenic genius, and the last I had heard, Mason had actually exploded. I never got the details: I assumed this was a metaphoric description, and maybe Mason had been committed to a state facility, or maybe he had leapt from a twenty-story building, or maybe he had been struck by lightning during an electrical storm. But given the volatility of Mason's cognitive states, I imagined that Mason had actually exploded, like in Cronenberg's film *Scanners:* his skull exploded like a shattered pumpkin, the pieces jettisoned as if a bomb had been planted in his cranium, with bone shrapnel and blood everywhere.

I was worried that if I kept up this high level of anxiety, one day I would spontaneously combust: I would walk down the street and suddenly burst into flames, becoming the literal embodiment of the proverbial flaming faggot. According to Ray Bradbury, books undergo spontaneous combustion at Fahrenheit 451. Perhaps humans do at a lower temperature, I thought, given the AIDS crisis: I saw all jumbled together greedy drug companies jockeying for profits; an arteriosclerotic government infected with bureaucracy; egomaniacal scientists vying for the Nobel prize with reckless disregard for those infected with the virus; sanctimonious bigots frothing at their mouths, spouting self-serving pieties on religious cable-channels; zealous media people stampeding to get that perfect sound-bite, keeping the general populace in their stranglehold; innocents buried in an information glut; ostriches with their heads in the sand; and rabid activists striking out blindly in anger at major institutions at random.

At other times I was so angry at the whole damn mess that I thought that under the pressure I might evaporate into steam.

In the final scene of Fassbinder's *Marriage of Maria Braun*, the eponymous heroine turned on the gas, paused deliberately for several minutes, then lit a match. The house exploded.

Was there a gas leak somewhere in the convoluted corridors of my own internal gastrointestinal system? Had the pilot been out too long? Would my eyebrows become singed at the onset of passion? Would I explode?

Or would I implode, my features gathering together as the gas whizzed out of me? Would I collapse like a dying star, a red dwarf? Would I contract into a black hole, a point of gravity, warping space and time, eventually leaving nothing but the memory of a strong indomitable force of suction? Would I disintegrate and disappear completely from this earth, leaving only dust, a wardrobe, and lipstick traces?

Something was fundamentally wrong with my life.

Every day I combed the obit columns of *The New York Times*

with an almost maniacal glee, looking for AIDS deaths. On the one hand, I was pleased that the conspiracy of silence had been broken, that through greater visibility, the community would wake up! pay attention! confront the crisis! but on the other hand, why should I be pleased? These people were dead. "What the fuck is wrong with me?" I thought. "I don't have a clue."

Formerly, I had constructed a complicated litany of qualifications for social situations: Would there be attractive and stimulating people there? Was I liable to get laid? If not, would the food be appetizing? the decor aesthetically pleasing? the venue within a ten-dollar cab ride from home? Now, everything was reduced to a single criterion: Was it good or bad for my T-cells?

En Route to Another ACT UP Meeting

I was halfway down the block, on my way to another ACT UP meeting, when I remembered that I had forgotten to bring my goddamned pills. I wondered whether I was irritated due to my natural dyspepsia or whether this was yet another side effect. I needed an alarm that would go off whenever I left my apartment without taking my beeper box. But how would I remember to reset this alarm? At this rate, I would end up with an infinite regress of mnemonic devices.

Every night I took a tablespoonful of naltrexone upon retiring, save for those nights when I forgot. I felt as if I were in some bad Brian De Palma horror flick the way I would suddenly bolt up in bed, as if after a horrid nightmare; but it was only that I had forgotten to take my nightly dose. Chastened, I would pad into the kitchen, wearing only the fuzzy rat slippers Sheila had given me three years earlier, open the fridge, take out the chilled bottle, and in the creepy light of the refrigerator bulb, gulp down a rough approximation of a tablespoon. I kept the bottle in the fridge because once the pharmacy had placed a sticker on it,

"KEEP REFRIGERATED AFTER OPENING," but this may have been a clerical error—it happened only once. Other erratic stickers on my many medications atop the refrigerator said, "WITH MEALS," "AVOID DAIRY PRODUCTS," "USE ALL MEDICATION UNTIL FINISHED," "TO BE TAKEN ON AN EMPTY STOMACH," "AVOID ALCOHOL," with little rhyme or reason. For the first few weeks the naltrexone had left me mildly stoned. Now the haze had lifted. The drug had no noticeable effects, save an occasional exceptionally vivid dream in Technicolor with Dolby stereo.

I stuffed the pillbox into my backpack, next to *The New Yorker* I had packed for the train, trudged downstairs again, and walked down Ninth Avenue, past the bulletproof door to what was once William's apartment building. Poor neurotic William, a perennial chorus member waiting for his chance for a lead in a Broadway show. I had followed him home one night five years earlier and had excruciatingly safe sex that even I viewed as excessive—comparable to masturbating on opposite sides of a Lucite wall. William was convinced that he had AIDS one full year before his mysterious illness was finally correctly diagnosed. I visited him twice at the hospital across the street. Two months later William canceled dinner at the last minute because it looked as though it might rain and he didn't want to risk exposing himself to the elements. I thought he was being a wimp. William died a month later.

I passed Worldwide Plaza, which was nearing completion. Howard, who had lived directly across from the parking lot that was transformed into the Zeckendorf complex, was spared the sound of the jackhammer. Howard had been a fanatic about the holidays. Once I went over to his house for a Halloween party. We carved pumpkins and watched Mickey Mouse movies. There were handcuffs on Howard's brick wall in the bedroom. Sex with Howard was too intense for me. He died at home, as he wanted to, a few months before they started bulldozing the foundation across the street. "It's important that I remember each time I pass his apartment," I thought. "Who else will?" Two years ago I passed by Bob Broome's house on my way to a trick's. The irony was killing me.

Every time I had a black-cherry seltzer I thought of Bob, who died in 1986. Black cherry was his favorite flavor. Every time I ordered Chinese takeout, I'd recall how Charles would save left-over rice to make fried rice. A few years back, Charles and three of his friends breezed into my apartment for a party, high on something, on their way to another party. For all their brio they looked like an entourage in search of a celebrity. Now two of the four were dead.

Soon the memories of the dead would overwhelm me. It would be impossible to go anywhere without thinking of the dead. New York was the city of the dead. I thought of Calvino's invisible cities and imagined being entangled in the stopped threads of shortened lives. Was I caught in the web of my past, spending all of my waking hours remembering my dead father, my dead tricks, my dead friends?

ALPHABET SOUP

The Monday ACT UP meetings could last forever. I had to have something to eat beforehand; it did my immune system no good to sit through a three-and-a-half-hour meeting on an empty stomach. I slid onto a round stool at the Village Den and ordered a large Greek salad. It arrived two minutes later in a bowl as large as the Adriatic Sea.

I picked at my salad and scanned the *Times* for the latest in fashion, leisure, homophobia, and death, and perhaps a story on the current drug-of-the-month. AL 721 ended up being the self-empowerment placebo of the year. Dextran sulfate didn't absorb into the bloodstream in oral form. Compound Q scared me with reports of extreme toxicity, even death; I preferred a more well-established letter: Compound W for warts, Preparation H for hemorrhoids. I wondered, "Does the entire alphabet signify?" If

I had the choice between overtraining and undertraining, I'd skip track practice. For the same reason, I was wary of pouring unknown substances down my gullet; I had taken high-school chemistry and knew from experiments that some cocktails didn't mix well. I looked at the latest smorgasbord of bogus drugs and saw a glass beaker stirred, not shaken, with a glass rod, over a Bunsen burner, bubbling, filling the room with clouds of colorful smoke. No thanks. I'd stick to Diet Coke.

So Many Meetings, So Little Time

Every Monday evening around three hundred rabid activists, politically correct lesbos, muscle-bound homos, demented radicals, crazed bimbos, fervent idealists, commie symps, pinko fags, concerned straights, and cynical queers both male and female met at the Lesbian and Gay Community Services Center, in a large, smokeless chamber. Meetings started at around 7:45 and usually ended by 11:00. I generally cut out, due to emotional and spiritual exhaustion, at around 10:00 P.M., with a sympathetic sore throat, although I had yet to open my mouth at the bombastic meetings. ACT UP meetings tended to raise the blood pressure. When some angry activists spoke, my T-cell count took a nose dive. One Brooklyn bisexual with ire in his throat would start at seventy decibels and jump in ten-point intervals every thirty seconds.

ACT UP had no leaders. Meetings were run according to a modified version of Robert's Rules of Order, democratic to the point of near anarchy. The facilitators tried to allow as full discussion as possible without letting things slide into complete chaos and to lower the level of vituperative and personal aggrievance to a tolerable level.

As with any other cause or activist group, you could organize your entire life around it. The Issues Committee met on Tuesdays, and the Coordinating Committee met on Wednesdays, and the Fund-Raising Committee met on Thursdays, and the Actions

Committee met on Fridays, and the Majority-Action Committee met on Saturdays, and the Outreach Committee met on Sundays, and the general group met on Mondays, and I've left out six or seven committees and subcommittees. So many meetings, so little time.

I entered the community center overcome with nausea. Outside the door, socialists were handing out copies of *Workers World*. Inside swarmed a mob of sexy young anarchists and knee-jerk radicals. I headed for the men's room, behind the table at the front of the room. There were usually a few chairs secreted behind the wall of urinals. I awkwardly dragged one through the morass of buzzing people to a relatively quiet section on the edge.

There was something inspiring about the crowd of three hundred gay men, lesbians, and straights "united in anger and committed to direct action to end the AIDS crisis." I felt a flush of pride to be a part of them. They were working night and day, researching drugs and bureaucratic processes, planning scenarios, leafleting, putting up posters, holding demonstrations, tying up phone lines, zapping fax machines, having die-ins in the middle of the street, writing letters, holding press conferences, doing everything in their power to stem the tide of death. The room in the community center was filled with energy.

It kept me sane.

I was especially impressed by the glorious lesbians at ACT UP. I was convinced that dykes represented the culmination of tens of thousands of years of evolution; it was clear that they were a higher life form. Lesbians had invented, patented, and codified the term "politically correct." If only I had real tits, I would give suckle and nourish them, as they had nourished me by their presence. I wanted to give them a suitable gift: a private concert with k. d. lang? a weekend with Martina? a bubble bath with Madonna? Alas, I was out of my element.

The meeting eventually began. There was about an hour of announcements, including a few about El Salvador resistance and the student rebellion in China. The Treatment and Data Committee gave their spiel on their most recent meetings with drug manufacturers. The lawyer from Lambda Legal Defense announced a meeting for the thirty people still charged from the recent City Hall demo.

I read a handout, Xeroxed from London's *Pink Paper*. Robert Gallo was quoted as saying we have no way of predicting how many people who are infected are going to develop AIDS. I thought he was lying again. "Would you buy a used virus from this man?" I asked myself. I didn't trust him; I didn't trust anyone. I thought that the AIDS virus was universally fatal, and all of the so-called good news was just false cheer, Pablum fed to us by the authorities.

What the fuck should I do? Tape the edges of my mouth up into the rictus of a smile?

A week before, I had gone to a health forum on slowing the progression of HIV infection. I was told, "Don't be consumed with your illness. Get on with your life." Sure. This was from an organization with thirteen-week peer-support programs in which the topics discussed included visualization, meditation, spirituality, and my favorite, "Death—A Meaningful Part of Life." It depended on which side of the grave you were on, I supposed.

BETTER LIVING THROUGH CHEMICALS

There was a housing presentation. A demo was announced for the following morning in Brooklyn at eight A.M. Then the administrator of ACT UP turned the floor over to a process queen with a procedural amendment to the working document. This would take some time.

I read another Xerox about the proposed cocktail therapies of the future: taking several drugs all at once, to intervene at several points of the HIV life-cycle. I hoped someone could come up with time-released multi-drug capsules. I wondered why this didn't work with AZT; there already were time-released vitamin

C pills and cold capsules. But then, as usual, my beeper went off. I opened my pillbox and chased the tiny pill around with my fat, nail-bitten forefinger, hoping not to jostle it and cause it to skip out into the next row like a Mexican jumping bean, for at $1.20 a pop wholesale, I couldn't really afford to lose it, and I would no doubt be misunderstood if I got down on all fours and crawled through the aisles at the meeting: People would assume I was missing a contact lens or orally fixated on the entire row in front of me. I then stuffed it into my craw, swallowed automatically, and contracted for the single dry-heave spasm I would feel in approximately half an hour if I didn't ingest something of substance in the interim. I hated it. Every four fucking hours. The only way I could stand it was by telling myself that it was only a temporary stopgap measure until something better came along. Sort of like a boyfriend. I half-hoped the AZT would exhaust its efficacy so I could stop it. The drug worked for maybe eighteen months, maybe two years—no one knew for sure. Eventually the dastardly virus would mutate or multiply, sneak past the drug's defenses, and I would be left where I started. By then there would be new, better, less toxic drugs available. Sure. And I promise I won't come in your mouth.

THE BLUE-LIGHT SPECIAL

I flipped through a copy of *New York Press*. On page 8 was a fifteen-percent-off coupon for AZT at a Village pharmacy. "This is ludicrous," I thought. "A sign of the times. Our materialistic consumer society has reduced the bizarre to the commonplace, the most expensive antiviral on the market to the banality of the blue-light special at K Mart." The coupon was also for discounts on Retin-A and Rogaine. I wondered whether using the coupon for one purpose invalidated it for the other. If one had to choose only one, would one grow hair, eliminate wrinkles, or save one's life?

The Widening Chasm

I read another promising article that predicted that AIDS was well on the way toward becoming a chronic, manageable disease, like diabetes. In my heart of hearts I knew the author was lying. When confronted with statistics that fifteen percent of those diagnosed with AIDS were surviving five years after diagnosis, I, the eternal pessimist, focused on the fact that eighty-five percent were dead. What was I going to do, celebrate the fact that if I got diagnosed, I would have an eighty-five percent chance of dying in the next five years? Take a gravedigger out to lunch? I didn't believe the optimistic voices, no matter how loudly they shouted. I was going to die. It was that simple.

Most people could not accept the premise that some day they were going to die. After years of despair, anxiety, false hopes dashed on the rocks, and the occasional IRS audit, I had finally made that astonishing leap of faith. How could I return to my earlier innocent state? It was as if I had crossed a fissure, a chasm. I couldn't jump back over the widening chasm.

Will It Help?

"And will it help matters," I thought, "if I get arrested at New York City Health Commissioner Stephen Joseph's office?"

Gordon Leaves a Message

I left the meeting at around 10:30 and took the subway home. I stood on the uptown IND platform with a "SILENCE = DEATH" button piercing the breast of my leather jacket. I dropped my backpack on a non-urine-soaked portion of concrete and bent over to retie my shoelaces. To kill time, I called my phone for messages. There was one, but the pay phone malfunctioned and I was unable to produce the proper tone to retrieve it. The train rushed in with a clattering of thunder. I chose a seat next to the door, under the subway map. I unzipped my backpack and extracted a sheath of Xeroxed handouts I had collected from the back table at the meeting.

I returned to my apartment, exhausted, at around eleven. The machine was blinking furiously, yet a double dash replaced the numeral that would represent the message count. I realized the power had momentarily gone off in the apartment, and the machine hadn't reset. I pressed "play" and heard nothing but static. Thinking that perhaps a message had been left later on the tape, I pressed "fast forward." I went to the bathroom to brush my teeth. When I returned, the tape had stopped. I rewound a few feet and pressed "play" again.

"Snap out of it!" said Gordon. "You can't let it ruin your life. Get over yourself, Mary. Snap out of it, B.J.! What you're suffering from is purely psychological. Stop this self-indulgent crap! You have no right to wallow in self-pity. Do you get off on this shit or what? Snap out of it!"

Gordon had died two years before. Was I dreaming this? I checked and rechecked the list of side effects, searching for mentions of buzzing noises, hearing impairments, hallucinations, and psychotic episodes. I found nothing.

Gordon died the day I took the HIV-antibody test. The next day I took a two-hour lunch and joined in an ACT UP demo outside the entrance of Memorial Sloane-Kettering Hospital with tears in my eyes. ACT UP had organized a seventy-two-hour picket to protest the fact that hardly any drugs were being tested, just AZT. I wanted to do something. Walking in circles for an hour was the best I could manage. By Sunday Gordon was nothing but bones and dust. Poor Gordon, ripped out of life at thirty-three. How many more had to die?

I played back the tape. Unlike in an *Alfred Hitchcock Presents,* it was still there. Gordon, directing my life from beyond the grave. What could be spookier? "Snap out of it!" Who does she think she is, Cher?

Then I remembered. Three years earlier, I had been dumped by some guy I had met at The Works. I had left a long, sloppy, self-indulgent message on Gordon's answering machine before going on a two-week vacation to Scotland. Gordon waited until the day before my return and had responded with this message. It lay at the end of my tape, after thirty-two other messages. It had never been recorded over.

Gordon was right.

I really didn't have any choice.

If I kept on despairing, I might as well have been dead.

There was plenty of time to deal with physical symptoms and problems down the line.

TAKING THE PHOTOS OFF THE WALL

I slowly removed the photographs from the wall.

The Javits Center photo went down. The photo of Susan Sarandon dancing in a ballroom against a backdrop of clouds, culled from *Interview* magazine, went down. The original ad for *Making Love,* from *The Advocate,* at least seven years old, went down. The photo of Joan Didion with her fingers at her temples, trying to stave off a migraine, went down. The naked man with the artful shadows covering his penis, holding aloft a towel from the Chicago Film Festival, went down. The original Limbo Lounge poster for *Vampire Lesbians of Sodom* ("More glamour! More excitement! More wigs!") went down. The cover from an Undergear catalog circa 1984 went down. The Hanna Schygulla cover of a pre–Tina Brown *Vanity Fair* went down. The " 'I Was a Teenage Intellectual' by James Atlas" cover of *The Atlantic* went down. The *Newsweek* gay-America cover went down. The *Playbill* cover from the original run of *Dreamgirls* went down. The postcard of "Starry Night" I sent to myself the day I got a mailbox at F.D.R. station for personal-ad responses went down. The poster of Ethyl Eichelberger as Lola Montez, five Fridays in October at Snafu, went down. The poster for *The Magic Flute* with the bizarre male torso, a python wrapped around his eyes and neck, under the illumination of a glaring naked white bulb, hanging, went down.

I had recently grown a beard for all of the usual reasons: to punish my face, to hide from the world, to alter my identity. Oddly enough, the last time a beard had spontaneously sprouted on my face was when I had been diagnosed HIV antibody-positive. I couldn't shave then because I had a rash. I went into the bathroom, turned on the light, and made my way to the sink. I turned the left spigot as far as it could go. A few moments later steam began to rise to the mirror. I opened the medicine cabinet and removed a Gillette TRAC II razor and a bottle of shaving cream. I covered my cheeks with foam, stuck the razor under the stream of scalding water, and shaved off my beard in slow, even strokes. In ten minutes it was gone. What remained was the face of one Benjamin Joseph Rosenthal looking half a decade younger.

THE PRIMAL REJECTION SCENE

I called my mother up in Rochester. I was done with stalling; I was going to get on with my life. No more secrets. No more lies. I dialed the area code, the exchange, and the phone number. After three rings my mother picked up, said, "Hello?" quizzically, and then *she hung up on her own flesh and blood, her only son.* Somewhat miffed and frustrated, I called her right back. *She hung up on me again.* I had had a lot of practice with rejection, being a practicing homosexual in Gotham City, but from my own mother? Until I realized, of course, that the phone was out of order. So I called my sister, Sheila.

"Did you tell her yet?"

"Nope."

"Benjamin, I thought about it. I'm no longer so sure. Maybe you should tell her."

"But her phone doesn't work! What should I do, send a telegram?"

Then Sheila, exhausted, had to go to bed too. She hadn't gotten a good night's sleep since the baby was born. Sheila said she'd call the phone company the following day and report it. She forgot. And my mother waited for four days before calling the phone company, *assuming* that someone else would have reported it.

VOYAGE OF THE DAMNED

Three weeks later I found myself on a Circle Line Cruise sponsored by Body Positive, referred to variously as the Love Boat, the Ship of Fools, or the Voyage of the Damned. I ran into Mark, whom I didn't recognize at first because he didn't have his hairpiece, although I thought it was because he shaved his mustache. Mark had tried AZT a year before and failed. His doctor went and died on him. Mark had approximately one T-cell for every ten of mine. Mark started screaming at me when I told him I was taking aspirin for the headaches, because they were contraindicated, according to the five-hundred-page pamphlet that came with the medication. My doctor told me that it was fine to take aspirin, so long as I avoided Tylenol. What was I supposed to do when two people were telling me what to do? Whom did I listen to? Whom did I believe? Especially when they were saying contrary things. Of course, it turned out that Mark and I had the same doctor, whom Mark switched to after the unfortunate demise of his previous physician, so what's a mother-fucker to do? Switch to Advil and other medications designed for the easing of menstrual cramps?

I decided that there was absolutely no reason to pursue the matter—the matter being Mark—further, because although he still presented a very attractive figure, there remained the T-cell criterion and Mark's failure to have a beneficial effect thereof. I

politely excused myself, dashed downstairs to the bar, ordered
an adult beverage that I quaffed immediately, and avoided Mark
for the foreseeable future. A bevy of glamour girls were seated
by the window, gleefully exchanging gossip and medications. A
beguiling architect began chatting with me; half an hour later we
had a rendezvous in the ladies' room and made out.

Minor Improvements

And eventually the side effects relented and wore off, although
not completely; there were still the occasional headaches and
slight nausea. But life goes on, doesn't it? And so did I. The
psychological paralysis passed. The gloom lifted, and what was
left was the normal state of discontent in which I had resided for
the past thirty-three years.

Untidy Endings

Roger was going to Yugoslavia with his mother on a holy pilgrimage to a tiny village where three women had daily visitations
from Mary, mother of Jesus. I didn't know why he felt it necessary
to go so far when there was supposedly an oil slick on the side
of the Elmhurst gas tanks in the form of Jesus.

Tom avoided his doctor and kept on putting off taking his
T-cell counts, preferring the route of homeopathy, herbal remedies, and healing crystals.

Mark's T-cells doubled after he dropped the experimental drug
Immuthiol and reverted to his habit of two martinis at dusk.

Richard lived in San Francisco with a lover. Richard had been
sober for seventy-five days. He went to AA daily. Richard has
had three bouts of pneumonia. He finally got tested. The results
were positive.

According to the ever-inventive *New York Native*, Gilda Radner may have died from Chronic Fatigue Syndrome.

The 100,000th case of CDC-defined AIDS in the United States was diagnosed in June; he received a supply of AZT and aerosol pentamidine, and a free nebulizer for one full year or a lifetime, whichever lasted longer.

Lonnie was dead.

Seymour was dead.

Howard was dead.

Bob was dead.

Charles was dead.

William was dead.

Gordon was dead.

And I was last seen laden with pills on a Trailways bus headed toward Canada, my Canada, clutching a copy of *Bob Damron's Guide* in one hand and a liberalized safer-sex guideline in my other.

·10·

The End of Innocence

DECEMBER 1989

"Lunch. Tomorrow. The traditional place. The regular time. Be there or be square. *Ciao*, baby." I played back the message. I had staggered home at 11:30 P.M. after the seventeenth pre-action meeting for the December "Stop the Church" demonstration. My answering machine blinked three times. New York Telephone wanted me to continue paying ninety-five cents monthly for a newly optional "wire maintenance charge." They had spent at least fifteen dollars badgering me with phone calls and mailings to convince me of this necessity. Someone on the ACT UP phone-tree called me about the demo at St. Patrick's Cathedral. Of this I was already aware. And Dennis was inviting me to lunch—probably for my birthday. I felt bad; I'd forgotten to send him a card five years in a row. I'd gotten so caught up in the activist shtick that I thought I hadn't even spoken to Dennis in the past four months.

Dennis used to be a Catholic priest. Now he taught ethics and ran an AIDS ministry. He popped up the next day in the reception room at my office at 12:40 on the dot. I pulled on a sweater and my leather jacket and bounded up the stairs.

"It's been too long," I said, hugging him.

"Think nothing of it."

"It's all my fault."

"No, I insist. It's all your fault," affirmed Dennis, smiling.

"OK, I agree. You're right. I concede the point to your superior wisdom, on the assumption that you'll pick up the lunch tab."

"Not so fast, José. If my recollection is correct, the last time you paid, it was back in aught seven, when we had that big blizzard, with a federal certificate of deposit from the Confederacy. But since it's your birthday, I suppose we can stretch the rules just this once."

"I would really appreciate a few T-cells for my birthday."

"Benjamin, I'm sorry, they were all out at B. Altman's. I made a special trip to the factory outlet out in Queens. No dice."

We took our seats in the nonsmoking section of a local pasta palace. There were twelve types of pasta and twelve varieties of sauces—mix and match at random, giving an even gross of possibilities. But first, Dennis inspected the wine menu. "I'll try the"—Dennis closed his eyes, placed a finger on the menu as if it were a dartboard, aimed, and shot—"the Pinot Grigio. A glass, please. I need something to drown my sorrows in," he confided. Dennis pantomimed a nose dive from a high-board into his wineglass. "I'm famished. *Je suis* famished."

"Let's order." A basket of bread coated in sesame seeds was placed at our table. Dennis lifted his glass in a salute to those not present, raised it to his lips, and sipped.

"Dennis, why just one glass?" Usually it was at least half a bottle. I had cut down from one beer a week to one a month in the interest of stopping my T-cells from dropping any further. "Is there something seriously wrong? Are you OK?"

He ran his finger across the top of the glass. There should have been some noise, but instead there was only silence.

"It's Chris. We're having problems." Dennis had been with Chris for practically ten years. I couldn't imagine them ever breaking up. "It started a couple months ago. We met for our Wednesday dinner in the city. He's usually pretty talkative. This time he's very quiet. He doesn't say a word. I have to ask him what's wrong three times. I go through the whole list. Is it his job? He nods his head no. Is it his family? He nods no again, looking down at his plate. Is it another crush? He nods yes, then starts crying. He says, 'It's more than a crush.'

"Chris has had these infatuations before. You know, we have an open marriage. I've had affairs. I'm in the middle of two as we speak, as a matter of fact. But I never fall in love.

"I haven't told Chris about them. I'm sure he can sense it. Although, for the first few years, I have an idea he just thought the open marriage was theoretical. So about once a year, Chris develops a crush on someone. They get friendly. And then he gets too aggressive, and the other guy will blow him off gently. He'll ask that perennial musical question, 'Why can't we just be friends?' They never get to the sexual stage. I think this is the first time it got physical. Usually it's all in his head, and then they reject him. He always gets depressed afterwards. He's very depressed. Part of me says, 'Poor Chris, I hate to see him so sad.' The other part says, 'That little shit, I'm glad he got dumped.' "

"Well, don't you think he'd be upset if he knew about your boyfriends?" I asked Dennis.

"He's not going to sexually blackmail me," replied Dennis, indignantly. "Benjamin, we haven't had sex for a year and a half. He *has* to know that I'm seeing other people. He was always less sexual than me. I won't let him manipulate me by withholding."

I figured that Dennis was exempt from the rules: He deserved everyone's love.

"I have two boyfriends. One is in Queens, the other in the Bronx," explained Dennis.

"What is this, *Enemies, A Love Story?*"

"We are in the midst of a holocaust, I need not remind you."

"Point taken."

"One's a doctor. The other fixes refrigerators. He's Italian."

"He's Catholic?"

"Natch. I don't know what he'd think if he knew that I used to be a priest. I haven't told him."

"Why bother with the past? Why ask for the moon when you have the stars?"

"We met at this place. It's called the Locker Room. It's on Fourteenth Street."

"Isn't that a j/o club?"

"You might call it that. I prefer to call it a venue for the ministration of myrrh and balms and ointments and the like. I'm sure Mary Magdalene would approve. And it doesn't cost, except the cover charge at the door."

"Still the active researcher, I see."

"I have purely a professional interest in these matters."

"Have I ever questioned your impeccable credentials?"

"Neither of them is in love with me." This, I didn't believe. Everyone was in love with Dennis, whether he liked it or not. This was a basic premise upon which the universe was founded, like nothing could travel faster than the speed of light, and the check was not in the mail.

Dennis looked up. "Listen." He pointed at the speakers near the ceiling. "Music from the heavens." He jerked his head up. "It's a heavenly choir."

"No, I think it's just the stereo." Classical gas. An aria. Voices from afar. Overweight women, breastplates and all, vying for the attention of a Teutonic god.

"But back to Chris. He says he doesn't feel the same about me as he used to feel. That happens. I used to have husbands confess that they no longer had sex with their wives and then they had masturbated four times that week." Dennis sighed.

"What penance did you give them?"

"Nothing. What's the point?" Dennis's eyes darted upward. He cleared his throat.

"It's been almost ten years. How long does the average marriage last, anyway?" I asked.

"Forever, according to the Vatican."

"I mean, according to the New York State Penal Code. I mean *The World Almanac*. What do they say in *Parade* magazine? Does Walter Scott have any insight in this matter? What about 'Dear Abby'?"

"I don't know."

"Maybe you could file a palimony suit and force him to stay attached for financial reasons," I suggested.

"I haven't seen him in weeks. We talk on the phone. We used to talk every day. Since our last conversation it's been a couple weeks. All I can do is wait it out. I told him I'd fight for him. I told him I still loved him. The complexion of love changes. You can't stay infatuated forever."

Dennis played with his food, distractedly. He arranged two strips of red pepper atop his salad into a cross, impaled them with his fork, and then scarfed them down.

"Poor Dennis. Chris will come around."

"I just have to be patient."

"One of my favorite virtues, next to cleanliness and godliness."

"I think you're confusing them with slovenliness and slothfulness."

"Don't forget gluttony," I added, preparing to chow down a rather large portion of vermicelli *carbonara* in a single swallow.

"So enough about me. What's doing with you? Where were you late last night? What dens of iniquity were you haunting? I evidently missed you on Fourteenth Street. I had you paged at the Toilet. I was told you were lying down in the trough and could not be disturbed."

"Another ACT UP meeting."

"You seem to be attending these meetings, dare I say it, religiously."

"I shudder to compare it to that," I responded.

"The camaraderie. The oratory. The spirit. The transcendence."

"The three hundred hot boys with pale skin, sideburns, skinny arms, six earrings, and tight black jeans."

"I'd genuflect any day," commented Dennis.

"So who said my motives were ever pure?"

"As the driven slush, no doubt."

"Listen, I'm in the center, and I'm always on my way to some twelve-step program—Phone Sexaholics Anonymous, Familial Guilt Anonymous, whatever. If only ACT UP didn't meet on the main floor! I can never make it to my meeting without being distracted. How can I pass through without stopping? We're having a big demo next week at St. Pat's, 'Stop the Church'!"

"I could go for that."

"It's cosponsored with WHAM, Women's Health Action Mobilization, not to be confused with the former group with George Michael, noted heterosexual song stylist. And they have these great psychedelic posters of Cardinal O'Connor as a public menace right out of *Vertigo*. He has demon eyes. Satan would approve."

"You're not perchance pissed at our most outspoken archbigot, I mean, cardinal?" Dennis was not fond of Mr. O'Connor.

"He's sticking his big snout everywhere. Here I am, an atheist Jew—"

"Whatever you do, don't sneeze in front of me. I wouldn't know what to say," interrupted Dennis. "Because 'God bless you' is obviously out."

"—and this asshole is getting in my way. Those fucking press conferences he holds after his Sunday ten o'clock masses. Who does he think he is—Geraldo? Why should he invade my private life? That son of a bitch is against condoms, even to stop the spread of AIDS. He won't allow any safer-sex education under his jurisdiction. This includes Catholic hospitals, hospices, shelters, and social-service centers. According to him, the only good homo is a dying one. He says he's full of compassion. I'd like to fling one of those bedpans he keeps on reminding us he changes in his face to see if he changes his tune. Mr. God-Hates-the-Sin-But-Loves-the-Sinner prevents sex education in the public schools. Christ, think of all those pregnant schoolgirls. I'm sure it was the immaculate conception. Or was it the virgin birth? I always get them confused. Earth to O'Connor, are you living in the real world?

"What really gets me is that he has power in this country, which was founded on the separation of church and state. His morality can go to hell. So anyway, this is the big one. I'm actually going to go into the cathedral on Sunday and get arrested. He makes me so fucking mad. Don't tread on me. Look: I've got tire marks all over my body from his eminence. I even bought some stage blood. I was kind of thinking of using it on my palms. You know, like Madonna."

"You're no saint."

"Well, maybe I am subliminally. I only buy Yves Saint Laurent cologne."

"I don't know about getting arrested. Think of it, B.J. Time in the slammer. You better practice dropping the soap in the shower. Sounds tough. Should I perhaps bake a vibrator into a cake?" Dennis was helpful as always.

"I think it's usually a nail file."

"Perhaps I could be called upon as a character witness at your trial? I hear they do wonders with latex in wigs these days. I've always wanted to be dressed like a nun. Audrey Hepburn. I would look so angelic."

"Not with that mustache, you don't."

"Yikes! I'd have to shave."

"Maybe you should join me. The potential for research alone should grab you."

"I can't. It's too risky."

"It would be great, considering your dark past."

"Shhh. It's my secret past. You don't want to let the cat out of the bag, do you?" Dennis pantomimed stuffing a kitten into a burlap sack. "Do it for me. I can't just now."

"You could always conduct a mass for Dignity on the steps of St. Patrick's."

"I have a feeling there may be a little interference from the police."

As usual, Dennis was right. That Sunday, hundreds of cops with billy clubs stood behind sawhorses and metal barricades in front of St. Patrick's. People were directed to enter by the side doors. Four to five thousand protesters massed a block away. Ignoring them, I slipped in easily at 9:25. A mass was in progress. The big one was at 10:00; I figured I'd beat the rush and get a good aisle seat. I saw a lot of other demonstrators. We had all entered separately, wearing an approximation of our heterosexual Sunday best—no telltale pink triangles today, no earrings for the boys, no leather jackets for the women. One activist was playing tourist: He had a subway map, a fake fur coat, and a Bloomies bag, filled with holiday purchases. Then, at 9:45, the ushers cleared the pews and forced everyone out.

O'Connor knew about the demo. The city had been stickered to within an inch of its life in the past few weeks. ACT UP and WHAM had leafleted the past two Sundays, detailing our quarrels with the cardinal and encouraging regular churchgoers to use other churches on that Sunday.

We left and lined up outside the side doors. We waited. Someone said a bomb threat was called in. Later, we decided that the cardinal had cleared the church so he could position his own zealots strategically. It was no coincidence that Mayor Koch was there. After a twenty-minute wait we entered, one at a time. Bags were checked. Some people were frisked and ejected. I sat down near a pillar. I pretended to gawk at the stained-glass windows.

My friend Michael sat across from me on the aisle, one row behind me. A few rows back a safe-sex porn star turned activist thumbed through his hymnal. I winked at him; he winked back. The tourist with his Bloomies bag was turned away at the door.

My group had decided to protest silently, lying in the aisle three minutes into the cardinal's sermon. An affinity group would read a statement and then join us. My watch didn't have a second hand. Unfamiliar with Catholic liturgy, I had no idea when the sermon would come.

Anticipating a possible disruption, the cardinal signaled the ushers to distribute printed copies of his speech. He noted that there might be some protesters in the congregation and began to speak. Was this the sermon? I wasn't sure. A minute passed, then two, then three. I looked around. The tension was palpable. I raised my eyebrows to Michael. He shrugged his shoulders, unsure. I took a deep breath. I nodded my head slightly. We slowly rose in unison, then went to the aisle and lay down, prostrate, imitating the order of the Carmelites. In a few moments the rest rose and joined us. The statement was read. Suddenly, there was shouting and screaming. The police had roughly dragged out a photographer; they were making preparations for arrests. O'Connor asked the entire congregation to stand and recite the Lord's Prayer. I heard a cacophony of shouts and curses. It was chaos. An usher stepped on the former porn star's hands. Someone next to me screamed, "I was molested at Covenant House, and I hold you responsible, Cardinal O'Connor."

"We are dying!"

"Act up! Fight back! Fight AIDS!"

"The Lord is my shepherd, I shall not want."

"Stop, you're hurting me!"

"You're killing us! You're killing us!"

I lay on my stomach, quietly ingesting it all. A few people at the front were taken away by the police through the exits near the pulpit. I waited, eyes opened, as the police approached. This was the end of innocence.

After what seemed like an eternity but was probably only ten or fifteen minutes, the police finally reached me. "You are trespassing. If you don't leave now, we will have to arrest you." This was the official warning; they were doing everything by the book. I could have just gotten up and left, but all of my friends were either inside at the demo or outside screaming their lungs out; there was nobody left to see a movie with, and moreover, there was nothing particularly interesting on television that afternoon. I remained motionless. Suddenly, ludicrously, I was lifted onto a stretcher and carried out to the front entrance by four burly cops, running. Where was the ambulance? What was their hurry? This was ridiculous. I smiled. I would have walked out, facing the spitting congregation, had they asked. Evidently, they didn't want to waste any more time. Did going limp on the police count as passive-aggressive behavior, or was it only like going limp in the middle of a sexual act? I wondered what my former therapist would have thought.

In the vestibule the officers placed the stretcher on the floor. "You can get up now. It's all over." I was alone. Then a policeman photographed me with my arresting officer. No time for last-minute touch-ups. Where was a comb when you needed one?

My arresting officer, a Hispanic a little shorter than I, with bright dark eyes and a black mustache, could almost have passed for a seventies clone. I would have offered him an ethyl rag, had I come supplied. I liked the looks of the steel handcuffs on his belt, but the nightstick was a little too much for me. He told me to put my wrists behind my back. I didn't squeal with delight; I felt that would be behaving inappropriately. Decorum was everything with me. He looped a pair of plastic handcuffs around them, not too tight but tight enough.

Then I was led to a van. Thousands of protesters shouted slogans and waved signs behind police barricades. I caught a glimpse of a sixteen-foot condom being carried like a snake by an affinity group. I joined eight activists in the van. Several had already slipped out of their handcuffs. It wasn't too difficult if they weren't too tight. Six more activists were placed in our van.

The van was dark. There were no windows; there was not much air. It was packed. There weren't enough seats for all of us. I had to play musical laps, which wasn't entirely unappealing, given my choices of a particularly dashing Jersey City performance-artist with coal-black eyes and thick bright lashes who looked great in a suit (I wondered what he looked like without one) and a tall, red-haired painter from the East Village. A Chelsea architect complained that his cuffs were too tight: He was losing circulation in his hands. The police refused to help, claiming they had nothing to loosen them. His fingers turned blue. A woman who was never seen in the same hat or pair of glasses twice sat across from me, wearing an elegant number with a tiny yarn puppet stitched to the top. The self-proclaimed loudest and fattest activist on the East (or any other) Coast took a nap, declaring that we were too boring a crowd to interest him. A wire-cage wall separated us from the cops in front. We could see a little out of the front. The door was open.

Later, I found out my closest friends were in other vans. One of them was stuck with a recent Ivy League graduate who spent the next few hours recounting his quite lengthy tale of the poignant disappointments of upper-class privilege. By the time they pulled up to the precinct station three hours later, his entire van had decided to file a civil class-action suit against the authorities and the egghead, claiming "cruel and unusual" punishment.

Our van circled the block, heading for a downtown precinct. Then we stopped and waited. Hours passed. After the church demo broke up, a small contingent decided to march down Fifth Avenue to Union Square for a rally for the homeless. Wasn't one demo a day enough? Some people were never satisfied. Our van slowly followed the demo, as if we had any room for additional arrests.

Downtown, we were led off the van, one by one. We were told to stand against the brick wall in the police station. I saw my fellow activists. The police photographed us again, one by one.

I hoped I could get a couple wallet-sized photos: I figured they'd make great party invitations. They cut our handcuffs with wire cutters. And then we had to remove our shoelaces and belts— like we were really going to hang ourselves. I could see it now: "Despondent homo AIDS activist offs self in lockup after controversial demo. Details at eleven." We emptied our pockets. One last chance to pass around breath mints (what could be worse than halitosis in the tank?) and Tic Tacs. There wasn't much use for a credit card in the clinker.

"I hope you don't mind if I keep my beeper and the pills," I said in a confident tone to an understanding police officer. A few moments later I realized that "understanding police officer" was an oxymoron. They took away my AZT because I didn't have the prescription on me. How stupid of me. Like I was going to overdose on AZT. Even more bizarre, the officers feigned ignorance of AZT; they claimed they had never heard of it. I was floored. Perhaps because AZT had become such a constant presence in my life, I assumed that everyone was aware of it. If I wanted to keep my pills, I would have to go to a hospital for the authorities to analyze them.

Then they told us we were going to be held overnight.

Would prisoners be trading me for cigarettes tomorrow?

A fellow activist whispered to me as we were being fingerprinted that the police were merely trying to intimidate us; we would be out by nightfall. I took two extra pills, hoping this wouldn't upset my stomach too much, and then surrendered my drugs. Then they took me back to my cell, which I shared with two exceedingly attractive young men who happened to be lovers too recently conjoined to even consider infidelity or threesomes. My luck. We discussed the typical New York topics: homoerotic art, apartment rents, the pros and cons of outing, the size of various activists' members and where they might be found at any given time, favorite tearooms. The cell's toilet did not have a paper strip sealing it fresh; there wasn't even a seat. When would I learn to be a real man and piss standing up? My friend Mark was in a large holding cell, with about twenty people total. They blew up condoms as balloons to decorate the room and spent the next few hours chanting. Finally, by five, I was released on my own recognizance. I had hoped Dennis would have come in clerical garb to bail me out.

"I can't believe they took away my AZT," I told Dennis on the phone the next day.

"Yikes! And to think you were after me to join you. It's doubtful that my thermos of Bloody Marys would have made it to the cellblock. I bet they would have confiscated that too and substituted inferior vodka and a powdered mix when I finally got released."

"I wonder what they thought my goddamned beeper was for?"

"Perhaps they assumed you were a kamikaze free-lance activist-for-hire, and that whenever you were needed at a demonstration supporting the violent overthrow of the government of the United States, boycotting Coors, or promoting lesbian love, the beeper would go off, with a phone number and an address. Was it brutal? Were you strip searched? Did someone's nightstick end up somewhere that it shouldn't have gone? Did they take away everything from you but your dignity?"

"Just our wallets and stuff. Oh, yeah, we had to take off our belts and shoelaces. Good thing I wore tight black jeans instead of baggy parachute pants. They used plastic handcuffs on us. This is not very ecological. I wonder whether they used disposable handcuffs to avoid contact with the deadly virus or because with mass arrests it's easier. You don't have to worry about getting the right handcuff key; you simply snip with wire cutters."

"So, how was life in stir?"

"It was fine, just boring. I was in a tiny cell with two other guys. They were lovers. We took turns playing Susan Hayward on Death Row. That stuff they use for fingerprinting is messier than carbon paper. My biggest fear was that they would serve us A and P bologna on white bread with no mustard. But they released us before dinner time, so they didn't have to feed us."

"Did you notice the hundred yellow ribbons I had tied to the Rockefeller Center Christmas tree to celebrate your release?"

"Why, yes, Dennis. That was very thoughtful of you."

"Don't mention it."

We were charged with four counts: trespass, criminal trespass, disturbing a religious ceremony, and resisting arrest. As if I had a chance to cooperate. The cops just tossed me onto a stretcher and carried me down the aisle. We had a series of meetings with our lawyers. I missed five mornings at work for court appearances. The first appearance was to postpone to consolidate our cases. The next time we handed in our written arguments to dismiss the case in the interest of justice. The third time, the prosecuting attorney handed in his arguments. The fourth time, the judge responded to our arguments, rejecting our pleas. Our lawyers met with their lawyers for intense negotiations. Seven months after the action in St. Patrick's, we appeared in court the final time. Most of us agreed to take ACDs (Adjournment in Contemplation of Dismissal), with three days' community service; six were willing to go to trial. The district attorney's office was rumored to be pushing for three years' probation should they get convicted. I ended up working with God's Love We Deliver, a volunteer organization that cooked and delivered meals to homebound People With AIDS. There was no hiding from God.

·11·

It's a Wonderful Life

APRIL 1990

What I want to know is, why did Ryan White have to pick the weekend I finally got around to telling my mother I was taking AZT to bag it? Was he maybe trying to help me as an object lesson? Ryan White was America's favorite innocent victim, which left me guilty, guilty, guilty. Verdict first, trial afterward, just like in *Alice in Wonderland*.

It was always *something*. I suppose it would have been cervical cancer if I told my mom the year when Gilda Radner bit the big one. But let's get real. Like most of America, I spent my life in chunks of ten minutes on the checkout line, greedily reading about the moment's sensation: Madonna's latest crotch grab on the cover of *Interview*, Dan Quayle's pathetic antics from the *Quayle*

Quarterly, the photo of Imelda Marcos's shoes from *New York Newsday.* Celebrity worship may be fatuous, but even atheists need something to believe in. My fantasy life was exclusively derived from the glossies: *People, Rolling Stone,* and *Exercise for Men Only.*

I was HIV-positive. So what else was new? I was just another example of the new nineties post-clone fag: no mustache, new Weimar Republic–inspired designer spectacles that cost one month's rent for my stabilized apartment, brush cut sans side-burns, a ten-year-old pair of worn-out Levi's, a Keith Haring T-shirt with the legend "IGNORANCE = FEAR / SILENCE = DEATH / FIGHT AIDS / ACT UP," and an arrest record as long as your arm.

I was completely typical; I'll give you an example. Remember the scene in *Starting Over* when Burt Reynolds had an anxiety attack in Bloomingdale's (who wouldn't?) and Jill Clayburgh asked for a Valium? Virtually everyone had one to offer him. Well, set your cinematographer's lens on me at the Spike on Sunday afternoon. Voice-over goes like this: "Goddamn it, forgot the beeper box. Could anyone spare a capsule of AZT?" In the next shot, slow motion, I'm being showered with tiny white cap-sules. What's the name of the flick? *Valley of the Dolls 1990? Gidget Gets the Plague?* This left me with two choices. For some reason I always ended up straddling the dialectic. Was I a top or a bottom? A cynic or a misguided romantic? I wasn't sure; may I please have another fifteen years to decide?

I didn't *think* I was schizophrenic. Still, I had two voices con-stantly arguing in my head. One said, "Why worry her? I mean, you're not even sick, maybe occasionally a little fatigued, but who isn't these days? So, you're taking poison pills. Big deal. Don't rock the boat."

The other responded, "You think your mother wants to find out when you're in the hospital or, worse yet, on your deathbed?"

The first replied, "Who says you're going to die? Think positive!"

The other said, "Listen, don't make bad puns at a time like this."

The first began, "Maybe she'd rather have everything all at once instead of disappointments like tiny cocktail hors d'oeuvres, one by one. Why constantly batter her with bad news?"

Which was the good voice? Which was the bad voice? And if I could tell them apart, which would I listen to, the one with the halo or the one with the pitchfork? Listen, my ears themselves were asymmetrical: One curled, the other didn't. My aural senses were inherently lacking. Was I extracted from the womb by a set of forceps clamped to the distorted ear? So how was I to decide? Just give me some guide to the perplexed and let me sit in some dark corner of someone else's soul for an indeterminate period of time and hope for the best.

I tried to decide by choosing the more difficult alternative. No pain, no gain. Was I confusing the dictum of the gym with the game of life? Was this the philosophy of a masochist? I knew it would be excruciatingly difficult to give Mom the news. I believe we last had a meaningful conversation on July 2, 1936. But wouldn't it be even more painful to refrain from disclosing this horrible, deep dark secret of mine for years? You see, I was a natural gossip. How could I possibly contain myself?

Why couldn't I have leukemia or some other more socially acceptable malady?

I'd practiced telling on everyone else: the census taker, Marlin Perkins of Mutual of Omaha's *Wild Kingdom*, last week's trick, the counterperson at Arby's, my proctologist, my third cousin once removed in Tampa, dead Laura Palmer of *Twin Peaks*, encased in plastic, the woman who stood behind me in the half-price TKTS line (I told her to skip *Cats* and try for *City of Angels*), the editors of *The New Yorker*, the men who installed my carpet from Macy's, and my father's grave. I'd sent telegrams, rented billboard space, used the electronic zipper in Times Square, leased skywriting planes, and written personal testimonials printed in

The Village Voice. I'd added my seropositive status to my résumé. I'd become so adept at telling that it was almost second nature when I met a prospective gentleman caller, hat in hand, bent at the waist, then springing up with a flourish, arm extended, my personal calling card gently placed into the receptacle of choice.

Why was Mom such a stumbling block? Was something Freudian going on?

The good voice (the bad voice?) told me, "Don't tell her on the last day of your vacation. Give her time to adjust, to get used to the idea, to ask questions." So the longer I delayed, the less likely I was to tell her, for I didn't want to be cruel. The bad voice (the good voice?) told me, "You should have written ahead. This is the sort of thing that shouldn't be done face-to-face. You could have included several helpful pamphlets and an extensive reading list." Sure. Ten years ago I told her I was gay with a letter. That did a lot of good. When I asked her about it a few weeks later, she said, "Bad news. You always get bad news through the mail." Then she had me talk to a gay professor she knew at the university who advised me to avoid the bar life (I stuck with gymnasium saunas instead).

I told my sister I was going to do it that weekend, so she could be on edge too. Sheila still wasn't sure whether I should or not.

My mother and I spent the Passover weekend frozen in suspended animation in front of the boob tube. I'd run out of things to say. Our conversations were always spectacular in their vapidity. Nothing was communicated. Everything I said was in code; everything I said was merely avoiding the issue. We talked about the weather, her aerobics classes, my job, and the latest Madonna video. Elton John sang "Candle in the Wind" at Farm Aid IV: "This one's for Ryan."

My mother asked a ceaseless stream of questions about day-to-day life, every little detail. Was this because I was so unforthcoming? Maybe we were comfortable only with the little details, the details that meant nothing, the details of life that meant nothing.

"Do you ask for plastic silverware in restaurants?" she asked. "I've heard that it's popular in the city."

"What for?" I inquired, completely appalled.

"I don't know. There was a hepatitis scare a few months ago downtown at the Lobster Grill. Fifteen cases. I read about it, I think, in the *Rochester Republican*. And then Regis and Kathie Lee had a segment on the latest trends in restaurant dining."

I remembered that a few years ago, she asked whether I donated blood anymore, like I used to do in college. Mom, I'm queer. Blood is *over*. We donate last season's designer originals to Bailey House. If you prick us, we may bleed, but we try to clot as rapidly as possible. How did I end up with the mother from another planet?

It was time to make the rounds. I went to visit my aunt and uncle on the other side of town. My cousin Marilyn was there, along with her boyfriend, Gus, with whom she lived in sin without benefit of clergy. They were planning on buying a house together. Marilyn told me that cousin Herschel was marrying a divorcée from the Midwest. I was not invited. Herschel once referred to me as "Mr. Excitement," for which I shall never forgive him. Once Herschel was married, Marilyn and I would be the only cousins who hadn't wed.

My beeper chose that moment to announce its presence, persistently, reverberating in the pocket of my leather jacket, on the back of which was an "ACTION = LIFE" sticker.

"What's that?" asked Marilyn.

"Oh, it's some drug that I've promised myself to tell my mom I'm taking, but I can't tell you until I tell her, and it will probably get her upset, and I've been putting this off for months, and I apologize for not telling you in such a tantalizing manner, but I figure if I dangle the truth, then I will be forced to tell, because it would be dishonest not to, and maybe it will be easier, maybe this will be practice, telling half of it. I hope you understand."

"Oh, that's quite all right," said Marilyn, more than willing to end the discussion right there.

"I hope you're not planning on jumping on the bandwagon and tying the knot too."

"We have considered it," said Gus, regretfully. His sixteen-year-old son from a previous marriage usually spent the weekends with them.

"The biological clock was ticking louder and louder, so we adopted a cocker spaniel last summer. It was pretty exhausting," said Marilyn. She was none too keen on additional progeny.

"We're waiting for a sign from God first. A virgin birth, water into wine, that sort of thing," said Gus.

"I think I get your drift," I responded.

"Not to worry," said Marilyn.

Later that night, back in front of what Harlan Ellison referred to as "the glass teat," I played out thousands of scenarios in my head. They all ended badly. The words were too thick to leave my mouth. I had cotton-mouth. Something was stuck in my throat. The residue of too many members?

It was very difficult to tell my mother things that mattered. Why? Because she didn't want to hear them? Because I didn't want to tell her? Maybe it was as difficult for my mother to communicate with me as it was for me to communicate with her.

I was sitting at the edge of my chair, the words at the tip of my tongue. I waited during *Arsenio Hall* for the appropriate commercial break. And of course my mother was tired; she was curled up half asleep in the chair in a position that her twelve-pound cat attempted but failed to imitate. She woke with a start and announced she was taking a bath and then going to sleep. Did I need to use the bathroom? There was no privacy in Rochester. With only one bathroom, showers, baths, and bowel movements were announced under the auspices of politeness.

The next day was Passover. Mom cooked up a storm of unleavened products, including a lemon-chiffon pie on a matzo-meal crust. I figured there was no sense in having her burn the sweet potatoes out of displaced distress, so I sat on my secret for the day. That evening was impossible, too. Not in front of the relatives. My cousin Bertha, nine and a half months pregnant and abandoned by her skittish husband, sat on the chair with easiest access to the facilities. My nephew, aged two, played with Sheila's hair at the table. Slouched in our chairs, we celebrated the festive meal (page 32 in our *Hagaddah*s, courtesy Maxwell House coffee) after sprinting through the four questions and the twelve plagues (Dare I add genital warts? It was all in Hebrew, so no one was the wiser), hiding the afikomen for Bertha's imminent arrival. Mom had triumphed again with the very best turkey, even though the button popped out during the preliminary cooking. The stuffing farcically used pieces of matzo in lieu of bread crumbs. Mom rushed in and out of the kitchen, the hinged door a blur, forcing second and third helpings on us before we had managed to take a stab at our first.

For the family photos, I set the auto timer and dashed to my proper place on the couch. Bertha, who did not wish to be photographed, wore a teddy bear on her lap to disguise the vast expanse of motherhood. Typically, I misjudged: Later, the picture revealed us huddled in fear in the lower right-hand corner, refugees recently released from cattle cars on our way to Dachau.

Sheila drove Bertha, who was exhausted, home at nine. I was still working on different conversational gambits that night as we watched the two-hour premiere episode of *Twin Peaks*. Again, we sat transfixed, in glazed idiocy, in front of the tube. "Mom, looks like I won't be needing that long-term investment-strategy seminar that cousin Mortimer recommended." No, too indirect. "Mom, guess what I have in common with Ryan White?" Too topical. "I'm sorry I contracted the deadly HIV virus, Mother, and I promise I won't do it again." Too apologetic.

We both went to bed after Carson's opening monologue. I felt defeated. I slept fitfully. I woke up at nine and refused to leave the bed for another hour and a half, in terror.

Sheila, who spoke to my mother not more than thrice daily,

called her at eleven to ask her how long it took to cook an ear of corn. Ten minutes later, on the last day of my vacation, I finally told her.

It was worse than I'd expected.

It was the worst five minutes of my life.

I casually palmed a tab of AZT and cleared my throat. We were in the kitchen. I had just eaten my last dish of fried matzo for the year. "Mom, I've been taking AZT for the past six months. Do you know what AZT is?"

"No." She stopped. She was at the sink, cleaning the frying pan.

"It's a drug that's supposed to inhibit the replication of the HIV virus. Do you know what HIV is?"

"No." She held the scrub brush in her left hand, the frying pan in her right. Soapy water dripped from the scrub brush. Behind her, through the window, the outside thermometer read 72 degrees. A red-winged blackbird whizzed by.

"It's the virus that people believe causes AIDS." I couldn't believe I was phrasing it in *New York Native* terms. Sure. And spermatozoa were the organisms that people believed caused pregnancy.

She knew what AIDS was.

"I found out I was HIV-positive about two and a half years ago. This doesn't necessarily mean I'm going to get sick."

She didn't look at me, as if I were a monster.

"But you tested positive for it," she spat out.

I looked back at her. She looked away.

"They're coming up with a lot of advances. They're making a lot of progress scientifically. Eventually, HIV infection will be a chronic manageable disease, like diabetes." In ten, fifteen, maybe twenty years. I'd believe it when I saw it in the pages of the *Journal of the American Medical Association*.

She sighed heavily, a sigh that took her sixty-two years to perfect. With harsh sadness, my long-suffering mother said, "It's a wonderful life." I realized that this was where I had learned irony.

It's a wonderful life-style, was what I think she meant.

I needed to leave immediately. Telling her days ago would have been hell. I asked her for the keys to the car. I was going to visit my grandmother at the Home. She handed them to me, head down. Tears did not stream from either of our faces. She'd get over it. It would take time. She didn't have a choice, did she? Knowing past history, we might never discuss it again.

Afterward, I was convinced I did the wrong thing.

Sheila later told me, "You're too hard on yourself. You were very brave to tell her. I could never have done it."

"I didn't expect her to be sorry or anything. Still. I had no idea it would be this painful. To get nothing."

My vision was a little blurry as I navigated down the driveway, sideswiping the hedges on the right. I coasted through several stop signs on the way and switched to a golden-oldies station. My right arm was a strand of dancing spaghetti, Maggie Smith flailing in time with "The Long and Winding Road." My left arm was tight on the steering wheel, in complete control. I blinked and wiped my face with my sleeve. The car behind me honked. I floored it and sped through the green light, drove another mile, passed the synagogue in which I had lost my faith ("BINGO EVERY WEDNESDAY" read the sign on the front lawn), and made a left turn to the Home for the Aged of the Jewish Persuasion of Central New York.

Grandma was in the dining room, tied in her wheelchair. A head nurse went around, inspecting the straps. "This one's too loose," she instructed the associate nurse. "How are you, Pearl? Do you want some apple juice?" She gave her a plastic cup. Grandma picked it up with both hands and swallowed greedily.

Grandma had been into bondage since she fell in bed and broke a hip. She had pneumonia on her ninety-second birthday the previous March. Her teeth were in, a perfect set of gleaming white false teeth. She was missing her glasses. The bags under her eyes were heavy. I spoke in English; she spoke in gibberish. I had no idea what she was talking about.

"Hi, Grandma. It's Benjamin, your grandson. I'm Selma's son. Selma was your daughter. She comes here every other day. Your other daughter, Maude, comes here on the other days."

"No, no one has come to visit me in a long time."

"So I finally did it, Grandma."

"The weather is cloudy today."

"I told Mom I was taking AZT. She didn't react too well."

She didn't know what the fuck I was talking about, which was fine with me, considering the state I was in.

"Nice to see you. No pretzels, please. Nothing like that. It's been hot. We went for a walk down the grass and had some ice cream later. I took the carriage. Reuben was six months old. He's my baby. He's my favorite. I know I shouldn't play favorites. Do you like to play bridge?"

My uncle Reuben had died six years before.

I was a little shaky. I had to sit down. I sat on the windowsill and rubbed my grandmother's arm. "I think I made a big mistake." I wondered who would die first: me or my grandmother.

"It's all right," said my grandmother. "The people here are usually nice. I don't like her. She screams all night long. Have you seen Saul? I haven't seen him for a few days."

Her second husband, Saul, had died fifteen years before.

"Maybe I'll figure it out later. I don't know."

"Nice to see you," she said. She closed her eyes. Her breathing became slow and rhythmic. She was asleep.

I walked down the hall to the elevator. Inside was a calendar of green construction paper, with all of April's holidays, birthdays, and social events. Hymie Goldstein would be ninety-five next Thursday. There would be a special kiddush in his honor that Saturday, after morning services, to be held in the chapel on the first floor. I signed myself out in the guest register. An aide was napping in the lounge. The activity room was closed.

I revved up the car in the parking lot and went to the mall. If every major city in the continental U.S. had a Chinatown, then every suburb had a mall named Shoppingtown. I picked up a copy of *The New York Times* in the Rite Aid drugstore. There was a tribute to Ryan White on the editorial page. I went to a pay phone, dialed the 1-800 Sprint number, ten digits of a number in central New Jersey (Dennis), and my fourteen-digit security code. No answer. I bought a dozen jam-filled, powdered-sugar, not-kosher-for-Passover donuts and collapsed on a wooden bench, cheeks smudged, facing the white fountain at the center of the split-level mall, midway between the two anchors, Penney's and Sears.

Back home, it was as if nothing had happened. Mom was gone, out at an aerobics class. Sheila came over with her son. We sat in front of the TV. Ryan White was on *Donahue,* a repeat of a show shot maybe eight months earlier. "I'm an innocent victim." He actually said it. I couldn't believe it. All this time I had assumed that this was a phrase used by the media, the ones who created the terms "wilding" and "outing," but not one that he would actually use reflexively himself.

My sister said, "Maybe we should change the channel?" I concurred. There was only so much you could take in one day. "Mom didn't ask any questions?"

"Not a one. Whatever happened to that natural curiosity that has so plagued mankind for years on end, leading to the invention of edible panties, compact discs, and flexible straws?"

"I love denial, don't you?"

"I would say it's complete." Denial. Or resignation.

"Maybe she'll talk to *me* about it," said Sheila.

"I hope so." Instead of further comment, I left a copy of the Body Positive newsletter for her to find, as if I had forgotten it.

This I related to Dennis back in New York City. "She'll probably burn it," he said. "Whoosh! Like they used to burn heretics at the stake."

"I don't know. Maybe she'll answer one of the classifieds: 'Straight biker-type seeks HIV-positive motorcycle mama.' "

"You're confused, B.J. She's the *mother* of an HIV-positive cycle-slut."

"I bet she'll burn the sheets, too," I commented.

"Polyester melts," Dennis pointed out.

"Thanks for the info. I'm sure she threw out the dishes."

"It's Passover, isn't it? No need to keep *trayf* or *chametz*. Maybe she'll go to some therapy group and work it out."

"My mother in therapy? Are you crazy?"

"B.J., I've got bad news. Remember our therapist?"

"Wollowitz? Sure."

"He's gone."

"Gone as in dead?"

"I'm afraid so."

"The usual way?"

"The usual way."

"Shit."

"I thought at first it might have been his heart. I remember he once told me he had rheumatic fever as a child and an enlarged heart."

"God damn it."

"Sorry I had to be the one to tell you."

"It's not your fault."

"But getting back to you, Benjamin, aren't you mad at your mother?" asked Dennis.

"Why should I be mad? I'm the one who fucked up." I accepted the blame but not the responsibility.

"Why aren't you furious?" asked Dennis.

It turned out that I was so furious, I was so incredibly angry, it took me an entire week to admit it. I was so concerned that I had done the wrong thing, that I had hurt my mother unintentionally, that I couldn't even recognize my own fury at her.

So I didn't call for a few weeks. She didn't call me. She wouldn't dare. I sent her dupes of the family photos I took. She wrote me a thank-you note that contained detailed descriptions of every restaurant meal she had had in the interim. Not a word about my condition. Then the day after Mother's Day I sent out cards: Mom got "Remember all of the aggravation I used to cause you when I was growing up? Well, I'm almost finished." I called her a few weeks later. We talked about the usual. She, dim as ever, remarked that it took a week for her to get the card, whereas my sister got her "Bitch! Bitch! Bitch! Thinking of you. Happy Mother's Day." card two days earlier. She knew I sent them both on the same day. The usual chitchat. Nothing ventured, nothing gained. And then, in closing, she used a new valedictory. "Stay well," she said. That I had never heard before.

Was she trying to say something? Was this her awkward way of recognizing, of facing up to it? I didn't know. I couldn't say. Whatever it was, it would have to do, for now.

·12·

The Rules of Attraction

JUNE 1990

Rule #1: Don't scare him away with unnecessary frankness.

"I'm in love with you desperately," I confess to Mitchell Goldstein, the sole remaining guest of yet another excessive party, at two in the morning. He stands with his back to the wall in my newly redecorated kitchen: pale green with lavender trim, and a single homoerotic calendar on the wall. Mitchell removes his hands from the pockets of his khaki pants and places them on my ass. We are exactly the same size. The pupils of his brown eyes are grossly enlarged. "Of course," I admit, "I'm in love with a thousand and one others at the same time; I don't deny it. Will you take me with all of my frailties, my flaws, my endless number of sins? I must confess them all to you." I start to massage his neck.

"I'm messy," I begin. "I snore. I tend to fart in bed. I have poor personal grooming habits. I don't cook; I defrost. I send my laundry out. I have all of the despicable habits of the petite bourgeoisie and none of the compensatory graces."

Mitchell Goldstein, whom I had personally recruited to help clean up, stifles a yawn. As usual, I started the evening with a modest selection of premium bottled imported beer and ended up with considerably more cans of a decidedly inferior quality. The apartment was littered with empties and makeshift ash-trays—butts floating in plastic glasses next to broken umbrellas and wedges of lime. Mitchell had arrived at nine, expecting to meet his close friend Bruce Morgan, an old unrequited crush of mine with flawless skin and sculpted body who had not only seen *Dangerous Liaisons,* the play and the film, but also read the novel in the original French. I had fecklessly invited Bruce in the hopes of rekindling a nonexistent flame. Absurdly, I had met him only once. Mitchell, a virtual stranger, buzzed the door in the guise of Bruce. I removed his jacket, tossed it on the pile on the bed, stuffed a glass of scotch into his hand, and pointed him toward the crowd in the bedroom. Bruce never arrived.

"Listen, I have to get this off my chest. Forget all the rest; it was just a sloppy bridge, a setup for my one true confession. Now, I'm telling you this because once, a long, long time ago, maybe it was six months ago, I met this *guy* as in *homosexual* on the subway—you know, your typical Joe Izod Lacoste College, with perfectly starched white cotton tennis shorts and a John F. Kennedy Junior part on the left side of the hair and a set of hairless bronzed calves bulging like the striations on a mandarin orange. Well, we didn't actually meet; it was more a series of nonverbal exchanges, a demonstration of contemporary semiotics as expostulated by Roland Barthes and Umberto Eco, which led, naturally enough, to my apartment, for he just *happened* to leave at my exit, or shall I say that in the heat of the moment I managed to lure him to my apartment—that perpetual red zone, with the flashing neon and portraits of male penises on the walls? This, of course, was before the new post-minimal me, with boring naked walls and sensible shoes." Mitchell places a strategic tongue in my ear. I ignore him.

"So it turned out Joe College wasn't on his way home as I had assumed. Joe, who resided in central Connecticut, was just going to the Adonis to see the type of movie where the cast consisted entirely of men in various states of undress and arousal and the timing of the next feature was irrelevant, to kill an hour before the next train. The events which transpired immediately after shall remain shrouded in a veil of discretion. Suffice to say that Joe missed his train, and even the following one, even though he took the rather extravagant and futile gesture of a taxi to the station. The following Wednesday he sent me a pleasant card with little or no prurient value. I called him up to thank him and explain myself. You must understand: I live under a constant black cloud of guilt, and every action I perform is under duress of that heavy black cloud of guilt. Not that it would matter, not as if we performed a single act that would have been questionable on the list of safe-sex practices approved by the Food and Drug Administration after seven years of exhaustive three-stage trials with extensive follow-up. I tell Joe on the phone (if he lived in the city, I would have done this properly, over Perrier and quiche at a suitable brasserie, but I don't want to drag him all the way into the city to find out, and I find I generally lose my nerve when I leave the island of Manhattan) that I'm HIV-positive.

"Here we reach an essential paradox. If Joe is sufficiently mature to appreciate my candor, he will undoubtedly understand that no risks were involved. A homo-in-the-know would realize that mosquitoes, food handlers, and the occasional close-mouthed kiss transmit nothing of danger. He'd say, 'What else is new?' or 'Now we have one more thing in common,' or 'I guess that means I should pencil you in for *this* weekend instead of next.' And if he isn't mature enough, chances are he will be unduly alarmed. Which would point me toward not telling him. But this, in fact, is *precisely* why I'm telling him: On the off chance that he freaks, I feel he deserves the opportunity to split for whatever irrational reasons.

"So I tell him, and he's completely shattered, because he lives in central Connecticut and he doesn't know five hundred thousand people who have died or gotten AIDS or tested positive. Moreover, he probably can't even distinguish between the three possibilities. When I wrote my friend the deranged Southern belle in Mint Julep, South Carolina, to tell her I was taking AZT, she responded with a heartfelt, sincere, and insanely misdirected letter saying how upset she was about the 'A'-word thing and bemoaning the fact that we probably wouldn't be able to spend the next fifty-seven years together; I eventually filed this in a folder titled 'Chronicle of My Death Foretold.' Joe was angry and upset, and there were the usual recriminations after I reassured him that he was in no danger from my mouth having contact with a prophylactic that just so happened to contain his erect member. Then he expressed sorrow at my horrifying fate, as if I had one leg in the grave already, as if I were in the final act of that Beckett play, buried in sand up to my neck. Of course, that was the last I ever heard from him, although I assume he checks the obits column of the *WhiteBread Connecticut Conservative* daily for my name." Mitchell begins unbuttoning his Urban Outfitters cotton print shirt. There is more hair on his chest than on his head. His nipples are so exquisite they make me curse my genetic makeup and consider using clothespins to enhance my own.

"So since then I've decided that I should tell everyone first—I mean, it's not really fair to wait until someone is so hot that he can't *just say no,* to wait until the pants are already down to the ankles and the shirts tossed on the couch in a muddled heap and the bulge in the Jockey shorts is quite unmistakable. It's not as if you can turn it on and off like a faucet and greet his thrusting tongue with the news that you're HIV-antibody positive and expect a rational decision on whether or not to proceed when his cerebral cortex has already been bypassed by his nipples and dick. So I figured I might as well tell you before it's too late, give you the out."

Mitchell pauses to think and responds carefully to this unexpected, unnecessary confession. "Oh, I just remembered. I have to see a friend. It's very important. If you'll excuse me. . . ." He feigns leaving abruptly. Then he turns, laughs, puts his arm on my shoulder, and says, "Which way is the bedroom, B.J.?"

Rule #2: Don't discard him because he has a loathsome profession. Someone has to bring home the bacon. Hopefully, this won't be you.

If he's a lawyer in mergers and acquisitions, be thankful he's not an actor. If he's an actor, be thankful he's not a salesman of computer hardware. If he's a salesman of computer hardware, be thankful he's not an exotic dancer. If he's an exotic dancer, be thankful he doesn't charge you. If he charges you, be thankful for the discount. If he doesn't give you a discount, try to find a lawyer in mergers and acquisitions.

Rule #3: Never sleep with a Republican.

"Are you absolutely sure you're not a Republican?" I ask Mitchell Goldstein in bed the following morning.

"I'm sure at least half of the attorneys at my firm are Democrats too."

"Have I heard of it? Is it called Gobble, Swallow, and Shit Them Out Before Lunch?" Mitchell is a corporate lawyer in mergers and acquisitions.

"I'm a vegetarian," he points out.

"How strange," I say, examining my toes.

"I'm your typical checkbook liberal," Mitchell says. I look into his eyes. The pupils are dangerously large again.

"I suppose you could call *me* a knee-jerk radical. I love the feel of steel handcuffs behind my back."

"S and M?"

"No, getting arrested for the cause."

"I'd like to show you where I live."

"Own or rent?"

"It's a co-op."

"Die, yuppie scum."

He dives for my crotch. I succumb in minutes.

Rule #4: Be flexible.

It's such a big production sleeping over with him, especially during the week. I select a shirt from my closet, leave it in the plastic wrapping but take out the cardboard backing, then place it in the backpack and put in the contact-lens boiler and cleaning solution and rinsing solution and soaking solution and carefully count out a day's worth of AZT and Zovirax, and then there's the morning's vitamins, All-Bee-Cee and zinc and A, and of course the beeper. I have to bring some Advil too; it turns out Mitchell, in perfect health, doesn't have any aspirin or an equivalent because he doesn't get headaches, and when he does, he prefers scotch. I don't even bother bringing the bottle of naltrexone over, because it's bound to spill and it's supposed to be refrigerated and it's a sugar-water placebo anyway, as far as I'm concerned. And I also need to bring a novel and a few magazines and my bills and a few letters so I'll have something to do at work the following day when I'm not making my sixteen thousand personal phone calls.

It would make sense to leave a spare everything at Mitchell's: an extra contact-lens cooker, along with solution, and enough drugs for an extended weekend visit. I could even keep a bottle of the night elixir there. But I don't. I'm not ready just yet.

It's bad enough to have a toothbrush there.

Rule #5: Don't sleep around.

"Why are there six toothbrushes in your bathroom?" asks Mitchell one Sunday afternoon at an absurd café in the Village that specializes in soups.

"There are six slots in the toothbrush holder; perhaps as nature abhors a vacuum, so does it abhor an empty toothbrush slot."

"And you call them guest toothbrushes?"

"Yes, all but the one I use regularly."

"Are they color-coded? Or do they have name tags?"

"I don't actually think they belong to anybody in particular."

"Why do you have so many toothbrushes?"

"Perhaps I am obsessive about my dental hygiene. Perhaps I'm just an old sentimental fool when it comes to toothbrushes, unwilling to throw them out. Perhaps I keep them around so my solitary toothbrush won't feel naked, alone in its holder, surrounded by emptiness. Perhaps I keep them around so I won't feel so lonely."

"Yet the guest toothbrushes are theoretically available for guests?"

"I suppose so."

"Exactly how many times have they been used in this manner?"

"I'd rather not say."

"Could you make a rough guess? A rounded estimate?"

"One is only used to clean my razor. Another is a chief alternate, for when my regular toothbrush is stiff with stale toothpaste because I hadn't rinsed it properly the last time I used it."

"And the rest?"

"I don't know."

"Are you aware that there are two more toothbrushes in your medicine cabinet, unopened, still in the package? Could you tell me why they are there?"

"I read somewhere that you should change your toothbrush every six weeks, to avoid reinfecting yourself with cold germs. I haven't yet decided whether this is true or merely a ploy by the

American Dental Association working in concert with toothbrush manufacturers throughout the world to stimulate sales."

Rule #6: Don't sleep around.

I like to sleep with people. I like to cuddle up in bed next to a warm body and drift off to sleep. Unfortunately, when you sleep over, they usually make you put out. I'm not always up for sex. Sometimes I get tired. My sexual excitation threshold is a little higher than it used to be. I no longer wake up with an erection every morning. This could have something to do with the drugs I'm taking, and it could have something to do with the virus that is replicating as we speak, and it could have something to do with the fact that I'm no longer seventeen and at my sexual peak. I really regret that I wasted my sexual peak masturbating when I could have hustled for large sums of money; the only drawback would be that I would be emotionally barren, but I'm already emotionally barren, so in retrospect, what did I have to lose?

It's easier to hit this sexual excitation threshold by sleeping with new and different and various people. Perhaps it's the shock of the new—the thrill, the excitement, the danger, the never knowing what to expect: ropes, whipped cream, or a rare bootleg recording of Bette Midler at the Continental Baths.

Rule #7: Don't sleep around.

I like to sleep in my own bed. Nobody else does. Is something subliminal going on here? I buy several completely extraneous and unnecessary consumer products for Mitchell's comfort: a bottle of Plax, a stick of underarm deodorant, a comb. Mitchell is bothered by the leaning tower of books, my overloaded Barnes & Noble bookshelves by the window that slope at a thirty-degree angle, threatening to collapse at any given moment, whereas I am proud of this apparent counter-example to the fundamental laws of gravity. The bed is too hard for Mitchell: The secondhand futon that I acquired from my overlibidinous friend George a week before he started going to Sexual Compulsives Anonymous meetings is worn thin. "It feels like sleeping on a board," says Mitchell, referring to the wooden platform directly below. My body is only a partial buffer; he still wakes with backaches.

"Don't complain. It's a lot better than the foam mattress I had for seven years," I respond.

I feel completely uncomfortable in his tenth-floor Fifth Avenue doorman co-op. Why must I always be dogged by that same set of Harvard Classics wherever I roam? I make a mental note to consider dating the illiterate. His books constitute a collection, including a first edition of yellowed complete works of Macauley, inherited from his grandfather. They are dusted once a month by a Nicaraguan housekeeper who speaks no English and becomes hysterical when she breaks an eighteenth-century piece of china standing in an antique display-case.

Like Antaeus, I have to have one foot on the ground to keep up my strength. When I go home, it's like putting my foot on the ground. I need daily contact. I have to go home once a day to check the mail, my bills and solicitations from charities and the occasional guilt note from a family member, and the phone messages.

I don't feel comfortable in a building with a doorman. When I announce my presence to the doorman, I feel like a thief, an inexpensive call boy Mitchell has summoned from the *Gayellow Pages*. I mention his name and floor. I feel even worse when the doorman recognizes me and doesn't bother to call Mitchell before sending me up.

I don't want to be alone in his apartment. I don't want to stay late and keep his keys when he has to wake up at six in the morning to catch a plane at LaGuardia to go on a skiing trip in Denver with his family. I wake up at six and share a cab with him and drop myself off at my own apartment and go back to sleep on my bed of nails. If I had stayed, not only would I have to face the doorman alone, I'd be stuck with his keys.

I don't want Mitchell's keys.

Rule #8: Frank expressions of emotion and discussions of feelings can help nurture the relationship.

"Are you afraid that I'm going to go down the tubes on you and die a horribly long drawn-out death in stages of despair, each succeeding stage worse than the previous, unimaginably grotesque, and that I'll lose my looks, my body, and waste away, and lose my sight and be nothing but a shell of my former self—only nastiness would be left, and then anger and then bitterness—and I would lose control of everything; or are you afraid that I might contaminate you with my deadly seed, that I might draw you into the circle of death and destruction, and that maybe I'm the black widow and you will be my latest victim, and that I will abandon you as it gets worse and then you will suffer unfathomable horrors, and I will be to blame, but you will blame yourself because you knew the facts before, and it takes two to transmit a virus, and even though we will diligently follow safe-sex guidelines—who knows?—maybe one day you will brush too diligently, and your gums will have a tiny microscopic tear in them, and a piece of saliva might enter, and then it will be over and done with?" I ask Mitchell on our third date, lying on his off-white sofa.

"Both."

"Oh."

Rule #9: Be patient.

It took me two years to come to terms with being HIV-positive. I decide to give Mitchell one month to get used to it. What's the point of having a relationship with someone who's mortally terrified of you? I figure I'm living in dog years. I really don't have all the time in the world.

I secretly resolve to dump Mitchell if I ever get ill.

Maybe plus signs should only sleep with plus signs, and negative signs should only sleep with negative signs? Mixed marriages are always more difficult: How will one bring up the corgis?

Mitchell can never understand my constant terror; I can never understand his complacency.

Rule #10: Practice safer sex at all times.

"Listen, Mitchell, I feel safe going down on you, but I get nervous when you go down on me. Irony of ironies, plus-signs can go down on negatives, but not vice versa. Since I'm positive, I don't really have to worry that much about catching it; I already have enough virus to last a lifetime, however long that may be. I mean, there's maybe a one in a million chance of getting the virus from sucking someone off. But in any event, how can I get from you that which you don't even have? Conversely, supposing you perform this act, punishable by up to ten years in prison in the state of Texas, on my person one thousand times—assuming we have the typical ten-year modern relationship and you go down on me about three times a week—that ups it to one in a thousand, which is one-tenth of one percent, which is enough to get nervous over, considering the fact that I don't floss. Whereas I think if I go down on you, the likelihood of transmitting the virus to you in this manner is more like one in a zillion, and we would have to have as much sex as the entire population of China does in five years to build up to the same one-tenth of one percent. In other words, even though I realize that this is an extremely difficult sacrifice for you to make, and you really hate this sort of thing, will you be so kind as to present me with your member, that I might draw sustenance from it?"

Rule #11: Don't ever ask what he's thinking; it's none of your business.

We are lying on Mitchell's off-white sofa after a hearty meal of stir-fried tofu and exotic vegetables available exclusively at Balducci's at five dollars a pound. I hold Mitchell from behind, in my arms. I rub his belly in soft, gentle motions. He smiles. I ask the question that I have always hated being asked and have promised myself never to ask: "What are you thinking about?"

Mitchell is evasive. "I don't want to say."

Now that my curiosity is piqued, I really want to know. "Come on."

"What are *you* thinking about?" he counters.

"That's easy. I'm just wondering about what *you're* thinking."

"I'd really rather not go into it," he pleads.

"You can tell me," I reassure him.

"I'm afraid you'll be offended."

"Me? Offended?"

"OK." I don't know why he gives in. "I was thinking about what would happen if you were in the hospital."

The invisible brick wall between us rises another foot.

Rule #12: Be cordial to his ex-boyfriend. Try not to sleep with him. He's bound to tell.

What do I say when Mitchell asks me if he's boring and he tells about how his ex-boyfriend Gilbert—who lived with him for two years, then dumped him, then through sheer perseverance worked his way back into his graces and lived with him for another year until Mitchell dumped *him*—thought he was too boring at times, and then he tells me that his ex-boyfriend Gilbert thinks his new boyfriend is boring at times? *Everyone* is boring after fifteen minutes. I don't know why I have such a short attention span. I'm glad I didn't grow up on Sesame Street; it would have been even shorter. There is only so much time I can spend with another person before my own thoughts take over, and they bore me terribly.

Mitchell is terrified that I will drop him because I told him that all of my affairs last less than three months, and in his case, to expect even less, because I am living in dog years these days.

One day I meet his ex-boyfriend Gilbert, whose name is still listed on the mailbox and in the building directory. Gilbert, with soft wavy hair the color of toffee and matching glasses, still has the keys to the apartment (better him than me) and had come over to let Mitchell in because Mitchell had left his keys in Denver on the family ski trip, confusing them with the keys to the rental. Gilbert, endowed with a sweetness that could cause insulin shock, stays long past his welcome, deliberately delaying his departure so that he can meet me, thumbing through the latest issue of *The New York Review of Books* and sipping zinfandel, although Mitchell does his level best to hustle him out.

I had called Mitchell from the gym, telling him I was on the way over. Mitchell doesn't tell me that Gilbert is there, because he is hoping that by the time I get there he won't be.

Gilbert is very cute, as expected. And of course, the first thing I think of is, why not sleep with the ex-boyfriend?

This way I will reassert some power over the situation. Mitchell will be completely disgusted that Gilbert has slept with his current boyfriend and in all likelihood never forgive him. But this is only one reading of the situation. The other is that Gilbert is bound to tell Mitchell, and Mitchell will, of course, dump me. This will end my turmoil: to have a boyfriend or not to have a boyfriend.

Why is this the first thing that pops into my head? Why do I want to hurt him? Sometimes he *is* boring. Boyfriends are *supposed* to be boring. How can anyone be exciting twenty-four hours a day?

Rule #13: Don't fall in love with a mysterious gentleman you met at the Eagle who lives in Key Lime, Florida, and came to New York for a sales conference. This is merely evading the issue.

"The problem is I don't miss Mitchell when he's away. I only miss people after they've dumped me, or when I am in the same room they're in. When Mitchell went on that one-week ski trip with his family, I didn't think about him once. Take that back. I dreaded his return, because it meant that I had to confront the relationship issue again. I dreaded him like I used to dread therapy. Could you pass me a beer?" I ask the mysterious gentleman I met at the Eagle who lives in Key Lime, Florida, and came to New York for a sales conference. We're in bed together, on the fifteenth floor of an anonymous hotel, cleaning out his prestocked expense-account mini-refrigerator. We've already eaten the honey-roasted peanuts, the glazed popcorn, and the cashews and macadamia nuts.

He hands me a Michelob Light. "We could always become lovers," he replies. I gaze into his black eyes. A scar is lightly etched onto his left cheek. "It's difficult for me to commit. I have several men pursuing me back in Florida. I could always tell them that I'm faithful to my New York lover."

"That's fine with me. You are undoubtedly the most attractive man I've seen in months. I think I need a lover who lives in a different state. We can run up long-distance bills and send each other presents through Federal Express. You can copy poems from your collection of English Romantics and claim you wrote them for me." The mysterious gentleman from Key Lime, Florida, reads poetry on planes. He has a condo on the beach and runs five miles a day. "I can send you suggestive Polaroids. We can even adopt a foster child in a foreign country together. Knowing that you are ultimately unavailable, I can fall desperately and hopelessly in love with you without risking commitment of a more serious nature. I can ply you with my charms, which are not inconsiderable."

"And what happens if I fall in love with you?" asks the mysterious gentleman from Key Lime, Florida.

"Oh, that's easy. I'll dump you."

"Aw."

"Come on, I'm being frank with you, putting my cards on the table. Now you can flirt with me with abandon, knowing that so long as you keep yourself in check, you'll never get hurt. You can take as many boyfriends in Key Lime, Florida, as you wish. You can refuse to return my phone calls. You can send back my extravagant presents. You can disappear, so long as you leave me a mailbox. I really don't care if my letters are forwarded to you. I can become devoted to your post office. Just make sure you don't fall in love with me, and our affair will last forever."

Rule #14: Let down your guard.

Mitchell is too nice and understanding for me. He's too amenable. I'm suspicious. What's up his sleeve? The sex continues to get better. This is something I don't understand. Aren't we supposed to gradually slip into habits of love, comfortable and pleasantly dull? I'll crawl under the covers of his soft and pliable white futon; I'm not really in the mood for sex (didn't we just have sex a week ago, on our last date?), but gradually, persistently, Mitchell convinces me. There's something wrong about this setup, though. Why is it he who always has to seduce me? Why am I never the instigator? Is there an element of masochism on his part? Is there also an element of the rapist aggressor? And am I so completely passive as to abnegate all responsibility for anything that may follow?

Rule #15: Be hopeful for the future.

"I'm going to be your last lover," he says.

"Don't say that. I'm terrified. If you're my last lover, that means I won't ever have another. Don't you see the finality of it all? The door of a bank vault slammed shut. *Finito.* No more. I can't breathe. Push back the walls. The ceiling is falling in on us. Life is a dead-end street. I'm in shackles, suffocating."

Rule #16: There is nothing to be afraid of in relationships.

I wonder: How can I make his life a living hell and make him reject me?

Rule #17: Lose your inhibitions.

Why haven't I fallen in love with Mitchell? We've been seeing
one another for three months, which is longer than my previous
record, with Richard, an alcoholic body-builder inclined toward
panic attacks in subways and unable to retain his erection unless
I remained absolutely still, a casualty of war in his deviant
imagination. Sometimes I wonder if Richard ruined me forever
for men.

If only I was able to fall in love with Mitchell. I don't want to
spend the rest of my life floating from crush to crush, yet I'm
afraid of any alternative.

Am I consciously preventing myself from falling in love? Am
I constitutionally incapable of falling in love? Or is Mitchell just
not the right person for me?

Rule #18: Don't compare him to some nonexistent ideal.

What is the perfect boyfriend? And how close is close enough
without compromising, without settling for less than I deserve?
For me, he is an AIDS activist with a perfect body who's also
HIV-positive but not sick and will never get sick, so although he
can comprehend my own anxieties, things will never turn tragic
for us. He works out and eats most of the things that I eat, and
he doesn't smoke, and he likes Madonna, and he can afford to
go out with me to dinner, and he doesn't hate my apartment. He
is great sex; he likes oral sex and doesn't mind not having anal
sex. He and I have the same sense of humor. I can never predict
what he is going to say at any given moment.

How shallow have I become? Why don't I just fall in love with
the mirror?

Rule #19: Spend time together.

"You're coming with me to the Hamptons this weekend," Mitchell informs me. I have been avoiding this for weeks with expla-

nations of weekend demonstrations, visits from out-of-town guests, and herpes attacks. I have run out of excuses.

I am terrified that we will run out of conversation.

Mitchell has a year-round share in the Hamptons. It is early March, and we will be there alone this weekend. We meet at Penn Station at 8:15 on Saturday morning because the trains run irregularly. We're returning on Sunday night. I bring a book of Augustan poetry that the mysterious boyfriend from Key Lime, Florida, sent me, his inscription and a Polaroid photo hidden in the jacket. We walk through historic cemeteries, shiver on the beach, go grocery shopping, and make a three-layer chocolate cake along with a coconut vegetarian curry. We listen to an FM jazz station, the sole station that we can both tolerate. Are we afraid of the silence? We write letters to friends. We sit on the couch and read mysteries. I take my drugs at regularly scheduled intervals. We miss the nine o'clock showing of *The Handmaid's Tale*. Mitchell has a two-hundred-page contract to go over for inconsistencies. I have an infinite checklist of things to do, and I am constitutionally incapable of finishing a single task outside of my home environment. Away from the apartment I detest, I am overcome with anxiety. I am convinced my apartment is being looted during my absence.

It's too cold to lie on the beach. We make slow, gentle love that night and sleep together like spoons. We go for another walk on the beach on Sunday. A hunk in silver tights jogs by. We both turn to look. Other men should not even exist for me, at least for the first three months of our relationship. Will I ever be calm enough to enjoy a honeymoon? We buy the *Times* and take the four o'clock train back to Manhattan. Mitchell naps as I fill in the crossword.

Rule #20: Don't sleep around.

"I think I'm busy this weekend. I may be seeing another one of my boyfriends," I tell Mitchell.

"Fine," says Mitchell. He refuses to get annoyed. He is insanely jealous; I can tell by the way he raises his eyebrows, although this is subconscious on his part. He isn't angry that I am seeing other men because he knows I am incapable of a deep personal relationship with him, so how could I possibly have one with someone else?

"You're not upset?"

"Do you want me to be? Are you trying to drive me away?" Mitchell suppresses his jealousy; Mitchell suppresses everything because he is afraid that I will drop him. I suppress everything because I don't want to reveal myself. I feel that I am constantly naked, and I don't want to take off another layer. I don't trust Mitchell.

"I don't know."

"B.J., are you that terrified of me?"

"Of course." I'm terrified of everyone.

"Do you want me to be mean to you? Maybe you're tired of having me treat you nice."

"Of course not. I'm not a masochist."

"What does that make me?"

Rule #21: Treat his possessions with the same respect with which you treat him.

One morning when I'm staying over at Mitchell's, I try to make the effort; I try to be nice. When I wake up, my breath is foul from the sugar-coated elixir I drank the previous night, the naltrexone, and I am irritable. One of the worst things about the AZT is that it is the first thing in the morning and the last thing at night. I can't forget it for a moment, so when we're lying together on the couch, I can't just relax and fall asleep; I always have to remain alert. It's almost as bad as contact lenses. Mitchell has the luxury of unimpeded slumber; I have to remember to blink every ten seconds so my corneas don't get scratched. Mitchell plods into bed after performing his optional nightly ablutions:

rinsing with Plax and brushing his teeth. I stop up the sink so I don't lose a lens down the drain, rub the cleaning solution on a lens in the palm of my right hand, spray the saline to rinse it off, stick it into the container, do the same with the left lens, and then stick the container into the socket. Then I bump my way into the kitchen for a glass of water and maybe a graham cracker, along with my midnight pills and elixir.

But I've always been ugly in the morning. Before ten A.M. my primitive brain translates the greeting "Good morning" to "Fuck you." I respond accordingly.

This morning, I am determined to be nice, to make the effort. I'm going to make tea for Mitchell. What does this entail? Not much. Turning on the gas under the glass teakettle while Mitchell takes his shower. OK. So I turn on the gas. Then Mitchell comes in and says, "You forgot to put in some water."

I thought it was full. Glass teakettles can be misleading. I say, "Oh." I lift the kettle, swear a stream of abuse because it's hot, get a pair of oven mitts in the shape of lobster claws, take it over to the sink, and fill it with water. It shatters into a million pieces. My brain is not functioning. The portion of my brain where particle mechanics is stored has not yet awakened. "Why didn't you stop me?" I ask Mitchell.

"I wanted to see what would happen."

"You were a physics major. Of course you knew."

"It doesn't matter. The teakettle cost maybe three dollars."

I feel like a heterosexual in an antiques store, all thumbs and no grace.

Rule #22: Don't rely on superstitious signs like horoscopes or dreams.

My dream: Mitchell and I are confined to a tiny room that gets smaller and smaller and smaller. Eventually we disappear.

Mitchell's dream: His father tells him that he is his sister's half brother. He realizes that his mother has slept around.

"I," I tell Mitchell, "am your mother."

Rule #23: Try not to fantasize about other people when you're making love with him, and don't tell him if you do, unless he's a better lay than they are.

I close my eyes and think of Dennis Quaid, Jodie Foster, and my mysterious lover from Key Lime, Florida.

"It would help if we talked during sex," says Mitchell.

"No comment," I reply, muffled, due to the fact that my mouth is presently occupied with some erogenous zone or protuberance or other such nonsense. I was always taught not to speak when my mouth was full.

"You look very pensive," remarks Mitchell.

I think I have the solution to our dilemma. All I have to do is pretend that Mitchell is my mistress and that the mysterious man from Key Lime, Florida, is my boyfriend.

Rule #24: Don't have strict qualifications for the position of boyfriend. Be flexible.

"Is activism another litmus test? If I don't go to Albany, does that mean I'm out?" Mitchell is more than willing to subsidize twenty activists' bus trips to Albany if that would excuse him from actually attending the latest demonstration. His liberalism extends to fondness for a particularly dysphonic recording by a black lesbian folk singer.

"There is one simple boyfriend test, I admit: the Jim Jarmusch litmus test. I absolutely refuse to date anyone who can abide the cinematic works of Jim Jarmusch, especially *Mystery Train*."

Rule #25: Communicate.

Block the 550 numbers from your phone, claiming you have children at an impressionable age and don't want their innocence corrupted. At least keep it down to fifty dollars a month. And if you *do* ever recognize his voice on the line, hang up immediately.

It's important that you both be friends as well as lovers. Talk on the phone daily. Talk about the weather. Talk about every-thing in your everyday life except for the tricks and the boys that you give back rubs to in the gym steam-room. Talk about your job. Talk about movies. Talk about common interests. Talk about the small things. Share the tiny details of your life. Talk about the books you read. Talk about your family. Talk about your traumas. Talk about your side effects. Have the same con-versation every day, with not much variation, because it's really white noise, pleasant white noise, intimacy.

Rule #26: Don't settle for half of happiness.

"OK. You win. I'm in love. Let's get married. Let's be a feature couple on the cover of *People* magazine. Let's be completely faithful with one another. Let's stay together forever and a day and never be apart and become partners in a business that requires constant attention and constant contact with one another—a hairdressing salon, say, or a sexual-massage pairs-only team with an ad in *Outweek.* Let's get high-powered jobs and come home and drink scotches and give one another foot rubs in our Upper East Side apartment decorated entirely in shades of grays and then spend the weekends in the Hamptons and maybe adopt a dog as a surrogate child and spend hours cooking gourmet meals and have tiny dinner parties and go to the opera and have discreet platonic affairs with twenty-three-year-old twinkie advertising executives-to-be with extensive wardrobes and go on skiing va-cations in the Swiss Alps and renovate a brownstone in Jersey City on the weekends and then sell it for a handsome profit, not that we need the extra income—it's just that we have time to burn. And then we can go to benefits in matching tuxes and sit in the orchestra and buy cocktails during intermission and con-verse with our boring friends."

"What makes you think I'm still interested?" asks Mitchell.

Appendix: After the Cure

1 9 9 6

The mood of the country is jubilant as hundreds of thousands of ecstatic fags and dykes gather spontaneously for ribald celebrations in Golden Gate, Griffith, and Central parks, with enthusiasm unrivaled since V-J Day at the close of the Second World War. For several days, the entire island of Manhattan becomes a clothing-optional zone. Joyous lezzies block traffic on the Golden Gate Bridge with an enormous dental dam, sewn together from all of the discarded units that are no longer necessary for safer sex.

Investigative reporters from *The New York Times,* tipped off by an anonymous leak, discover that for the past ten years government scientists at the NIH in Bethesda, Maryland, had been formulating possible AIDS-treatment drugs by using a random dip of a silver-plated chromium spoon into a convection-heated vat of Campbell's alphabet soup and then synthesizing the resultant three-letter acronyms.

The FDA had been planning on conducting fifteen years of double-blind placebo studies testing the new cure against inert phosphorized jelly beans when their Rockville facilities are destroyed in what the authorities term a suspicious blaze. ACT UP/Rockville disclaims all responsibility.

Lambda Legal Defense initiates a class action suit against Burroughs Wellcome for its excessive pricing of AZT. When the books are finally opened under the Freedom of Information Act, Lambda finds that the main active ingredient of AZT is Flintstone vitamins.

In a gesture of good faith, William F. "Tattoo You" Buckley, Jr., who has been held hostage at an undisclosed location for the past eighteen months, with no reading material at all save the complete works of Gore Vidal, is released. ACT UP/Rhode Island disclaims all responsibility.

Jesse Helms, John Cardinal O'Connor, Andrew Dice Clay, and Axl Rose remain at large. Rumors persist that they had been kidnapped and held in a tiny cell and were being punished merely by being subjected to one another. ACT UP/Chelsea disclaims all responsibility.

Sexual terrorists put poppers in the air circulation of the Sears Towers. ACT UP/Chicago disclaims all responsibility for the action.

After the cure is announced, Charles Ortleb, publisher of the *African Swine Fever Virus Weekly* (formerly the *New York Native*), now insists that ASFV causes polio and fetal alcohol syndrome.

Susan Sontag writes her twentieth sequel to *Illness as Metaphor:* Following the highly acclaimed *Eczema, Seborrhea, and Psoriasis and Their Metaphors* and the controversial *Discourse*

Analysis, Deconstructionism, and Their Metaphors, the eagerly awaited *Logorrhea as Metaphor* is published.

GMHC announces that it will conduct special clinics for those who forgot exactly how to have sex during the epidemic.

Gay activists plan on regrouping in Washington in October for a plenary session to reassess goals and priorities. Foremost on the list of demands is the reclamation of the Fire Island Pines from the breeders. The ever-controversial Darryl Yates Rist will deliver the keynote address, "Tearoom Sex in Mid-America: Rest Areas of Interest."

Larry Kramer forms an organization dealing with our most pressing health concern since the AIDS epidemic: DSBU (Deadly Sperm Build-Up). Three months later he will be forcibly removed from the board of directors, at his own request.

Louise Hay shifts her focus from healing tapes to mall and elevator music.

Cher comes out with a new perfume: Trash. Calvin Klein switches from underwear to lubricant design: His ads in the glossies practically slide out of the magazines. Simultaneously, he licenses slightly more graphic and extended versions of his commercials as videos, available for purchase.

With the drastic drop in condom use, officials from the Trojan corporation donate to the artist Christo enough leftover latex to wrap the Empire State Building.

Enterprising capitalists convert aerosol-pentamidine nebulizers to filtrate nitrous oxide and other recreational drugs.

Healing Circles become sites for circle jerks.

Instead of AIDS benefits, promoters sponsor events to recapitalize unsafe-sex emporiums. Prominent former AIDS activists mud-wrestle wearing only jock straps.

It is no longer necessary to be a walking pharmacopeia. Men stop exchanging recipes for AL 721 at the Spike. Leather bars revert to their former functions: aesthetic debates on current opera divas, critiques of fashion shows, and the occasional pickup.

Throughout the country, people stop drinking their own urine for medicinal purposes, unless they are so inclined by personal preference.

The Advocate stops running advertising for items claiming to be the latest cures: a Chinese cucumber carved into a facsimile of Jeff Stryker's most notable feature, aloe-vera malt shakes, do-it-yourself home acupuncture kits, hydrogen-peroxide enemas, macrobiotic window boxes suitable for fire escapes, stress reduction through ergonomically designed pornography, and so on.

Gay men, thankful for the altruistic deeds lesbians performed for them at the height of the epidemic, return the favor by running day-care centers at women's music festivals, donating sperm for turkey-baster fertilization, marching for abortion, and lending their sisters their favorite dresses.

Antibody-positives and -negatives, who had become socially stratified during the epidemic, once again commingle to the pleasure of all.

There were times back in the dismal eighties when we thought that the crisis would never end. I remember dark hours when queens lost their reason and fled to the subcontinent, never to be heard from again. Were it not for the inspirational bass beat of Miss Gloria Gaynor's "I Will Survive" reverberating through the antechambers of our collective unconsciousness, many would have given up in despair. But the nightmare is now over. The disease has been vanquished. And now, if you will excuse me, I have an engagement with an as-yet unidentified prospective boyfriend at some unseemly cocktail lounge near the docks. Wish me luck.